REUNION...

The scenery held Nesta entranced. It was a day of sunshine and shadows. Banks of bubbling white clouds swirled over the twin summits of Glyder Fawr and Glyder Fach. The view up the valley from the hollow of Cwm Dyli, with the high peaks of Snowdon grouped around it, stretched to infinity. The mountain air was clean, tangy and invigorating.

By the time they reached Gwyndy Farm, the day had proved so memorable that Nesta was loath to spoil everything by returning to reality.

'It's what we came for,' Gwilym insisted as Nesta paused uncertainly at the gate. 'No harm in just asking if he is here or whether she has seen him recently, now is there?'

Nesta still held back.

The mental image she had built up of her father was a satisfying one and she was fearful of destroying it. In her mind she knew exactly what he was like. She often held imaginary conversations with him and knew what he would say or do in any situation.

She had placed him on a pedestal and she was afraid that turning her dream into reality might ruin it forever . . .

Also by Marion Harris in Sphere Books:

SOLDIERS' WIVES
OFFICERS' LADIES

NESTA

The Heart of the Dragon:
Book One

Marion Harris

SPHERE BOOKS LIMITED

SPHERE BOOKS LTD

Published by the Penguin Group
27 Wrights Lane, London W8 5TZ, England
Viking Penguin Inc., 40 West 23rd Street, New York, New York 10010, USA
Penguin Books Australia Ltd, Ringwood, Victoria, Australia
Penguin Books Canada Ltd, 2801 John Street, Markham, Ontario, Canada L3R 1B4
Penguin Books (NZ) Ltd, 182 – 190 Wairau Road, Auckland 10, New Zealand

Penguin Books Ltd, Registered Offices: Harmondsworth, Middlesex, England

First published in Great Britain by Severn House Publishers Ltd, 1988
Published by Sphere Books, 1988

Copyright © 1988, Marion Harris

Printed and bound in Great Britain by
Richard Clay Ltd, Bungay, Suffolk

Except in the United States of America,
this book is sold subject to the condition
that it shall not, by way of trade or otherwise,
be lent, re-sold, hired out, or otherwise circulated
without the publisher's prior consent in any form of
binding or cover other than that in which it is
published and without a similar condition
including this condition being imposed
on the subsequent purchaser

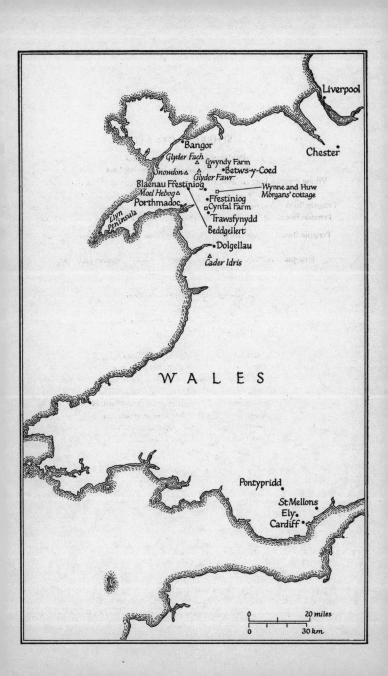

Liverpool

Chester

Bangor

Glyder Fach △
Snowdon △   △ Gwyndy Farm
               Glyder Fawr   • Betws-y-Coed
Blaenau Ffestiniog △
Moel Hebog △   ┌ Wynne and Huw
Porthmadoc   │   Morgans' cottage
                      □ Ffestiniog
Llyn   □ Cynfal Farm
Peninsula   • Trawsfynydd
                      Beddgellert

                • Dolgellau
                △ Cader Idris

W A L E S

                      Pontypridd •

                        • St Mellons
                      Ely •
                      Cardiff •

                    0   20 miles
                    └──┴──┴──┴──┴──┘
                    0   30 km

'Someday he will marry me . . . and *then* I will give him a son!'

A punishing wind sprang up from nowhere, tearing the words away from Eleanor Greenford's trembling lips.

It had come whistling along the dock road, past the grim warehouses, lashing at the fair-haired, slender, seventeen-year-old girl who was leaning on the bridge, a parcel, clumsily wrapped in a copy of the previous day's *Cardiff Echo*, clutched to her chest. The tears that misted her huge violet eyes began trickling slowly down her pale cheeks, leaving dirty blotches on the newsprint as they landed on the parcel, almost obscuring the date 'Friday 13th May, 1921'.

With a heavy sigh that shuddered right through her body Eleanor pushed the bundle away from her, clasping her hands tightly over her ears so that she wouldn't hear the splash as it hit the water.

She watched with morbid fascination as the fast-flowing current sucked the package into mid-stream, carrying it down-river to where the tide would take it out into the Bristol Channel.

She swayed as she turned away, her legs felt weak and there was a hollow sickness inside her stomach as she clutched at the rail along the top of the bridge. She was back in Tiger Bay, in the dismal, dirty room in Margaret Street, lying on the narrow, hard bed, her knees held tight to her chest, a grey-haired, wrinkled face hovering above her as a searing pain tore at her insides.

A tram rattled by on its way to the Pier Head, its clanging reverberating in her ears. She had five minutes before it passed again on its return journey. Five minutes in which to force her trembling legs to carry her to the stop at the corner of the road. Once she was on the tram she could sit still until it reached Crwys Road. By then she hoped she would feel strong enough to walk the short distance home.

The thought of drifting off to sleep in her own soft bed helped to dull the nagging ache. And when she woke all the pain, and unbearable soreness, would be gone, she told herself.

The clanking of the approaching tram brought her mind back to the present. As it ground to a halt she moved forward, forcing herself to climb aboard. She clutched the steel pole and, swaying precariously, hauled herself up on to the platform.

'Had one too many, cariad?' the conductor grinned as he tugged the bell cord, signalling the driver to pull away.

He grabbed her arm and helped her inside. She sank down on to the slatted wooden seat and closed her eyes, waiting for the feeling of nausea to subside before she handed him her fare. The swaying, bumping motion was sending such agonizing jabs through her lower back that she had to bite hard on her lower lip to keep herself from crying out.

'Are you all right, then?'

Eleanor opened her eyes as someone sat down alongside her.

'There's pale you are . . . not feeling too good, eh?'

'Headache,' Eleanor mumbled.

'Must be a cracker. I used to get them when I was your age. Cleared up completely after young Iori was born.'

Eleanor opened her eyes again and dutifully peered at the bundle the woman was holding in her arms.

'Little beauty, isn't he,' the woman said proudly, pulling aside the shawl so that Eleanor could see the baby's plump cheeks flushed with sleep, the dark lashes spread like tiny fans, the parted pink lips.

'He's lovely . . .' the words choked.

She leaned back, closing her eyes. What had she done? One day her baby would have looked like that. The vision of the newspaper-wrapped bundle floated through her mind. As soon as the paper was sodden by sea water it would disintegrate, like an onion shedding its skin. The meagre flesh on the unformed tiny body would become food for the gulls and fishes. She shuddered, drawing her blue coat more tightly to her body.

Struggling with handbag and shopping, the woman with the baby moved to another seat. Eleanor pretended not to notice. She sat staring out of the window, shocked each time she caught sight of her own reflection in the glass. Devoid of their violet lustre, her eyes were two sunken holes in her gaunt face. And her shoulder-length hair hung like lank straw.

She left the tram at the corner of Crwys Road, hurrying past the imposing Victorian houses with their tiled vestibules and stained-glass door panels, hoping she would not meet anyone she knew.

As she turned into Coburn Street, where the front doors of the tightly packed terraced houses opened straight on to the pavement, she squared her shoulders and held her head high.

Some children were playing on the corner with whips and tops. As she walked past, a small boy who was sitting on one of the stone window-sills called out, 'Afternoon, Miss Greenford.' And because he was in the class she taught at St Joseph's, she was forced to reply.

Her own front door was ajar. As quietly as possible Eleanor slipped inside and was already half-way up the stairs when her mother called out, 'That you, then, Mrs Rossiter?'

'It's me, Mam,' Eleanor replied, clutching at the banister rail for support and hoping that in the dimness of the hall her mother would not notice how ill she was looking.

3

'Eleanor! I was expecting you back home yesterday. What happened?' She came out into the hallway, smiling with relief. Then her round face became anxious as she stared at her youngest daughter. 'My God, what is it? You look terrible.'

'I'll be all right. I just want to go and lie down. I . . . I've got a headache.'

'Headache, is it? You look more like you have the flu than a headache. Go on up to bed and I'll bring you a hot drink. I hope it is just flu, my girl, and not some awful foreign illness. Alice Roberts may be your best friend but I don't like you staying there overnight. All those seamen coming into the pub from foreign parts and bringing heaven only knows what diseases with them . . .'

'I never go down into the pub, you know that perfectly well, Mam. Alice has a sitting room upstairs.'

'Doesn't matter. You breathe the same air. That's how these diseases spread. Too late now, you've caught whatever it is you've got. Just look at you shivering away there. Get along upstairs and I'll bring up a hot-water bottle and a drink. I wonder if I ought to call in the doctor . . .'

'No! Stop fussing. I . . . I'm all right. Just a bit of a headache, that's all.'

'Well, get up to bed and we will see how you are in the morning.'

As she peeled off her clothes, Eleanor saw that the check skirt she had been wearing, and also the lining of her blue coat, were both blood-stained. Quickly she pushed them to the back of the cupboard she used as a wardrobe. She knew she ought to sponge them with cold water right away to be sure of getting the marks out but she felt too weak to bother at the moment. Anyway, there was always the chance her mother would catch her and then she would have to explain how they came to be in that state.

Before getting into bed, she spread a towel over the bottom sheet for fear of marking it. She was shivering uncontrollably as she lay back against the pillow and pulled the bedclothes up around her shoulders.

'Come on now, get this down you,' her mother urged, coming into the room with a mug of hot milk. 'I'll just pop this hot-water bottle in by your side. I have wrapped a piece of flannel round it so that it won't burn you.'

'I'll take it,' Eleanor told her, holding the bedclothes tightly around her. She knew that if her mother turned them back she was more than likely to spot the towel and ask why it was there.

As soon as she had finished the hot milk, Eleanor handed the mug back to her mother, who was hovering at the bedside, concerned about how ill she looked.

'I'd stay there until morning, if I were you,' Mrs Greenford murmured. 'I'll come up later and see if you want anything.'

'Thanks, Mam.'

As she snuggled deeper into the bed, pulling the blankets up over her shoulders, a feeling of relief washed over Eleanor. If only she could sleep, she thought. Her body and head ached, but her mind was churning with questions and answers, reproaches and excuses, as she went over the happenings of the past two days and the events leading up to them. Always she came back to the same point. What would her parents say if they ever found out?

The thought of having to conceal her sin for evermore weighed heavily. She had committed a crime against both God and man and, worst of all, she couldn't ask for forgiveness.

How was she ever going to explain to her mother that she wasn't going to confession next Friday night . . . or ever again, for that matter. Yet how could she do so without telling Father O'Neil what was on her conscience. Not that he would tell her mother, of course. Anything said in the confessional was a guarded secret. But he would know. And she would know that he knew. She would see the sad, accusing look in his eyes every time he spoke to her. The unspoken reproach would be unbearable. How could she, a good Catholic girl, a teacher at St Joseph's school, have done such a thing?

It would break her mother's heart if she knew, Eleanor thought sadly. Her mother was such a good woman. Not pious or sanctimonious, but pure in heart and thought. She was always eager to help others, whether it was hot broth when they were sick, or passing on clothes to those less fortunate than herself, families who had lost their man in the war.

She knew her mother had often forgone the rent on the two rooms they sub-let, just because their lodger had been on short time, or needed the money to pay some other debt.

Her father was just as kind-hearted. He would mend his own shoes with a piece cut from a worn-out bicycle tyre, or a piece of lino, so that he could give an out-of-work neighbour with young children to feed a few shillings from his wages.

Eleanor sighed. It was as if they were always saying 'thank-you' for their own good fortune. Perhaps it was because when they had been younger they had suffered such hardships.

She never tired of hearing them talk about the 'old days'. Her father's voice still had a trace of the soft Dorset dialect. When she had been small, bedtime stories had always been about the gentle, rolling countryside where he had lived as a boy.

'That's where I met and courted your mother,' he would say, smiling happily at the memory. 'My Susan was the prettiest girl in the village with her blue eyes and fair hair. We walked out together for nigh on four years before we wed.'

'And was it a grand wedding?' She always asked, even though she had heard the story countless times.

'It were that. Tables loaded with good food laid out behind the church. The sun was a-shining and everyone was there. The proudest day of my life when I walked down the aisle with my Susan on my arm. Real love match and no mistake.'

'Get away with you, James,' her mother would smile, colouring up. 'Tell her about the cottage.'

'Just like a fairy-tale. A little stone cottage with roses round the door and its garden full of vegetables and flowers. And the loveliest purple lilac you ever did smell.'

'And were you both happy?'

'Happy, we was in heaven. Then the babies started coming. First Gwen and then Betty, two of the prettiest little maids you ever set your eyes on, and we was over the moon. Then our John was born and our cup of happiness was full to the brim.'

When her father reached this part of the story, Eleanor would feel the tears prickling and a lump rise in her throat.

''Twas the turn of the century things began to go wrong. The old Queen died and it was the start of unrest. The farm where I was in charge of the smithy was sold and, before we knew what was happening, we were turned out of the cottage. Just imagine it, our home and livelihood gone.'

'So you came to Cardiff,' Eleanor would prompt, because she wanted to hear the rest of the story and couldn't bear to see the misery in his eyes.

'Yes. I was told that a good blacksmith would soon find a job in the dockyard. And I did, though 'twas a struggle at first. All we could afford was just one room in a back-street in Tiger Bay. Imagine what my poor Susan had to put up with, trying to look after three young children in those conditions. Still, we managed somehow and pinched and saved until we could afford to move to two rooms in a house in Splott.'

'And then you moved again and I was born.'

'Yes,' he smiled fondly at her. 'On 17th November 1903. That was a Red Letter Day and no mistake! We had just moved into this house here in Coburn Street and, even though we had to let two rooms to help to pay the rent, it was still a great achievement.'

They still let two rooms, but now it was because the house was larger than they needed since her two sisters and her brother had all left home. Her parents talked some-times about going back to Dorset but Eleanor doubted whether they ever would. They might not be Welsh but their hearts were in South Wales and all their children lived nearby.

She turned uneasily in her bed. She would be the last to leave home. She was the youngest of the family, and had always been treated as rather special. Her two sisters, Gwen and Betty, had both worked at James Howell's, the big department store in Queen Street, but because there had been more money to spare she had been able to stay on at school and train as a teacher. When she qualified, Father O'Neil had made sure she got a job at St Joseph's and she had been there now for almost a year.

She had been quite content with her life, and hadn't even considered the future, not until she had met Rhys Evans.

The very thought of his name conjured him up in her mind. The tall, lean figure, broad-shouldered and slim-hipped with dark, magnetic, slate-grey eyes under straight dark brows and the thick crop of dark hair which to caress felt like plunging your hand deep into a bear's pelt.

His mouth was firm as if chiselled out of granite from the same block as his square chin and well-shaped nose. But it was his voice, rich and dark and with a lilt like music, that had first captured her attention.

She had met him when she had been visiting Alice at The Hope and Anchor. Of all the countless people her parents had rented out rooms to, Alice Roberts and her family were the only ones who had become friends. Eleanor and red-headed, buxom Alice had taken to each other from the first day the Roberts moved in.

Like her mother, Eleanor often wished that The Hope and Anchor was not in Tiger Bay, but in all the years she had visited it she had never been accosted. The Lascars, and other foreign seamen, might stare but they never spoke or attempted to touch. That was why she had been taken off-guard the night a group of young sailors started making a nuisance of themselves as she was walking down Adelaide Street to catch a tram home. They had just come ashore and had already been drinking. Rhys had been with them but he had immediately stopped them pestering her. His lilting, sonorous voice had fascinated her.

'Give the girl a chance, you're frightening the life out of her,' he had said in a firm voice.

He had disengaged himself from them and stood by her side, mutely assuring her of his protection should any of them try to touch her. But no one had argued or attempted anything.

'Thank you,' she smiled shyly after they had disappeared down the road.

'I had better see you home. It isn't very safe for a young girl, as pretty as you are, to be out on your own as late as this,' he told her gravely.

It had been the start of her first romance.

Alice had been wildly excited by the secret liaison when Eleanor had taken her into her confidence and eager to act as a go-between. Eleanor had made her solemnly promise not to mention Rhys to either of their parents in case they might raise some objection.

'I might be almost eighteen but Mam and Dad still think of me as the baby of the family, even though our Gwen got married when she was not much older,' she sighed.

'They would certainly be up in arms if you thought of taking such a step,' Alice agreed.

Eleanor wriggled deeper under the covers, clutching the

9

hot-water bottle closer to her. Its warmth spread a relaxed glow through her body, easing the gnawing pain, and she let her thoughts once more drift back to Rhys Evans.

He was so different from anyone she had ever known. She had been entranced by the wonderful stories he had spun, tales told to him by his father, legends of Wales with its towering mountains, beautiful valleys, lakes, castles, waterfalls and wooded groves. A land of myth and magic, where dragons, heroic deeds and ancient battles mingled together.

She had thought it strange that he had gone to sea when he was so passionately fond of his homeland.

'I had to,' he told her. 'I couldn't bear the thought of working in the slate mines. I wanted to be where I could see the mountains and breathe clean fresh air.'

'You should have gone and worked on a farm.'

'I would have loved to do that but my father wouldn't hear of it. Felt it was letting the side down. All our family for generations had worked in the slate mines.'

'So you ran away to sea.'

'That's right! I left home and walked for days, following the mountain ranges. I tried to get work on the farms I passed but they all had the same story. Now that the men were all back from the war there weren't enough jobs to go around.'

'So what did you do?'

'I'd spent my last shilling on a meal and, as I was eating it, a chap came and sat down and started talking. He only had one arm, he had lost the other when his boat had gone down. He made going to sea sound so exciting that it made my mind up and I knew it was the life for me.'

'My brother, John, was at the Dardanelles during the war,' Eleanor told him. 'He was only eighteen. I remember how upset our Mam was when she heard the Turks had mined his ship. He was in the water for sixteen hours before he was rescued, and then he was in hospital for a long time afterwards.'

'It's a different life now . . . anyway, I'm in the merchant navy. We carry cargoes all over the world, take one lot out from England and bring back another from Africa or South America or even Australia.'

'And are you going to be a sailor all your life?'

'No. When I've saved enough money, I want to start my own sheep farm in North Wales,' he told her, his eyes shining. 'I've plenty of time, I'm only twenty. I'd like it to be in the Nant Gwynant Valley, somewhere near the foot of Moel Hebog, the Hill of the Hawk. It's beautiful there, high mountains all around you. On a clear day you can see Snowdon etched against the skyline and even when its top is wreathed in cloud it still has a magical quality.'

As she drifted off to sleep she remembered the legend he had told her about Prince Llewellyn who had lived in a palace near there in the thirteenth century. He had gone out hunting and left his faithful dog Gelert to guard his baby son. When he returned, the dog's muzzle was smeared with blood and the cradle overturned. In a great rage he slew the dog, assuming that it had killed the child, only to find afterwards that the baby was alive and that the hound had protected it from a marauding wolf.

In her dream, Rhys came home to find she had destroyed their baby. She became drenched with sweat, shaking with fear, cowering beneath the bedcovers as he towered over her, his slate-grey eyes glistening, dark brows knitted, chiselled lips drawn back in anger as he plunged a knife into her.

She woke screaming with pain. Her relief as she slowly realized that it was morning and that it had been no more than a dream ebbed as she sensed something hot and sticky trickling down her thighs. She pushed back the covers, then gasped with horror. She was lying in a pool of blood.

At the sound of her mother coming upstairs, she quickly pulled up the bedclothes and feigned sleep.

Mrs Greenford put the cup of tea she was carrying down

on the bedside table before bending down and placing her hand on Eleanor's brow.

'How do you feel? Your forehead is quite clammy.'

'I . . . I still feel a bit shivery,' Eleanor smiled weakly.

'Drink your tea while it is hot,' her mother ordered. 'I'll find another blanket to put on your bed. You stay there today and if you are no better by tomorrow then I'll call the doctor.'

Eleanor sat up cautiously, holding the bedclothes tightly beneath her arms, afraid her mother might see the bloodstains.

'Do you want something to eat? A bowl of porridge?'

'No!' The very thought of food made her feel queasy. 'I'll just try and sleep.'

'You do that. Your Dad and me are off to Mass but we shouldn't be gone very long.'

Eleanor nodded and lay back, closing her eyes. She waited impatiently for her parents to leave the house so that she could investigate the state of the bed and try to clean things up.

2

It was a mellow sunny day in late September when Rhys Evans' ship put into Cardiff docks. After being away for well over a year it was good to step ashore and once again breathe the air of his beloved Wales.

His trip had been a long one. He had sailed the Atlantic and the Pacific, he had visited South America and Australia and seen a great many strange sights and new places, but, for all that, he was glad to be back. The vast oceans of the world were all very well but nothing was comparable with the grandeur of the mountains, the scent of the pine forests, or the brooks and waterfalls in the green countryside of his own homeland.

After his papers were checked at the dock gates he made his way to Adelaide Street. Eleanor had been constantly in his thoughts all the time he had been away. He had meant to write to her but had never done so, partly because he felt it was unfair to expect her to wait complacently while he was roaming the globe.

Now he was impatient to see her again. The memory of their last time together had stayed in his mind like an enchanting dream. It had been something to think about when he was on watch, with only the stars for company, the ship churning along in the dark ocean. The memory had been like a precious jewel, polished by constant handling, a talisman he pinned his hopes on when he tossed and turned in his hammock, too tired to sleep.

Although he knew where Eleanor lived, he decided it might be prudent to ask her friend Alice to take a message to her rather than go to her home. That way, if she was no longer interested in seeing him, they would both be spared the embarrassment of a face-to-face encounter.

It was mid afternoon and The Hope and Anchor pub was closed, so he went to the side door and rapped sharply. It was a long time before anyone answered. The Roberts family were used to sailors, eager to spend their long-earned money, hammering to be let in. When Mrs Roberts finally appeared at an upstairs window, her voice was edged with irritation.

'The doors will be open at five o'clock and not before,' she called down to him.

'I'm not after a drink, I want a word with Alice,' Rhys shouted back.

Mrs Roberts pushed the sash window up higher and leaned out to see him better. 'She'll be behind the bar at five. You can talk to her then,' she snapped.

'Please let me speak to Alice, Mrs Roberts. I was hoping she would deliver a message for me before she starts work . . . to Eleanor Greenford.'

'Wait there.'

The window slammed shut. Rhys paced anxiously up and down the pavement waiting for Alice. To his relief, she not only remembered who he was but seemed delighted to see him.

'I was afraid you might have forgotten me after such a long time,' he remarked as she planted a kiss on his cheek.

Her green eyes shining, she shook her head so vehemently that it set her red curls dancing. Rhys Evans was not the sort of man you forgot easily, she reflected. She guessed why he had called and felt envious of her friend. She wished someone as attractive as Rhys would come looking for her after being away for over a year.

'How is Eleanor?' he asked eagerly. 'You two are still friends?'

'She's all right,' Alice said laconically.

'Does she ever mention me?' he asked cautiously.

'Yes . . . sometimes.'

It was only with a great effort that she stopped herself from assuring him that Eleanor constantly talked of him, confident that one day he would return.

'Do you think she will want to see me again?' Rhys asked hopefully.

Alice was evasive. She was afraid to say very much in case she blurted out the truth about what Eleanor had been through since he had sailed away.

'I can't answer for her but I'm pleased to see you,' she said, smiling up at him coquettishly.

'Well, that's good to know,' he told her, grinning broadly and giving her a playful hug. 'Will you let Eleanor know that I have docked . . . and that I'm longing to see her.'

Alice hesitated for the merest second. She would have liked to tell him that Eleanor had forgotten him, or that she was going out with someone else, and then hope he might take her out instead, but she couldn't bring herself to do so.

'Where do you want to meet her?'

'I don't really mind. Look, why don't you ask her to come back with you? Do you think she would?' he asked eagerly.

'I doubt it.' She touched his arm placatingly as she saw him scowl. 'She won't finish teaching until four o'clock, and she must go home and let her Mam know where she is going now, mustn't she?'

'Yes. I suppose you are right.'

'Better make it seven o'clock. I'll tell her you will be here.'

'Couldn't you wait for her . . . to make sure she comes,' he persisted.

'Don't talk daft! The pub opens at five and my Mam will expect me to be here behind the bar pulling pints.'

'But you will go and see Eleanor first.'

'I've said so, haven't I?'

'Shall I walk along to the tram with you?'

15

'Come on, then. If we stand here gassing much longer I won't be back for opening time.'

He would have liked to have gone with her to meet Eleanor but something in Alice's manner made him cautious. To expect Eleanor to greet him with open arms, after not hearing from him for over a year, was asking a lot, he supposed.

The three hours of waiting until seven o'clock seemed interminable.

After he had booked in at the seaman's mission in Bute Road and left his kitbag there, he went to a cafe for a meal and sat drinking endless cups of tea to pass the time.

At six o'clock, he walked down to the Pier Head and hung around where he could watch the trams coming in, he was so impatient to see her again. He had met a lot of girls during his travels, white girls, coloured girls, half-castes, but none of them had got under his skin like Eleanor.

Even though he was only twenty-one, and intended to stay at sea for a while longer, he felt it would be great to have a wife like Eleanor to come home to. He wished he had written to her. She would have probably liked to have had a card from him, a picture of one of the strange places he had visited, something with a foreign stamp on it.

The trouble was he wasn't much of a one for letter-writing, he didn't even write home ... but then, that was different. His mother had forgiven him for running away, and always welcomed him with open arms, but his father still treated him as an outcast.

Rhys sighed. He had known he was a misfit, ever since the day when he had put on his first pair of long trousers. They had been handed down from his brother, Bowen, who was almost three years older than him. For all that, though, they had ended mid-way down Rhys's calves, a good four inches above his ankles.

All the Evans men were small and wiry, their wives big-bosomed and buxom. 'Built more like our Mam than our Dad,' his sister Wynne had sniggered, as she watched him struggling to get his broad shoulders inside Bowen's jacket.

He had also differed from the other men in his family in not wanting a job in a slate mine.

His father, grandfather and countless uncles, as well as his own younger brothers, all seemed to feel the same way about the great grey quarries where they worked, whether it was at Penrhyn, Bethesda, Dinorwic, Llanfair, or Llechwedd.

These harsh, awesome expanses of slate seemed to impress the rest of the Evans family in the same way as the towering heights of Snowdon and Cader Idris, or the tumultuous waterfalls at Dolgoch, inspired him.

His rows with his father over his future had been long and bitter. Only his mother seemed to understand how much he loved the countryside and how he yearned for the green grandeur of the mountains in summer and felt overwhelmed by their stark magnificence in winter when they were capped by snow.

But she knew better than to contradict her husband!

'It's no good, Rhys,' she sighed. 'His heart is as hard as the slate he hews. Do as he asks, boyo. When you are older perhaps you can go your own way then. There is talk that things will be changing in the mines very soon. They do say that the troubles at Penrhyn will never be properly settled, and that the unrest has already spread to Dinorwic. I don't understand it all, mind you, but your father seems to be very bitter about what is happening. Don't go against him, you know you can't win.'

But although Rhys might not have his father's unrelenting love of the slate quarries, when it came to knowing his own mind he shared his father's iron will. He didn't argue with his father. Instead, he left home.

His new life had been incredibly hard.

He had missed the mountains. When his ship was tossing

in the middle of the ocean, and storm clouds bubbled overhead, he could sometimes envisage the long ridge of Cader Idris, or the snow-capped top of Snowdon, in the great cloud masses. And then his heart would ache to be back there.

It was where he wanted to be now, just as soon as he had seen Eleanor. He checked the time and his spirits sank when he saw that it was after seven.

He decided to go back to The Hope and Anchor just in case Alice had a message for him. As he strode along the busy dock streets he wondered if perhaps Eleanor was doing something tonight, something she couldn't put off.

When he found she was already at the pub waiting for him, he could hardly believe his good luck.

'I went to the Pier Head to meet you,' he told her as his eyes feasted themselves on her.

'I came the other way. I took a tram to James Street and walked over the bridge,' she explained.

She was just as he remembered her. Slender, yet with softly rounded breasts and hips. Her wide-set eyes of deepest violet glowed like amethysts, framed by softly waving, shoulder-length, fair hair. And a welcoming smile that conveyed so much more than mere words.

'Why don't you two go into the Parlour Bar,' Alice suggested. 'Nobody uses that until later in the evening, so you'll have it to yourselves.'

The moment they were alone, Rhys gathered Eleanor into his arms. His lips were hot and hungry as they sought hers.

She stiffened, but his ardour swamped her resistance. The fire that he had kindled all those months earlier flamed anew, and her lips parted with a small cry of pleasure before his mouth engulfed hers.

When they drew apart, her violet eyes were misted with happiness. She ran a hand over his strong jawline and lean, tanned face as if remembering every bone and plane. His own strong hand trapped hers, holding its palm to his burning lips as his slate-grey eyes searched hers questioningly.

Was she still his? He wanted to know but was unsure how to frame the question. The very fact that she had come at once to see him gave him hope, as did her unstinted welcome.

'I . . . I meant to write,' he muttered hoarsely.

'You are here now, that is all that matters,' she said softly. Her cool fingers rested momentarily on his lips, hushing his excuses.

He caught her close again, his excitement mounting as she hugged him impetuously.

Alice, arriving with the drinks he had ordered, brought them both back to reality. They moved apart, grinning at her sheepishly.

As Eleanor sipped her port-and-lemon, she wondered if she was in some sort of trance. She had dreamed so often that one day this would happen, that the ship Rhys was on would dock in Cardiff again and that he would come looking for her. She had even imagined herself falling into his arms, just as she had done now.

On other occasions, remembering all she had endured after he had sailed away, she had been determined to have nothing more to do with him.

Yet now that he was actually sitting next to her, so close that she could feel the heat from his body, she couldn't conceal her feelings. She knew that he was the only man in the world she wanted.

Was this the weakness of the flesh that Father O'Neil preached about, and warned his flock to be on their guard against, she wondered guiltily.

As Rhys drained his glass of beer he knew that, now he had met up with Eleanor again, he didn't want to lose sight of her for one moment. His mind was in a turmoil. He was torn by the choice between spending all his shore leave in Cardiff or going home to North Wales as he had originally intended.

'How long before you sail again?' she asked, as if sensing something of what was in his mind.

'Ages. I've booked a bed at the seaman's mission for tonight. I intended going home to North Wales tomorrow. Why don't you come with me?'

Eleanor shrank back as though he had struck her, and Rhys was startled to see the anguish in her eyes before her lids dropped.

'No!' she whispered, the colour draining from her face. 'No, I couldn't do that . . .'

'Why not?'

Memories of what had happened the last time they had been alone together, and the terrible consequences she had been faced with afterwards, burned in her mind.

She wrestled with her conscience, knowing that this was the moment when she should tell him about the baby but afraid to do so in case it turned him against her.

She toyed with her drink, until her stomach heaved at the blood-red colour and she pushed the glass away.

Rhys waited impatiently for her answer. He couldn't understand her reluctance when only moments before she had seemed so pleased to see him.

'I just couldn't . . . it wouldn't be right . . . my parents would be shocked . . . they don't even know you!'

Colour suffused her face as the words tumbled out.

'Drink up, then, and you can take me to meet them.' His hand reached out and squeezed hers.

Eleanor looked apprehensive. Her mother had no idea she had a boyfriend. To suddenly walk in with Rhys would call for explanations. She needed time to think about what she would say.

'Come on!' he broke into her thoughts. 'They've got to meet their future son-in-law sometime!'

'Their what?'

'I'm in love with you . . . I'm going to marry you,' he breathed softly.

Eleanor stared into his dark eyes, mesmerised by his words.

He leaned closer and, as his mouth covered hers, she gave herself up to the sweetness of the moment, wondering if perhaps it was all a dream. The sharp prickling sensation of his chin stubble against her skin told her otherwise.

She felt her senses throbbing. All the feelings she had submerged for so many months rose to the surface. The blood pounded to her head, waves of excitement set the tops of her toes and fingers tingling. As Rhys gathered her closer, pressing her so hard that she felt her nipples hardening against the roughness of his uniform, she felt weak with desire.

All her determined resolves never again to let any man have his way with her vanished. She loved Rhys more than she had ever thought it was possible to love another human being. She felt an overwhelming sadness that she had destroyed their baby. If only she had been sure that he was coming back, she thought regretfully.

'What's wrong?'

She was suddenly conscious that Rhys had stopped kissing her. He was holding her away from him, a questioning look in his dark eyes.

'Nothing. I . . . I thought I must be in a trance. All the time you've been gone I've dreamed of you coming home to me. Then, as the months passed and there was no word from you, I thought you had forgotten me.'

'Never! You've been in my thoughts every day.'

'You never wrote to me.'

'I'm not much of a letter-writer.' He gathered her into his arms again. 'I'm better at "doing" than "writing",' he whispered, as his mouth descended fleetingly on hers.

'I . . . I wasn't even sure you cared,' she whispered, tremulously. Her eyes softened and her smile widened as she looked up at him.

'I love you . . . I always have,' he told her earnestly. 'I want to marry you.'

21

Eleanor gave up fighting. Rhys had come back to her, that was all that mattered. His tenderness obliterated the deep hurt that had festered inside her ever since the abortion. He was just as handsome, and as caring, as the memory she had treasured all these long dark months. What more could she ask for, she thought with a happy sigh.

For a brief moment she was tempted to tell him about the baby. To be able to tell him what she had done, to confess and rid herself of the overwhelming burden of guilt that weighed so heavily on her conscience, would be such sweet relief. Only the fear that Rhys might be horrified, might even turn against her, kept her silent.

Her mother always maintained, 'least said, soonest mended', and some inner caution warned her that it was the right way to handle the situation.

Perhaps this was what the Church meant by Purgatory, a state of torment and pain here on earth, not, as she had previously thought, a place where the soul suffered after death.

Any other misdeed and she could have confessed, begged forgiveness, wiped the slate clean with prayers, fasting and acts of contrition. This sin was too great for that. It was something she would have to conceal for as long as she lived. If what her mother had taught her and all the Church claimed was true, then she was sure that someday she would be punished for what she had done. God would wreak retribution in his own good time.

'Come on, then!'

She drained her glass. 'I'll just let Alice know we're going.'

As the tram from the Pier Head bumped its way through the city, Eleanor cuddled up against Rhys trying to imagine what her parents would say when she walked in and said she was going to be married.

3

Eleanor refused to listen to any of the pleas, entreaties or admonishments from her mother, Father O'Neil or the rest of her family. Only if Rhys had wanted to postpone their marriage would she have taken any notice, but he was as eager as she was that it should take place before he was due to sail again.

To everyone else it might seem like a whirlwind courtship but to Eleanor it was the culmination of a dream.

Father O'Neil was disturbed both by the haste with which the wedding was to take place and by the fact that Rhys was not a Catholic.

'Why the hurry, my child?' he exclaimed sorrowfully, his rheumy green eyes searching her face. 'Have you thought what you will be doing by marrying outside the faith . . . ?'

'We want to be married before Rhys has to rejoin his ship.'

'Can't you wait until his next shore leave? That would give him time to take some religious instruction.'

'He isn't a heathen, Father. He was brought up to go to chapel regularly . . . he's told me so.'

'It is not the same thing at all. You've never seen these fiery Welsh preachers, bellowing forth about hell, brimstone and damnation. God forbid that you ever should. I would like time to convert him to the true faith, or at least instruct him in the ways of it.' Father O'Neil passed one of his hands across his forehead, pushing back his thinning grey hair in a worried gesture. 'Does he know that your children must be brought up in our faith?'

'We haven't talked about it,' Eleanor said, flushing with confusion.

'Just as I thought!' His thin lips tightened ominously.

'You are rushing into this marriage, my child. Take time to think it over. Pray to the Blessed Virgin for guidance. You are making a lifetime commitment, remember.'

Even when her mother added her remonstrations to those of Father O'Neil, Eleanor still remained adamant.

'If Father O'Neil doesn't want to marry us at St Joseph's, then we will go to a registry office,' she announced defiantly.

'There's no need to talk like that, my girl,' her father told her sternly. 'We've nothing against this young man, it's just that we would like to get to know him a bit better. You've told us nothing of his prospects or what sort of home he can provide for you.'

'I was going to stay here until Rhys has finished at sea,' Eleanor stated. 'You and Mam don't mind, do you? There's plenty of room now that all the others are married. Be better renting out rooms to me and Rhys than to strangers,'

'Have you spoken to your mother about this?'

'Not really. I was waiting for Rhys to get back from North Wales. I just took it for granted that she would agree.'

The week Rhys was away visiting his own family passed in a flash. The house in Coburn Street was bursting to the seams with activity. From first thing in the morning until it was time for bed, people were dropping in to see if they could help with the arrangements.

'This haste is positively indecent,' Mrs Greenford sighed. 'It takes all the joy out of planning. There certainly isn't going to be time for me to make your wedding dress.'

'Borrow mine,' Betty suggested. 'It should fit you. We're the same height and size.'

'Thanks, but I'm buying a dress. I've seen exactly what I want in Howell's window.'

'You can't have a ready-made wedding dress!' her mother exclaimed. 'Whatever are things coming to?'

'The dress I've seen is in cream tussore silk with a panel of embroidered lace down the front. It's ever so pretty. I can wear it for best afterwards.'

'Where do you think you'll be going that you'll need a long dress?' Betty said derisively.

'It's not a long one, it's the new mid-calf length. I've already bought some cream satin shoes, trimmed with little bows at the front, to wear with it. They're ever so posh.'

'Aren't you going to wear a veil, then?' her mother frowned.

'Do you think I should? I hadn't really thought about it,' Eleanor admitted.

'You must have a veil,' her mother insisted. 'Betty will lend you hers.'

'Mine is white. It wouldn't look right with a cream dress.'

'I'll ask Gwen if I can borrow hers. The number of years it's been lying around it has probably gone cream with age.'

'That would be something old, all right,' Betty agreed. 'You know what they say: something old, something new, something borrowed, something blue! I'll lend you a blue garter . . .'

'Yes, well, never mind about that, what are you doing about bridesmaids and their dresses?' her mother asked.

'My Dilys has set her little heart on being a bridesmaid,' Betty said eagerly. 'And I bet our Gwen is expecting her Gwladys to be asked as well.'

'I'm not having any bridesmaids . . . they can be flower girls if they want to,' Eleanor added hastily, seeing the expressions of dismay on the faces of her mother and sister.

'It's not the same,' Betty argued. 'They will be so disappointed.'

'Perhaps you'd like me to have some page boys. We could dress Gwen's Idris and your Richard up in blue velvet suits!'

'I shall ask Father O'Neil if Richard can be one of the altar boys. He will probably allow our Gwen's two boys to serve as well since it's a special occasion. Be nice that, having both your sisters' boys in attendance.'

'It's all getting out of hand,' Eleanor muttered. 'I wanted a quiet wedding, not a lot of fuss. And who is going to pay for it all?'

'You are the last of our daughters to get married,' James Greenford told her, placing his arm around her shoulders. 'I'll do as much for you as I did for the other two. I just want you to be sure that you are marrying the right man, that's all.'

'We had no idea you even had a sweetheart,' her mother added in puzzled tones. 'If only you'd brought him home to meet us . . .'

'He's been away at sea for over a year,' Eleanor reminded her.

'Are you positive you still love him. . . after all that time?'

'Yes, Mother.' Eleanor assured her. 'I have never been more certain of anything in my life,' she added, planting a kiss on her mother's soft round cheek.

'And he's going back to sea again almost right after you are married?'

'I am afraid so! That is why I want to stay on here.' Her violet eyes darkened. 'You don't mind, do you, Mam?'

'Of course not . . . where else would you go? It will give you a chance to save up and get a home together for when Rhys comes back for good.'

The discussions and arguments about whether Eleanor was doing the right thing, or not, in rushing into marriage lasted right up until the eve of the wedding. Then, as if by magic, everyone seemed to be in complete accord.

There was only one minor setback. Rhys returned to say that he had been unable to persuade his parents to make the long journey from North Wales, so they would not be at the wedding.

As she walked down the aisle on her father's arm, Eleanor had never seen St Joseph's looking more lovely. Michaelmas daisies and chrysanthemums added great splashes of colour to the sombre grey walls and the pews were packed with family, friends and neighbours. The class of children she taught were all there, the girls wearing white pinafores over their dresses, the boys looking well scrubbed, their hair plastered down with water.

It was the first time she had seen Rhys in a suit and, for a fleeting second, as she took her place alongside him at the altar rail, he seemed like a stranger and she felt a moment of panic. Then, as she looked into his slate-grey eyes and read their message of love, her moment of self-doubt faded away.

The party afterwards was a boisterous family affair that spilled out on to the pavement, with friends and neighbours joining in the fun.

Mrs Greenford and her two eldest daughters had been baking all week and the table groaned under the lavish spread of pies and cakes and cold meats. The men drank beer but for the women there were home-made wines which Susan Greenford had been hoarding for just such an occasion.

Rhys, lean and handsome in his dark grey, double-breasted suit, stood head and shoulders above the other men. Eleanor's mother looked at him with a mixture of admiration and caution. Although both her other daughters had been married in their teens, Susan Greenford still regarded Eleanor as the baby of the family, someone who still needed her protection. Perhaps it was because she had led a more sheltered life than either Betty or Gwen.

Susan had always felt proud of the fact that Eleanor was a teacher. She knew Father O'Neil held her in very high regard. He was always saying how good she was with the children.

She wondered what would happen now. If Rhys was

going back to sea again in a week or so, then would Eleanor stay on at St Joseph's? They hadn't even discussed it. She wasn't even sure if Father O'Neil would consider it right and proper to have a married teacher.

Susan Greenford sighed. It had all been so sudden. Eleanor hadn't even got a bottom drawer together, nothing at all to set up home with and no savings worth talking about.

Seeing them together, Rhys so tall and handsome with his broad shoulders and shock of thick dark hair, she could understand Eleanor falling for him. But looks weren't everything. A kind heart, consideration and understanding when things went wrong, counted for far more.

She knew she had been more than lucky on that score. Her James was a gentle giant. He had worked hard ever since she had known him and even now, when he was into his sixties, he was a fine figure of a man. His brown hair might be thinning but his hazel eyes were as bright and sharp as ever. She could remember when he was as lean as Rhys. It was the years of heavy work as a blacksmith in the shipyards that had broadened him, she mused. But it hadn't changed his kindly manner. His huge hands could be as gentle as a woman's, his tone, except on the rare occasions when he was riled, was always warm and friendly.

He had always been a good provider, bringing his pay-packet home unopened, expecting nothing more than a few shillings back for beer and tobacco. She had managed their money well, there had always been food on the table and clothes on their backs.

In the early years it had sometimes been a struggle, but now, as she looked round at their children, their two eldest daughters with their husbands and children, their son, who had been married barely a year and whose wife, Mairo, was expecting their first baby any day, she felt a sense of pride and satisfaction.

Eleanor would be the last of their children to marry, but in a way, provided she had chosen well, it would be comforting to know that they were all settled.

It was after midnight before Eleanor and Rhys made their way up the narrow staircase to the middle-bedroom. Eleanor felt suddenly nervous. They had spent so very little time together since he had come ashore that they were still almost strangers.

Remembering how she had rushed to see him like some love-sick schoolgirl, when Alice had said that Rhys had called at the pub and wanted to see her, she wondered whether perhaps her family had been right and she had been too impetuous.

Perhaps if he had changed, grown fat or coarse in his ways, she wouldn't have been swept off her feet in quite the same way.

But he hadn't. In fact, he had looked even more handsome than she had remembered.

As soon as she had looked up into his eyes all the feelings she had tried so hard to suppress over the past year rose to the surface. Every tender moment that had passed between them was rekindled. Her skin had burned for his touch, her body had ached for his embrace. It had been like a fever raging through her.

Even if he hadn't mentioned marriage she would still have wanted him. The trauma of the abortion, and the anguish and heartache she had known afterwards, seemed inconsequential. Just seeing him, feeling his hand on hers, seeing the desire in his piercing grey eyes, had roused her to fever pitch.

Yet now, in the confines of the bedroom, she felt overwhelmed and confused. Rhys seemed to tower over her and she felt a sudden urge to escape. At that moment she would have given anything to be across the landing in her own small bedroom.

Perhaps if they were in there, amongst surroundings that

were familiar to her, she would not feel so frightened. This room, with its heavy furniture and oppressive drapes, seemed cold and unfriendly.

She tried to speak but her voice was a husky croak. Panic sent a singing through her ears. As Rhys drew her towards him she felt powerless to resist.

Hesitantly, she looked up into his dark grey eyes as he drew her into the circle of his arms. Her heart thudded as she saw again the message of love that she had seen earlier in the day, when she had stood at his side in St Joseph's.

As his mouth descended and his firm warm lips touched hers, the thumping beneath her rib-cage eased. The tension melted. With a sigh of sheer happiness, she gave herself up to the delights of his embrace.

As his lips, hot with desire, moved in a series of rapid kisses over her eyes, cheeks and throat, she stretched up to run her hands through his thick dark hair.

Knowing Rhys wanted her as much as she desired him, all her apprehension disappeared. She wanted to prolong their lovemaking, so that she could remember each caress, every moment of ecstasy. In a few days' time he would be back at sea, and then, for them both, there would only be memories.

As he began to undo the fastenings at the neck of her dress her nervousness returned. Supposing she had been wrong! Her memories of those wonderful moments in his arms, that had filled her thoughts during all these months of separation, may have been just a figment of her imagination. And could she please him?

Waves of panic made her limbs tremble.

From downstairs came the muffled sound of merry-making and she longed to be there amongst it, putting off the moment she wanted so much yet which now she was afraid to experience.

'There's still people about ... in the house,' she whispered agitatedly.

'They won't come up here . . . they won't disturb us,' he assured her softly, his breath warm on her cheek as his mouth sought hers.

Gently but confidently, he removed her dress. His lips burned into her skin as they travelled down the nape of her neck to her bare shoulders. When he crushed her hungrily against the hardness of his body she was taken by surprise and allowed herself to be pressed down on to the bed without any further resistance.

4

'So you're off to North Wales for your honeymoon! There's lucky you are,' Alice Roberts smiled enviously as she watched Eleanor filling a brown-fibre suitcase with clothes.

Overcome by curiosity about Eleanor and Rhys, she had slipped away from the pub when they had closed at midday on Sunday, the day following Rhys and Eleanor's wedding, and paid a surprise visit to the Greenfords.

'I've never been on a real holiday before,' Eleanor told her, starry-eyed and bubbling with excitement.

'You've been to Pontypridd to stay with your Betty.'

'Not quite the same thing now, is it,' Eleanor laughed.

'And you are going to visit Rhys's family?'

'We'll be *staying* with them.' Her violet eyes widened, 'I'm scared stiff! Supposing they don't like me.'

'Bit late for them to find out,' Alice joked, her green eyes glinting with amusement. 'They should have come to the wedding, and then when Father O'Neil asked if anyone had any reason to object they could have spoken up.'

'Alice, don't! Supposing they had done that! I would have died of shame.'

'Well, they didn't, did they? And they are probably just as worried about having you to stay as you are of meeting them. Once they see that you haven't got two heads, and that when you stop shaking you are really quite nice, they'll lose their hearts to you just as Rhys has done.'

'You're making fun of me again, aren't you?'

'No I'm not. Your trouble is that you are far too shy. Instead of creeping into your shell, why don't you try to meet people half-way? Be bold.'

'I'll try. I wish you were coming with us.'

'Rhys would like that, I'm sure. Where is he, by the way?

'He's gone to find out the time of the train. It seems we change at Chester and get a train from there to North Wales. I've never heard of the place where his parents live. Its right up in the mountains, near the slate quarries where his Dad and brothers all work.'

'It sounds a bit like Pontypridd, so you should feel at home.'

'It's meeting his family that I'm worried about . . .'

'Don't start on that all over again. I've told you, speak up for yourself. You're as good as them. And just remember, Rhys picked you out of the whole world . . . and he didn't have to marry you either.'

A dark flush stained Eleanor's cheeks, her violet eyes sharpened as they met Alice's green gaze.

'You won't . . . you won't ever mention that other matter, will you, Alice?'

'I won't talk about it to a living soul, not even to Rhys . . .'

'Promise!' Eleanor pleaded, grabbing at Alice's arm.

'I've said I won't,' Alice answered tetchily. 'Forget it . . . I have.'

'I don't suppose I'll ever manage to do that,' Eleanor sighed. 'I'll carry the shame to the grave.'

'You are nutty,' Alice told her with a fond smile. 'Who would care, even if they knew? Most women have secrets of that sort but they don't dwell on them. Just forget it. When you married Rhys yesterday you wiped the slate clean and started a new life.'

Her guilty secret haunted Eleanor. She longed to tell Rhys, but she was afraid he might not understand her reasons for getting rid of the baby. He had come back to her, just as he had said he would, so he was bound to feel hurt that she hadn't trusted his word.

Rhys put her mood down to a mixture of excitement

and nervousness over visiting his family and did his best to reassure her.

Once they were on the train, Eleanor became totally absorbed by the view. As the great steam locomotive huffed and puffed its way to Newport and then northwards to Abergavenny, she sat entranced, her face glued to the window.

Then, as the rhythmic motion and noise of the train lulled her senses, she settled back against Rhys's shoulder and slept until they were pulling into Chester.

'We have almost an hour to wait for our next train so let's see if we can get something to eat,' he suggested.

The railway buffet was crowded but they managed to find two seats at a corner table. The hot meat pie and cup of strong tea revived them both. The rest of the journey seemed to pass all too quickly for Eleanor.

As the train slowed to a halt and Rhys lifted their case down from the luggage rack, she once more felt mingled dread and curiosity at the prospect of meeting his family.

Her premonition of doom increased as she stepped down on to the platform and looked around her. For a moment she couldn't understand what was different, then slowly she realised that everything was a bluish grey. It was as if they had left the sunshine behind in Cardiff and entered a massive grey cloud. The sky was dark and foreboding, and it was hard to tell where the sky ended and the grey stone buildings began. Their dark slate rooftops seemed to melt into the glowering sky, and disappear into a hazy mist.

'Here we are then, this is Blaenau Ffestiniog,' Rhys announced. 'The Llechwydd slate mine is about a mile up the road. It's only a hundred yards or so to the house,' he added as they started off down the hill.

With each step she took, Eleanor felt more and more depressed. Everywhere she looked was the same blue-greyness, not only the houses and garden walls but the road and pavements, fence posts, steps leading up to the fronts of the houses and even the signs over the shop fronts. And all around them, like an enormous protective barrier, shielding them from the rest of the world, were the towering mountains, their tops disappearing into the low grey cloud.

'You're cold! That's probably because you've been sitting down all day,' Rhys commented when she suddenly shivered uncontrollably. 'Soon be warm again once we get to the house and you've had a cup of tea.'

As Eleanor had expected, the house had a similar colour aura to the rest of her new surroundings. The only spark of colour was the front door. It had been painted in a vibrant shade of deep blue which even the film of fine grey dust couldn't dim completely.

'We're here, Mam,' Rhys called out, pushing open the unlocked door and leading the way into the dark narrow hallway.

As Eleanor entered the room at the back of the house she was conscious that it had the same blue-greyness as the outside world. Not only was the floor paved with huge slabs of grey slate but even the window sill was of polished slate. In front of the black range, with its shining steel fender, was a rag rug in varying shades of grey, the occasional splash of red on it looking like blobs of blood that had been accidentally spilled.

'Hello, then.' Rhys stood just inside the doorway looking round. 'This is Eleanor,' he said, pulling her forward.

No one spoke.

For what seemed an age, a sea of faces stared at her. Eleanor tried to say something but her voice choked in her throat. Now that her eyes were used to the gloom she saw that, in addition to Rhys's mother and father who were sitting on either side of the hearth, there were two younger men in the room. From their age and appearance she surmised they must be Rhys's brothers.

Mr Evans, a thin, craggy man with dark eyes and a severe, hard mouth, sat hunched forward, his bony hands outstretched to the red glow. Mrs Evans was an imposing bulky figure, her salt-and-pepper hair drawn back in a bun that emphasized her aquiline nose and pointed chin to a forbidding sharpness. Over her high-necked, grey dress she wore a spotless, lace-trimmed, white apron. Her blue eyes were shrewd and critical and Eleanor felt herself colouring under their scrutiny.

'We've just got off the train,' Rhys said, placing his brown trilby down on the table. 'Been travelling all day. A cup of tea would go down well.'

'I had better make you one, then.' His mother stood up, smoothing down her apron. 'You never said as you would be home again so soon,' she added reproachfully.

'Seeing you didn't feel you could make the journey to Cardiff I thought we ought to come up and see you all,' Rhys answered. 'I knew you would want to meet my new wife, just as Eleanor wanted to get to know all of you.'

'Better come and sit down,' one of the young men said, standing up and offering Eleanor his seat.

Eleanor settled herself on the straight-backed wooden chair, wondering what to say or do. The coldness of their welcome was plain and she longed to be back home in the warm heart of her own family. Alice's words 'they are as frightened of meeting you as you are of meeting them' echoed in her mind. As she looked up from under her lashes she knew that just wasn't true. These people were hostile not scared. They didn't like her and they were making no effort at all to hide the fact.

Covertly, she studied Rhys's two brothers. Both were thin, pasty-faced men with their mother's sharp nose and chin. The smaller of the two, the one who had offered her his chair, had a thin moustache and was smoking a cigarette in quick hard puffs as if angry or nervous.

She was wondering just how much longer they could remain so dour and silent when the front door swung open with a crash and a heavily pregnant girl of about her own age waddled in.

36

'Someone has just told me our Rhys is back again,' she exclaimed. Her round face beamed and her deep-set blue eyes shone with excitement. 'And you've brought your wife!'

Before Eleanor knew what was happening she found herself being hugged and kissed by the bubbly newcomer.

'This is my sister, Wynne,' Rhys explained. 'She got married last year ... and she hasn't wasted any time as you can see,' he grinned as he regarded her rotund shape.

'Baby's due next month,' Wynne smiled happily at Eleanor. 'Huw, that's my husband, wants a boy but I say it doesn't matter what we get just as long as it's healthy.'

'Did you want something, our Wynne?' Mrs Evans asked, coming into the room with the teapot in her hand.

'A cup of tea seeing as you've made one,' her daughter grinned. 'I was doing a bit of shopping and Gwynfryd Williams told me she had just seen our Rhys getting off the train. Said he was dressed up like a dog's dinner and that he had a smart young lady with him. I thought it must be Eleanor, so that is why I popped in.'

'Shouldn't you be at home getting your husband's tea on, my girl?'

'Huw is working overtime. Need the money, see,' she patted her extended stomach fondly. 'Surprising what the first one costs. No hand-me-downs, see. Have to buy everything new for it. Had quite a lot of things given me, mind. People always seem to make a fuss over the first. After that they have to take pot luck.'

Eleanor smiled and nodded understandingly. She felt an instant affinity with Rhys's sister, she was so friendly and warm.

Wynne's inconsequential chatter eased the atmosphere in the room and even Mrs Evans seemed more relaxed as she spread a white tablecloth and laid out cups and saucers, a plate of bread and butter, some home-made jam and a plate of bakestones.

'Pull up your chairs then,' she said as she poured tea into the cups, passing the first one over to her husband, who remained sitting by the fire.

Although she sat at the head of the table, Mrs Evans took nothing on to her own plate. She sat there watching, her glance resting frequently on Eleanor.

'Where are you sleeping tonight, then?' she asked Rhys as she refilled his cup.

He looked at her startled. 'I hadn't given it a thought. Here, I suppose.'

'Out of the question,' she said firmly, pursing her lips. 'We've no spare bed.'

'I sleep here when I come home other times,' Rhys said in surprise.

'Yes, but you share a room with Tudor and Hwyel. You can hardly do that now you have a wife,' his father stated.

'Couldn't we use Wynne's room?'

'It's Hywel's room now.'

'Well, couldn't he go back in with Tudor . . . just for a couple of nights?'

As Rhys looked questioningly at his brother, Eleanor saw Mr Evans shake his head signalling for him to refuse.

'Our Dad's boss,' Hwyel muttered uncomfortably. 'If he says no, then that's it.'

'But . . .' Rhys gazed in astonishment at his father. 'We only came so that you could meet Eleanor . . .'

'You should have let us know and asked if it was convenient,' Mr Evans said, giving him a long level look.

'Are you saying we're not welcome . . . that you don't want us to stay?' Rhys said, bewildered. 'But this is my home . . .'

'No, not any longer. You are a married man now, Rhys. You must fend for yourself.' Caradoc Evans took the stubby blackened briar pipe from his mouth as he turned from the fire. His dark eyes were unfathomable. He stared first at Eleanor and then at Rhys.

'This stopped being your home when you went away to sea,' he said vehemently. 'Come back to the mines and you can come home again, otherwise you are no son of mine.'

Having delivered his bald, uncompromising statement, he drew forcefully on his pipe and turned back to the fire, hunching his shoulders as if to shut out everyone in the room.

Eleanor looked down at her plate, blinking back her tears. How could they be so horrible to Rhys. She couldn't bear to see the hurt look on his face. He had been so eager for her to meet his family, so sure that they would welcome her with open arms, and instead they were treating him worse than they would have done a complete stranger.

An overwhelming sense of despair flooded over her. The excitement of seeing Rhys again, the frenzied preparations for their wedding, the excitement of the event itself, followed by the long tiring train journey had drained her.

She closed her eyes, trying to shut out the harsh grey atmosphere around her, and thought of her own soft feather bed in the room she had known all her life in Coburn Street. At that moment it would have been sheer bliss to find herself back there.

She looked across at Rhys, wondering what they would do now. Her precious savings were safely stitched inside her corsets. There was probably enough to pay for them to stay the night at a hotel. That is, if there was a hotel in Blaenau Ffestiniog. On their walk from the station, all she had seen had been rows and rows of grey terraced houses.

She opened her eyes, startled as Wynne pushed back her chair and said loudly and defiantly. 'You can come back to my place, our Rhys. There's a bed there for you and Eleanor.'

'That will do!' Caradoc Evans growled threateningly. 'You stay out of this. None of your business, my girl.'

'And what I do in my own home is none of yours, our Da. I've left home too, you know! Come on,' she turned to Eleanor with a warm smile. 'It's a tidy walk, so we had better be going or I won't have Huw's meal on the table when he gets home.'

5

As soon as Rhys went back to sea, Eleanor found herself reverting to her old routine, and at times she wondered if her marriage had been merely a figment of her imagination. Then she would look down at the gold band shining on her left hand, and remember the nights when she had lain in his arms, and feel a comforting sense of satisfaction.

She went back to St Joseph's wrapped in an aura of joy. Father O'Neil had at first voiced strong disapproval because one of their teachers was a married woman.

'In your case I suppose we can make an exception, seeing as how your man is away most of the time,' he admitted reluctantly. 'We'll have to wait and see how things go, though. I'm not promising anything. It depends on how often you are going to be asking for time off.'

'Rhys will be away for eight months, perhaps longer.'

'Now, is that so,' the old Irish priest murmured thoughtfully. 'Well, in that case, perhaps we can safely say you can stay on until the end of the school year in July. After that, it will depend on what the bishop thinks as well as what this new husband of yours decides he is going to do.'

'Rhys is talking of coming ashore for good when this trip is over. I do hope he does,' Eleanor said wistfully.

'Well, there you are then. There's no knowing where he will want to settle when he leaves the sea. He may even want to go back to his own home in North Wales.'

'I hope not. I would sooner stay in Cardiff.' Eleanor suppressed a shudder as she remembered the chilly greeting she had received at Rhys's home.

'You are a married woman now, Eleanor, so you will have no choice but to do your duty by your husband and go wherever he wants to live,' Father O'Neil told her gravely. 'All the same,' he went on thoughtfully, 'if you did settle here, then perhaps in time I could convert him and see that you both followed the true faith.'

He held up a hand as Eleanor was about to speak. 'We'll talk about it again, some other time.'

Her friendship with Alice was deeper than ever. She confided in Alice about the way the Evans family had greeted her, and Alice had been galled by their attitude.

'Pity you bothered to go all that way to see them,' she fumed. 'First and last time, eh?'

'Well, I don't know about that. Wynne was ever so nice. Even though her baby is due at any time she made us very welcome. And I quite liked her husband, Huw. Strange really, he was a quarry worker too, yet he was quite different. He was a warm, cheerful sort of man. He didn't sit brooding or staring into the fire, he laughed and joked about things.'

'The others sound a right lot of old miseries,' Alice laughed. 'It's a good thing Rhys left home before he got like them.'

'He went to sea because he couldn't bear the thought of spending the rest of his life working in the slate quarries. And now that I've been up there I can understand how he feels.' She suppressed a shiver. 'I can't explain it, Alice, but just everything was grey. The sky, the sides of the mountains, the houses and even the people. There was a grey dust everywhere. And they used slate for everything. Roofs, doorsteps, even the garden fences! I couldn't live there.'

'You'd better persuade Rhys to stay at sea then, and you can go on living here in Cardiff.'

'What good would that do, I should never see him. No, when he comes home next summer I want him to get a shore job, so that we can settle down in a place of our own, like other married couples.'

By Christmas, Eleanor knew that she was once again pregnant, and she didn't know whether to be pleased or dismayed.

'Rhys won't be home until about June, we'll have no time at all together,' she grumbled, as she told Alice.

'He'll certainly see a change in you,' Alice chuckled. 'He leaves a slim young bride behind and comes back to find a wife who is the size of a house.'

'Do you think I should warn him or let it be a surprise?'

'An awful shock you mean. Tell him now, and at least he'll have time to get used to the idea.'

'Supposing he doesn't want children. Mind you, he did seem happy that his sister was having a baby.'

'Not his responsibility though, was it?' Alice commented sagely. 'I'd tell him right away if it was me. You should have done so last time.'

'Alice, you promised we'd never mention that again,' Eleanor said sharply, the colour draining from her face, leaving it pinched and drawn.

'I wouldn't . . . not to anyone else,' Alice assured her.

'I don't want it mentioned, ever again . . . not even between us,' Eleanor snapped.

'Have you told your mother this time?'

'Not yet, give me a chance. I'll wait another month, until I am completely sure.'

'You'd better tell her as soon as possible, just in case things don't go as they should,' Alice warned, her wide mouth tightening.

'What do you mean?' Eleanor asked in alarm.

'You don't want to talk about it,' Alice retorted with a shrug.

Fear gripped Eleanor's heart like a cold hand but she said no more. Alice was making mountains out of molehills and she refused to play along. Nevertheless, when she began to feel sick as she got out of bed each morning and found herself unable to eat any breakfast, and waves of nausea assailing her at odd hours during the day, she remembered Alice's ominous warning.

Mrs Greenford made light of Eleanor's condition. She had borne four children herself and already had eight grandchildren, so the thought of one more filled her neither with excitement nor misgivings.

'First babies can be troublesome,' she told her youngest daughter. 'Still, they do say that if you are sick and feel bad early on then you have an easy time when it comes to the birth.'

'Did I ought to go and see the doctor?'

'Whatever for? Having a baby isn't an illness. Go and see him when it quickens, not before.'

'When is that?'

'At about four and a half months. You'll soon know when it starts to move.'

'But I keep feeling sick . . . and faint.'

Mrs Greenford nodded her head understandingly. 'That's the way of it, I'm afraid. Try loosening off your corsets, that may help. It's early days yet, you're often sick in the mornings for the first two or three months. After that things go well enough, just as long as you don't go lifting anything heavy.'

'Do you think I should tell Father O'Neil?'

'Give it a while,' her mother frowned. 'You won't start to show until you are about five months gone, not with the first.'

'But he will need time to find a replacement teacher.'

'Well, tell him at the end of the Christmas term. That should give him plenty of time. You won't need to stop work until Easter.'

'You . . . you're not cross, our Mam?' Eleanor asked hesitantly.

'Cross! Why should I be cross? That's what you get married for isn't it, to have children,' her mother said in surprise.

'And it will be all right to go on living here until Rhys gets fixed up with a shore job?'

'Stay here as long as you want to.' Mrs Greenford gathered Eleanor into the warmth of her arms and hugged her. 'Be lovely having a baby about the place again. Our Gwen's lot are growing up so quickly, even young Bronwen is walking, and with Betty being in Pontypridd I don't see much of her three. John's wife has her own mother to help with baby Glyn, so it will be like old times to have a row of nappies blowing on the line.'

The rest of the family seemed to share their mother's delight at the news. They were full of advice about what Eleanor should and should not do. They also offered to help out by loaning her a crib, and a pram, and some of their own babies' outgrown clothes. Remembering what Wynne had said about the cost of providing everything new for a first baby, Eleanor accepted their offers gratefully.

She found it comforting to be able to talk to them about the symptoms she was experiencing. Alice was a wonderful friend but she had no practical knowledge about what having a baby entailed. All her information was based on what she had read or picked up from other people.

'I still think you ought to tell the doctor, or your mother, about your abortion,' Alice insisted, when Eleanor seemed to have more and more discomfort as her pregnancy advanced.

'I thought we agreed never to mention that ever again,' Eleanor scowled, reaching for a cushion to wedge against the small of her back to ease the terrible aching.

'I'm sure you shouldn't be having this much discomfort,' Alice persisted doggedly.

'What do you know about it?' Eleanor snapped.

'Not as much as you,' her friend agreed. 'I know one thing, if I looked like you then I'd be off to the doctor in two shakes. Have you looked in a mirror lately? If Rhys was to walk in here now he wouldn't recognize you.'

'I'm not all that big,' Eleanor protested.

'I'm not talking about the size of you, I'm talking about how haggard and drawn you look. Anyone would think you were about forty.'

'Thanks very much, you're a great help,' Eleanor snapped.

'Well, it's the truth and it is time someone told you. Pregnant women are supposed to look positively blooming. You look the opposite, and if your family don't tell you then I'm the only person left to do so.'

'I'm tired because I'm still teaching,' Eleanor muttered.

'About time you gave up then, isn't it?'

'I'm going to at the end of the month.'

'Three weeks away! You're asking for trouble, so don't say I didn't warn you.'

'When I stop work, I'll have a lie in every morning, and rest for two hours every afternoon. I won't even travel on any bumpy old trams down to Tiger Bay. If you want to see me you will have to come to Coburn Street.'

'Now you're talking sense,' Alice laughed. 'I'm going to see you keep to that,' she vowed.

Even the enforced rest didn't seem to help. Eleanor was in constant discomfort. Her back ached whether she was lying down or standing up. She couldn't sit for more than ten minutes without being seized either with pains or cramps. Anything other than the very plainest of foods made her feel sick. She would waken with a headache that grew worse as the day progressed, until in the end there was nothing for it but to go to bed with a vinegar compress on her forehead. She would lie there in the darkened room feeling sorry for herself and wondering how she was ever going to get through the next few months.

Rhys had sounded pleased by her news but he knew nothing of how she was suffering. His letters took a long time in coming, and similarly hers took ages to reach him, so she said nothing about the many discomforts for fear of worrying him. Instead she prayed for his return.

He had said he would be home about the end of June. As the warm spring days advanced into early summer she began to mark off the days. Now that it was warmer and she was able to sit outside in the small strip of backyard, she felt considerably brighter. The sun's heat seemed to ease some of her aches. As her eighth month of pregnancy drew to its close she looked brown and in reasonable health, although her face and neck were still thinner than they should have been.

Alice was a regular visitor. After the pub closed at three o'clock she would catch a tram from the Pier Head to Cathays and arrive hot and breathless. She brought her lunch with her, and insisted on sharing it with Eleanor.

Sometimes it was freshly baked bread and a wedge of tasty cheese. Other times it would be a meat pie, still hot when she arrived. She always brought some fruit to tempt Eleanor's appetite. Strawberries when they were in season, bananas, oranges, and once a luscious pineapple that a sailor had brought into the pub.

Picnicking in the sunshine and listening to Alice's cheery chatter became something Eleanor looked forward to. And, also, Alice always had the very latest shipping news.

'This time next week *The Magpie* should be putting into dock,' Alice told her towards the end of June.

'I don't think I can bear the thought of Rhys seeing me like this,' Eleanor puffed. It was a roasting hot day and, even in the loose-fitting pink smock that she wore to try and conceal her bulk, she was hot and uncomfortable.

'Just look at my ankles! They're the double the size they should be.' She extended her legs in their broad-fitting, low-heeled shoes for Alice's inspection.

'My God! What does the doctor say?'

Alice leaned forward and gingerly touched the shining skin, horrified as her fingers made a deep indentation, as though she had pressed them into dough. 'Surely they shouldn't be like that!'

'There is something wrong with my kidneys, or so the doctor said.'

'Can't he do anything about it?'

'It will go right by itself once the baby is born,' Eleanor told her complacently. 'That's why I've had so much backache lately.'

'Are you sure?' Alice asked, chewing uneasily on her lower lip.

Meeting the accusing gleam in her friend's green eyes, Eleanor looked away quickly.

'Don't start on about that again, Alice,' she said belligerently. 'You promised . . .'

'I know I did, and I won't go back on my word. I do think you should tell your doctor about the abortion, though. It's not fair on him. If he knew the whole story he might be able to do something more to help you.'

'It's not worth bothering about it now,' Eleanor said stubbornly. 'Another week or so, and the baby will be here.'

'The doctor wouldn't say anything to your mother,' Alice persisted. 'They take an oath, the same as a priest . . .'

'I've never told Father O'Neil,' Eleanor muttered miserably.

'I thought you trusted him.'

'No, not over this. I don't trust anyone . . .' she raised her head and stared fixedly at Alice. 'Except you. You are the only other person in the world that knows what happened . . . and you've promised.'

'I know,' Alice sighed. 'I won't let you down.'

A week later she was to regret her promise.

6

Some people said it was the hottest July on record. Eleanor lay on top of her bed, lethargic and bathed in sweat. Her swollen body seemed to be one gigantic ache. Twinges radiated from her spine, down her legs and arms as though she was in the clutches of some gigantic octopus.

Mrs Greenford looked in from time to time to renew the cold compresses on her forehead and to bring her cool drinks.

When Gwen had called earlier that morning she had begged her mother to send for the doctor.

'I don't like the look of our Eleanor, not one little bit,' she said anxiously when she came back downstairs. She took her own baby, Bronwen, from her mother and sat down on the sofa, holding the two-year-old on her lap.

'She's been like that for days. Just lying there with her eyes closed,' Mrs Greenford confided. 'Our Betty came all the way from Pontypridd at the beginning of the week to see her and Eleanor could barely make the effort to talk to her. Betty had young Chris with her and you know what a little imp he is. The noise he made nearly drove Eleanor mad. I brought him on downstairs and left Betty up there with her for a few minutes but she didn't say much.'

'No, all I can get out of her is that she wants Rhys to come home before the baby is born.'

'I know,' Mrs Greenford sighed. 'After Betty went home, Eleanor just lay there with her hands clamped over her ears and tears streaming down her face.'

'Has she had any labour pains?' Gwen asked anxiously.

'Not that she's said. Mind you, she seems to be in some sort of pain most of the time, so I doubt if she would know if she had gone into labour or not.'

'I think you should send for the doctor. It can't do any harm to let him have a look at her.'

The doctor's reaction was swift. Within the hour an ambulance had arrived and Eleanor was taken off to hospital.

Mrs Greenford was beside herself with worry. There had been no word from Rhys for almost a month. *The Magpie* should have docked sometime in June. She knew Alice had told Eleanor that his ship had been delayed by engine trouble but even that had been several weeks ago.

Unable to settle at home, Mrs Greenford decided to go and see Alice and her mother and tell them what had happened.

She arrived just after three, as the last customer was leaving. Mrs Roberts took her through to the living room at the back where the kettle was singing on the hearth.

'It is wonderful to see you, Susan,' Mrs Roberts enthused. 'You are just in time to have a bite to eat with us. I keep meaning to come and visit you but I never seem to find the time. I'm rushed off my feet when we are open. All I can think of is taking my shoes off and having a bit of a rest in the afternoon before it's time to open up again.'

'I came to let Alice know the latest news about Eleanor.'

'Oh! Has she had the baby?'

'Not yet. They . . . they've taken her to hospital.'

'Alice said she was having it at home,' Mrs Roberts commented as she bustled around, laying out food on the pristine white cloth she had spread on the table in front of the window.

'Pull up your chair, Susan,' she invited. She reached down a tea-caddy from the mantelpiece and spooned some of the contents into a teapot and poured the boiling water over it.

'Nothing for me,' Susan Greenford held up a hand. 'I must be getting back.'

'You may as well have a bite and a cup of tea while we talk. I bet you have had nothing since breakfast time.'

Susan Greenford smiled dismissively. 'That's true enough. Not much appetite, I'm too worried about our Eleanor.'

'You still need food to keep your own strength up,' Emily Roberts told her firmly. 'Come on now, sit over there opposite me and we can eat and talk at the same time.'

'I thought Rhys was a nice enough young chap,' she said conversationally, as Susan seemed to hesitate.

'Oh he's all right, I suppose. I've not seen enough of him really to get to know him. They went off to see his family in North Wales right after the wedding.'

'But Eleanor seems happy enough?'

'Lonely.'

'That's understandable. Good job she is still living at home with you. Come along now,' Emily Roberts cut a wedge of cheese, buttered a chunk of bread and placed a spoonful of pickle on the plate alongside it, 'you must try and eat something.'

'I think I need the tea more than food,' Susan smiled.

'Would you like something with it . . . a drop of whisky or brandy?'

'No, of course not. This is fine.'

'Right, here you are then.' Emily poured a cup and pushed it across the table.

'Is Alice not in? I came to see if she knew when Rhys's ship might dock. It seems she told Eleanor that it was held up by engine trouble, but she didn't say which port they had put into. I thought I might get her to come down to the shipping office with me and see if there was any way we could get a message to Rhys.'

'She should be back any minute. She went up to the Hayes to do some shopping. Come on, eat up, and have another cup of tea. She might be home again by then.'

The hot tea and food not only revived Susan but helped to calm her.

'I ought to be getting home. I suppose I should have

gone to see Eleanor, not come down here on a wild goose chase,' she reasoned.

'I tell you what,' Emily Roberts beamed, her florid face full of concern, 'you go to the hospital, that will put your mind at rest. As soon as Alice gets back I'll send her down to the shipping office to see if they can get a message to Rhys.'

'If his ship has engine trouble . . .'

'They might be able to get him on to another one. Leave it to Alice. She has a way with her, that girl. Now go on with you!'

The visit to the hospital did anything but set Susan Greenford's mind at rest. The long antiseptic corridors filled her with foreboding. The directions from the man on the reception desk were so rambling that in her confused state it took Susan a long time to find the right ward.

'You can't see her,' the Sister on duty told Susan sharply. 'She is much too ill to have visitors.'

'Couldn't I just peep through the doors, just to set my mind at rest,' Susan pleaded.

'Quite impossible. She has been taken into the delivery room and only staff are allowed in there. Come back later this evening and we may have some news for you.'

'But is everything going all right?'

'She's having a baby. Surely you must know what that means,' the Sister replied tartly.

'I do. I've had four of my own, and eight grandchildren, so I know all about having babies,' Susan flared, her blue eyes shooting fire. 'All my babies have been born at home, so I can't understand the need for her being brought in here.'

'In this case there are complications. Perhaps if you had told your doctor a few months ago that your daughter had had an abortion, things would have turned out differently,' the Sister snapped, giving Susan a withering look.

'An abortion!'

All the way home Susan Greenford tried to make sense of what she had been told. It couldn't be true. Eleanor was such a quiet God-fearing girl, she couldn't have kept something like that a secret. And who could the father have been?

As the tram lumbered along Cathedral Road she tried to recall the last time Eleanor had been off-colour. Apart from school holidays, she had never taken a single day away from St Joseph's.

When she left the tram and began to walk along Salisbury Road towards Coburn Street, her bewilderment was replaced by anger. They had made a mistake at the hospital. They must have been talking about someone else. It couldn't have been her Eleanor. She should have insisted on seeing her.

The empty house was depressing. Susan went up to her daughter's room as if expecting to find some sort of answer there. The room was neat and tidy, except for the unmade bed, but oppressively hot.

She opened the window, then sat down, gently rocking the wooden crib with her foot. Why couldn't Eleanor have had her baby here, just as they'd planned? Everything was ready and waiting for it, she thought, staring at the mound of white nappies, the lace-trimmed baby gowns and the white shawl she had finished crocheting only a few evenings earlier.

Niggling doubts now replaced her anger and she began to accept that something was wrong. The aches and pains Eleanor had complained about all the time she had been pregnant, and the way her feet and legs had swelled up, weren't natural. She hadn't looked too well for months.

Gwen and Betty had both been the picture of health right through each of their pregnancies. They'd put on weight, but then that was only to be expected. She had herself with each of her own babies. Most women did, that was Nature's way.

Yet Eleanor had seemed to get thinner, her face and neck quite gaunt, except for her legs which had swollen enormously, Mrs Greenford thought worriedly.

By the time Alice called, she had worked herself into a frenzy. When she started going into details about what they had said at the hospital, Alice was in too much of a rush to stay and listen. Afterwards, Susan wondered if Alice knew more than she was telling.

The abortion!

Of course, that was it, she thought aghast. Alice knew something about what had happened. Her mind worked overtime as she brooded about all the implications. If Alice knew, then was Rhys to blame? Had Eleanor been pregnant before they were married!

Struggling to keep calm, she tried to remember if Eleanor had been ill during the past year. One minor touch of flu around Whitsun but that hadn't amounted to much. She had looked washed out for two or three weeks afterwards but . . .

Her thoughts were cut short by her husband's homecoming. He listened gravely to her outpourings.

'Leave my meal until later,' he told her. 'I'll get washed and changed and we'll both go back to the hospital.'

There was a different Sister in charge of the ward.

'It's providence you've come,' she told them, 'she's been asking for you.'

As they followed her prim starched figure down the ward, James took Susan's hand in his, giving it a reassuring squeeze.

Eleanor lay flat in the bed, her face drained of colour, huge black circles under her eyes.

'Hello Mam!' She smiled weakly. 'Have you seen the baby? It's a girl.'

'Not yet,' Susan told her, taking her hand. 'I didn't even know it had been born,' she added gently.

'She's lovely. Dark hair like Rhys. You never told me

there would be so much pain, though,' she sighed tremulously.

'Your Da is here,' Susan said softly, moving aside to let her husband come nearer to the bed.

Again Eleanor's bloodless lips parted in a feeble smile.

'Rhys . . . where is Rhys . . ?' she whispered, with a small catch of breath.

'His boat hasn't docked yet. Alice promised to go to the shipping office and see if they can get a message to him.'

'He won't get here in time . . . not now.'

Her hoarse whisper seemed to hang on the air as her body quivered and then went still.

Susan Greenford felt a terrible foreboding. She looked up at her husband, silently imploring him to do something. For a moment he seemed unaware of what had happened. Then, when he spoke to Eleanor and there was no response and he saw the tears flooding down his wife's face, he swept aside the curtain and shouted for the Sister.

'At least you got here in time,' the Sister said gently as she checked Eleanor's pulse and then pulled the sheet up over her face.

'You mean you expected her to die?' James Greenford groaned. His hazel eyes darkened as he stared at the Sister disbelievingly. He clenched and unclenched his massive hands in a paroxysm of anguish.

'There were complications. As we explained to Mrs Greenford, if we had known that your daughter had . . .'

'I haven't had time to talk to my husband,' Susan interrupted. 'We came here the moment he got home from work. I'll tell him all about it later.'

'Why can't I hear it now?' James Greenford protested stubbornly.

'It will make no difference, not now,' Susan said sorrowfully. 'There were problems . . . women's troubles, not something you talk about openly.'

'You mean you knew she would have difficulties in having a baby . . .' James Greenford looked bewildered.

'Not until it was too late. Come on,' she slipped her arm through his, pulling him away from the bedside. 'We had better be going home.'

'There will be funeral arrangements to be made, and there are papers to be signed,' the Sister reminded them.

'Can they wait until tomorrow? We'll come back first thing,' Susan said wearily.

'And what about the baby?'

Susan and James Greenford exchanged troubled looks. They had both been so concerned about Eleanor that neither of them had given thought to the baby.

'If there is no one to take the baby we can transfer her into a home. Later on we can make arrangements for her to be adopted.'

'You can do what?'

James Greenford's roar of anger had heads turning. Susan laid a restraining hand on his arm but he shook it away irritably.

'You kill my daughter and now you want to rob me of my grandchild,' he yelled. 'What was wrong with her that brought all this on. Childbirth is natural, a God-given right. There shouldn't be any complications, not unless you lot in here bungled things.'

'James, James. Let's go. They did all they could,' Susan implored, clutching his arm and trying to pull him away.

Her lips trembling, she frowned at the Sister, shaking her head, silently pleading with her not to say more.

She didn't want her husband to know that Eleanor had already had an abortion, not yet anyway. Some day she might tell him, when the hurt of losing Eleanor had passed, but not now.

'If you wish to collect the baby, then come back tomorrow. Bring in her clothes any time after midday. You will have to see the Almoner. There will be papers to be signed.'

Susan nodded her agreement but she felt overwhelmed with the enormity of what they would be taking on. She and James were both in their sixties, much too old to start bringing up a baby. Right from the start, it would have to be bottle-fed so there might well be problems rearing it.

The thought of endless sleepless nights, from now until it had finished teething, was daunting. And there would be nappies to change and wash, the ironing and starching of tiny baby clothes, as well as constant care and attention.

Yet, they couldn't let Eleanor's baby go into a home or be adopted by strangers. Gwen and Betty both had toddlers of their own so it wouldn't be fair to expect them to take on another baby.

She was so immersed in her own problems that when they reached home she didn't recognize the man pacing restlessly to and fro in the street outside their house. Not until he grabbed her by the arm, his grey eyes flint-sharp with anguish.

'Rhys!' Her heart contracted with pain. If only he had got there sooner Eleanor might have rallied after her ordeal.

'How is Eleanor? Where is she? One of your neighbours said the hospital . . .'

The words poured out in a torrent. Rhys was under such strain that he was almost incoherent.

'You are too late!'

'I came the moment we docked . . .'

'You might as well go back again, our Eleanor doesn't need you now,' James Greenford barked, his mouth a hard uncompromising line.

Rhys stared at his father-in-law uncomprehendingly, but the older man offered no word of explanation. His massive shoulders were bowed as he turned and went into the house.

Rhys looked so bewildered and dejected that Susan felt sorry for him. It was not his fault that things had gone so

57

wrong. Or was it? If it was true that Eleanor had already had an abortion, then surely Rhys must have been responsible. She wondered if he knew. She sighed. It wasn't something she could ask straight out.

'You'd better come inside,' she told him as she followed her husband into the house.

'When can I see Eleanor? Which hospital is she in?' Rhys asked impatiently as he followed her into the back living room.

'I expect you could do with a cup of tea. I know we both could,' Susan murmured. She moved the big iron kettle from the trivet in front of the fire over the glowing coals.

'I won't stop. I'd sooner go and see Eleanor right away.'

'Sit down. There's no hurry. She won't be going anywhere,' James Greenford muttered bitterly as he slumped into his armchair.

'She'll be wanting to see me. Alice left a message to say it was urgent.' He looked from one to the other. 'What about the baby . . . has she had it?'

'Yes, but we haven't seen it yet,' Susan Greenford said quietly. 'Tomorrow, we're fetching it home.'

'Tomorrow! They're letting them out that soon?' His grey eyes brightened. 'I thought she would have to stay in hospital for at least a week, perhaps longer.'

'It's just the baby we'll be bringing home,' Susan Greenford said, searching desperately for the right words to break the terrible news about Eleanor.

'You may as well tell him, he's got to know sooner or later,' James Greenford growled resentfully.

'Know what?' His grey gaze searched their faces hungry for news. 'Is anything wrong?'

'Eleanor . . . Eleanor didn't recover from the birth,' Susan Greenford said her voice breaking.

Rhys sat stunned.

There was an uneasy stillness in the room, emphasized

by the ticking of the clock on the mantelpiece. James Greenford was staring into the fire as if he couldn't bear to look at his son-in-law. Susan Greenford pleated and re-pleated a corner of the red chenille cloth that covered the table, sniffing back her tears.

With an effort, she finally rose to her feet and began to brew the tea. The rattle of the china as she laid out the cups and saucers splintered the silence.

'When?'

'When what?' Susan Greenford's face looked pinched and drawn and she seemed to have shrunk into a small round ball.

'When . . . when did it happen? When did Eleanor . . . ?' Rhys hesitated, stumbling over the words. He shrugged helplessly. He couldn't bring himself to say 'die'.

'This afternoon,' James Greenford told him. 'We saw her just before the end . . . she was asking for you. She wanted *you*, not *us*,' he added bitterly.

'And the baby . . . what is it?'

'A girl. They wanted to put her out for adoption. My grandchild!' His voice became an agonized growl. 'Over my dead body!' He slapped a giant fist into the palm of his other hand. 'We're going back in the morning to get her. They killed our Eleanor but they're not going to take her baby from us.'

7

The train journey to North Wales was torture for Rhys. Sitting there hour after hour, staring out unseeingly at the countryside flashing past the window, his thoughts were of the same journey he had made less than a year ago. Only that time Eleanor had been with him.

He still couldn't accept that she was dead. The grim funeral had seemed a mockery. Her family had regarded him with such hostility. As if he was to blame! Even Alice, who had always been so warm and friendly towards him, had seemed bitter and withdrawn.

It probably hadn't helped that Eleanor's baby had been kept in the hospital. When he had gone with his mother-in-law to collect it the next morning they had been told that it had a respiratory infection and would need specialized nursing for a week or so.

They had taken him to see the baby but he found it hard to believe that he was now a father. The baby was long and thin, with a blotched face and a shock of very dark hair. Its eyes had been tight shut, as if it refused to come to terms with the world.

He had found himself unable to discuss the baby or its future with Eleanor's parents. That was why he was going home. He wanted to talk things over with someone close to him. He needed advice from his own family, not from strangers.

'Back again already!' his mother exclaimed in surprise when he walked in. 'Where is your wife, then? Hasn't she come with you?' she asked sharply, sensing trouble.

She had thought a lot about Eleanor and decided that, though she was pleasant and pretty, she was not the right wife for Rhys. She had thought her prissy and certainly not good enough for her son. There were plenty of lovely girls in Blaenau Ffestiniog who would have jumped at the chance of marrying Rhys. They were girls who spoke the Welsh and whose families had been born and bred amongst the mountains. Eleanor was a city girl, a stranger.

'No, Mam, Eleanor's not with me. She won't be coming again . . . ever.'

'You mean she has left you!' There was dread in her voice. Her judgement had been right after all.

'I suppose you could say that. Eleanor is dead! She's left me a daughter though.'

'*Marw! Duw! Beth digwdd?*'

Gwyneth Evans was so taken aback that her words 'Dead! My God! What happened?' came automatically in Welsh.

'She died giving birth to our daughter.'

'And the baby?' Her mouth was pursed, her blue eyes shrewd and wary.

'She's still at the hospital. I don't know what I am going to do about her. They talked of adoption . . .' his voice choked and faded.

'That might be the best thing . . . poor little soul. Well, we couldn't have it here,' she added defensively. 'House full of men this is, no room for a young baby, and a girl at that.'

Rhys passed a hand through his dark hair. 'No,' he agreed, 'I suppose not. I did wonder if our Wynne . . .'

'Don't you go lumbering another baby on to her,' his mother said sharply. 'She's like putty, agree to anything. She has more than enough to do looking after the one she has. No, with you at sea, the best thing is to have it adopted. That way you will be sure it gets a good home.'

'It's a baby, for God's sake, not a dog we're talking about,' Rhys said heatedly. 'It's your granddaughter!'

'A dog would be less trouble. Could always have it put

down if we found it too much trouble,' Mrs Evans stated emphatically. 'No. Your Da would never agree to the baby coming here. We've brought up one family and that's enough. Anyway, I've enough to do looking after three men.'

'Well, that's it then.' Rhys stood up, his face a grim mask. 'You will let Dad and the boys know about Eleanor . . . and the baby?'

'I'll tell them, though I don't suppose it will interest them overmuch.'

'You're a hard lot,' he said, staring at her angrily. 'Your own grandchild and you are not even interested in what happens to her. I'll not forget this in a hurry.'

He walked away from the terraced house that had been his home, vowing silently that he would never return there. He felt too enraged even to go and see his sister, Wynne.

His determined strides took him towards the steep Crimea Pass. As he climbed, he looked down on the grey slate town he was leaving behind him and felt as though he was physically severing his bond with Blaenau Ffestiniog.

Near the top of the pass, he took the Betws-y-Coed road. A few miles outside the town he struck off left, taking the track at the foot of Moel Siabod that led towards the Snowdon ridge.

It was the sort of bright, clear day he loved. As he approached the towering range, wispy clouds were pirouetting around the peaks. And, as always, he found that the awe-inspiring grandeur put his own problems into perspective. As he trudged up the Pyg track, breathing deeply of the clean sharp air, feeling the heat of the July sun on his back, he tried to come to terms with Eleanor's death.

He found it hard to believe that he would never again be able to stroke her softly waving hair or see the warmth and love in her deep amethyst eyes. She had been his ideal woman, radiating kindliness and charm.

It had been these very qualities, the opposite to those of

her friend Alice, that had first attracted him. He had grown up surrounded by girls who were dark-haired and dark-eyed. Eleanor's fair prettiness had captivated him from the first moment he had seen her.

Her warmth and gentleness had been bonus qualities. Her sweet voice rang in his head when he was on solitary watch at sea. He remembered her wisdom and her light-hearted banter but, above all, he remembered how soft and desirable she was when he held her in his arms.

Those moments had been too few. A brief interlude two years ago, moments which he had remembered vividly, again and again, as he traversed the world. Then his home-coming and his incredible good fortune to find her still waiting, still wanting him.

Asking her to marry him had been the most impulsive thing he'd ever done. After a year's separation they hardly knew one another. It could have been disastrous. The mental image he carried could have been a figment of his imagination, a dream conjured up in the dark watches of the night.

Their honeymoon had been brief but they had enjoyed every minute spent together. Taking her to North Wales could have ruined everything, since Wynne had been the only one to hold out a welcoming hand. The few days spent with Wynne and Huw at their cottage had proved unforgettable.

Eleanor had been awed by the grandeur of Snowdon and the Glyders, intrigued by the legend of Moel Hebog, spell-bound by the beauty of the waterfalls and lakes. Looking at it all through Eleanor's eyes had given him a new insight into the land he loved.

Their honeymoon had been brief, yet he had not been disappointed. He had found she exceeded even his wildest expectations. When his leave ended, he had gone back to sea brimming with contentment, anxious to complete the trip and then find a shore job so that they could spend more time together.

When Eleanor had written telling him that she was expecting their child he could hardly put pen to paper for excitement. The wonderment of it all filled his thoughts night and day.

His frustration when they had been delayed in Tangiers with engine trouble had been so great that he had planned to jump ship. He had tried desperately to find another vessel bound for Cardiff, Liverpool or any other British port. His plans thwarted, he had been forced to contain his impatience and wait for *The Magpie* to be repaired.

He hadn't even felt apprehensive when he found Alice's message waiting for him. He merely surmised that, because the baby was almost due, Eleanor was anxious to see him. She would hardly venture down to Tiger Bay in her condition, so it seemed natural that the summons should come from Alice.

Alice should have warned him what to expect, he thought angrily. He was still puzzled by her attitude towards him. She had seemed delighted by their decision to marry, yet at Eleanor's funeral she had seemed distant, reluctant to be seen talking to him. Another one who blamed him for what had happened to Eleanor, he thought morosely.

The few brief words they had exchanged had been guarded and she had avoided his eyes. It was almost as if she was covering up some guilty secret and he wondered if there was something he hadn't been told. He resolved to go and see her as soon as he got back to Cardiff.

He sat down on the scrub turf that edged the side of the track and stared moodily at the scene around him. Snowdon towered in awesome grandeur. Away to the left, the undulating land rose in craggy peaks, while immediately below him was the grey blue of a lake and in the distance he could see the sprawl of Blaenau Ffestiniog and the harsh grey stains where the slate quarry cut into the green apron of the mountainside.

The old feeling of resentment against those responsible for such desecration flared up anew. For every ton of finished slate that left the mines, at least fifteen tons of waste were left behind.

His hatred of the mine-owners, of his father and brothers for helping to create such slag heaps, seethed in his mind and began mingling with his hostility towards those who had let Eleanor die, until he found himself in the grip of a cold, shaking fury.

A sudden gust of wind warned him that a summer storm was about to break. He looked up to see that the top of Snowdon was wreathed in rain clouds. Knowing the mood of the mountain range, he set off downhill, slithering and sliding over the loose shale.

It wasn't until he was almost at the base of the mountain, drenched by raindrops the size of pennies, that he remembered he hadn't even brought a change of clothes with him. It hadn't seemed necessary since he had been expecting to stay with his parents and knew he already had plenty of clothes there. Now, after their bitter exchange of words and his mother's complete lack of sympathy or understanding about his situation, he couldn't bring himself to go back there.

He wondered if Wynne would put him up for the night and decided it was worth a try.

Wynne was overjoyed to see him.

'Just look at you! Like a drowned rat. Come along in and peel that lot off before you catch pneumonia.'

Shivering, he huddled over the fire trying to dry his wet hair with the towel she handed him.

'Never did have enough sense to come in out of the rain, did you, boyo?' she teased as she came back into the room with a bundle of Huw's clothes in her arms. 'Probably look like a scarecrow in these, trousers half-way up your legs and a shirt big enough to go round you twice. Still, they'll do while I dry your things out and no one's going to see you.'

'While you are getting changed, I'll fetch Trevor. He's about due for a feed. You haven't seen him yet, have you?'

She was back in a few minutes, a wriggling chubby bundle in her arms. 'Here,' she handed the squirming baby to Rhys. 'Hold on to him while I put your clothes to dry.'

He took the baby gingerly, holding it round the middle as if it was a cat he was about to put out of doors.

'You'll have to do better than that when you get your own little one,' Wynne laughed. She took Trevor from him and sat down in a low chair, undid the front of her dress and began feeding the baby. 'How is Eleanor?' she asked, looking up once the baby was suckling contentedly.

Rhys couldn't speak. The sight of the fat gurgling baby had rekindled the soreness in his heart. As he watched Wynne feeding Trevor, her mouth parted in a loving smile as she gazed down at the child at her breast, he felt overwhelmed with sadness and despair. He would never see Eleanor feed their child, never watch that glow of mother-love that transformed even Wynne's homely features into something radiant.

Choked, he got up and walked over to the window and stood there staring out unseeingly.

'Does it embarrass you to see me feeding Trevor?' Wynne asked awkwardly. 'I can go into the bedroom.'

'No. Don't talk daft!'

'What's wrong then?' she asked frowning.

'It's Eleanor.'

'Not ill is she?'

'She's dead!'

Wynne took the baby from her breast, rested him against her shoulder, rubbing his back. His milky burps were the only sound in the room.

'Dead? What do you mean ... how ... an accident?' Her voice trembled with concern.

'She died having the baby.'

'*Duw annwyl!*'

66

'Dear God! Yes, that's my feelings. If there is a God, then why does he do something like this? And she was a believer, a devout Catholic,' he added bitterly.

'Oh, our Rhys, what can I say?'

She placed the half-fed baby down on the rug and came and stood by his side, taking both his hands between her own.

'Were you there?'

'No,' he shook his head miserably. 'She died just before I docked. I went to the hospital to see her body. She looked so lovely, they'd brushed her hair out and it was as if she was lying on a golden pillow . . .' he stopped as a lump came into his throat. His massive shoulders heaved and tears welled over as his whole frame shook with sobs.

Wynne gathered him into her arms as if he was a small boy, rocking him to and fro, crooning words of sympathy until the paroxysm of weeping subsided.

'I'm sorry. I shouldn't have done that,' he reached out blindly and stroked her head. 'Blubbering like some great child.'

'You needed the release. You'll feel better now.'

She patted his shoulder understandingly. 'Keep an eye on young Trevor while I make a pot of tea.'

As she handed him a mug of strong tea she asked gently, 'Did Eleanor lose the baby?'

'No. The baby is all right. It's a girl.'

'Well, where is she?'

'Still at the hospital. She's developed some sort of chest infection and has to stay there for a few days.'

'Have you seen her?'

'Just for a few minutes. Skinny as a rabbit with a shock of dark hair. Now . . . now that I've seen your Trevor, I can't wait to get back,' he grinned sheepishly.

'How are you going to look after her?' Wynne asked, her voice heavy with concern.

'I don't know.' His grey eyes were bewildered as they

met hers. 'I've told our Mam but she doesn't want to know.'

'Well, she is getting on in years. A young baby needs a lot of care and attention, especially if it has a weak chest. I could probably take her for a while . . . if Huw would let me.'

'Our Mam said I wasn't even to mention the baby to you,' Rhys said bitterly. 'Said you had enough on your plate as it was.'

'Someone has got to look after her . . .'

'The hospital suggested adoption,' Rhys interrupted. 'Mam seemed to think it might be the best thing . . .'

'Let her go to complete strangers!' Wynne exclaimed horrified. 'Your own flesh and blood!'

'Eleanor's father wouldn't hear of it.'

'I should hope not. Will they take the little mite?' she asked hopefully.

'I don't know. Eleanor's mother is in her sixties, the same as our Mam. Be something of a handful for her.'

'Does Eleanor have any sisters?'

'Two, but they've got broods of their own.' He stood up, pacing fretfully. 'I just don't know the answer. I promised Eleanor that I would try and get a shore job when this trip was over but now, with her gone, I feel too restless to settle anywhere. Anyway, there doesn't seem any point, not now.'

'Except for the baby!'

'But I can't look after her on my own.'

'Perhaps Eleanor's family could keep her for the time being, just to give you a chance to get straightened out,' Wynne suggested.

'Maybe. I'll talk to them. I know they don't want her to be adopted. In fact,' he passed a hand through his shock of dark hair with an air of bewilderment, 'I'd taken it for granted they would have her, until I heard our Mam ranting on. Until then I hadn't given much thought to the trouble looking after a small baby would be.'

'Only if you feel resentful about it,' Wynne said softly. 'If you love the child then you don't notice the work. Let's hope that Eleanor's Mam will help out. Anything is better than letting the little one go to strangers. That's the last thing Eleanor would have wanted!'

8

'That child is going to grow up a spoiled brat, you mark my words,' Betty Jenkins announced sourly as Nesta stood in front of her, a bright-eyed three-year-old, twirling to show off the pretty crocheted dress her grandmother had just finished making for her.

'Nonsense!'

Susan Greenford's mouth tightened and her gentle blue eyes filled with tears. It seemed that no matter what she did for Nesta one or the other of her daughters was ready to criticize. Even John's wife, Mairo, grumbled that Nesta was dressed better than her Myfanwy.

'How can you say that?' Susan Greenford's voice sounded hurt. 'I pass all Nesta's little dresses and coats on to you the minute she has grown out of them. Your Myfanwy is nearly two years younger so they should fit her perfectly.'

'Oh, I'm not saying you don't,' Mairo sniffed. 'But it's not the same, is it? They're second-hand.'

'And Nesta has to have hand-me-down things as well,' Susan told her sharply. 'Our Gwen passes on lots of her Bronwen's clothes.'

'She's a very lucky little girl then, isn't she?' Mairo gave an acid smile. 'That Alice Roberts is always giving her things, too.'

'Yes, well, she was Eleanor's best friend . . .' Susan Greenford sighed and lapsed into thought.

The mention of Alice's name always brought back troublesome memories, things she would rather not dwell on. She had never got to the bottom of what Alice knew about the abortion Eleanor was supposed to have had and which had been the root cause of the complications when Nesta was born. Several times she had tried to talk to her about it but Alice always avoided the issue.

She often wondered if Rhys knew more than he admitted. When she had once tentatively broached the subject he had seemed as bewildered as she was. Yet, even so, she was not fully convinced.

She had noticed that there was a coolness between him and Alice at the christening but that could have been because Alice had refused to be godmother.

Rhys had agreed that for Eleanor's sake the baby should be baptised as a Roman Catholic and raised in the faith. He had asked if Alice could be one of the godmothers, to which Susan had agreed, promising to ask Father O'Neil's permission since Alice wasn't a Catholic. Before she had a chance to do so, however, Rhys told her he had been to see Alice and she had refused anyway.

He tried to explain away the estrangement between him and Alice as grief because she and Eleanor had been such close friends.

'She seems to blame me in some way,' he had said ruefully.

His words had been so frank, spoken so openly, that Susan Greenford was quite sure he knew nothing about the abortion.

And since Eleanor was gone, and nothing that was said or done could bring her back again, she had let the matter rest.

Rhys had only been home once since the christening. Nesta had been barely eighteen months and still teething.

'Does she always cry at night like this?' he asked worriedly, when he padded downstairs at three in the morning to find Susan walking the kitchen, trying to soothe the fractious child.

'It's her teeth, poor little love,' Susan told him. 'Here, you hold her a minute while I mix up some honey and cloves to soothe her sore gums.'

'You go on back to bed,' Rhys told her when the mixture failed to have any effect. 'I'll stay down here with her until she goes off to sleep.'

For the rest of his shore leave, Rhys was the one who saw to Nesta when she was fretful. For Susan it was like a holiday, and by the time Rhys went back to sea for another year-long trip Nesta's molar was through and she was sleeping quietly the whole night long again.

Susan had made the new dress that Betty was being so critical about, because Rhys was once more due home. Nesta chattered constantly about her Da-da, although Susan was sure that she had no idea who he was. How could a baby who had been only eighteen months old remember someone? She only hoped Rhys would realize this and make allowances if at first she was shy and refused to have anything to do with him.

Her fears were groundless. When the knock came on the front door Nesta's little legs couldn't carry her down the passage fast enough. Her cry of 'My Da-da, my Da-da,' was loud enough to be heard out in the street.

As Susan opened the door Nesta flung herself at the giant of a man who stood there, her tiny arms hugging his knees and almost toppling him over in her exuberance.

As Rhys swung her up into his arms she squealed with excitement, patting his face with her chubby hands, showering him with kisses.

Susan felt a lump rise in her throat as she watched them. The child was so obviously overjoyed to see her father, Rhys so unashamedly proud of his lovely little daughter.

Throughout his leave they were inseparable.

Rhys took Nesta out each day to the park, he took her shopping for new clothes and toys. At home, he couldn't do enough for her. He helped to dress her in the morning, he bathed her and read to her at night before she went to bed.

When his leave came to an end, Susan was worried about

how Nesta would react. If Mairo, Gwen and Betty thought she had been spoiled before, then by now, after so much attention from Rhys, she must be utterly ruined, Susan thought.

James agreed with her.

He was a man who normally kept his own counsel but he grew increasingly worried as he saw the ever-growing closeness between Rhys and Nesta.

He idolized his granddaughter but in a quiet protective way. He was always ready to talk to her, or cuddle her when she climbed on to his knee after tea each night, and he had missed her company while Rhys had been at home.

Like his wife, he was sure there would be trouble once Rhys went back to sea. The child was bound to miss him and he wondered how they were going to explain away his absence so that she wouldn't feel he had deserted her.

Happily, their fears were unfounded.

'I'm off back to sea tomorrow, little one,' Rhys told Nesta as he tucked her up in bed on the last night of his leave.

'On a big ship. Like the ones we went to look at?'

'That's right. And I'll be gone for a long, long time.'

'Can I come with you?'

'No, I'm afraid not,' he stroked back the heavy dark hair from her brow. 'You'll be a good girl for Grandma?'

She nodded gravely, staring up at him with huge dark eyes.

Next morning, as he hoisted his kitbag on his shoulder, Nesta stood silently at Susan's side. She had already kissed him goodbye, hugging him so tightly that he had thought he would be choked by her strong little arms. As he turned the corner of the road he looked back, waving his hand in a final farewell. She hesitated for a minute, then as her grandmother bent down and said something to her she blew him a kiss and waved until he had disappeared from sight.

Susan had expected tears, tantrums even, but there had

been none. Nesta accepted her father's departure stoically, as if she knew it was inevitable. For a few days she was exceptionally quiet. Then the old pattern of life was restored with her nightly cuddle from her grandfather, and her request for him to tell her a story after she was tucked up in bed.

It was the same each time Rhys came home. Once he was there, they spent every minute they could together, totally immersed in each other's company. When he returned to sea there were never any tears, just quiet acceptance of the situation.

One month after she was five, Nesta started school. She was in the infants class at St Joseph's, the school where her mother had once taught. She learned quickly and once she could read spent most of her time with her nose in a book.

'You ought to send her out in the street to mix with other children more,' Betty told her mother. 'Right mardy little coward she's getting to be. Selfish, too. Doesn't want to share any of her things.'

'She's just quiet and not used to boisterous games,' Susan defended. 'She plays on her own most of the time.'

Mairo had grown less critical of her young niece as Nesta had grown older. Her own daughter, Myfanwy, was a tiresome child and it was a relief to her when she visited her mother-in-law that Nesta would play with the younger girl, keeping her happy while she enjoyed a well-earned break.

'Let Nesta come over to our place for a week in the school holidays, if you like,' Mairo told Susan. 'The change would be good for her and give you a bit of a rest.'

'She would probably enjoy that,' Susan agreed. 'That is if Rhys isn't home from sea. I've had a letter from him to say he hopes to be home sometime in July and that he would like to take Nesta up to North Wales to see his folk. She is going on seven, you know, and none of them have ever seen her.'

'No, nor ever sent her a card on her birthday or at Christmas time. Funny folk they must be. That Alice Roberts takes more notice of Nesta than they do.'

'Yes, Alice is good to her, there's no denying that,' Susan admitted. 'Never misses her birthday or Christmas. Beautiful things she buys for her. Nesta loves going out with Alice. She talks about nothing else for days afterwards.'

'Takes her mind off her father being away so much, I suppose.'

'She misses him though. Worries me sometimes the way she sits and thinks about him. Makes up stories about where he is and what he's doing. It's almost as though she was there with him. She remembers every little detail of what he tells her about his travels. If she was a boy I'd be on edge in case she ran away to sea looking for him.'

'He's never got married again. Funny really, because he's a nice-looking fellow,' Mairo murmured thoughtfully.

'Never had the time, has he? He spends every minute of his leave here with young Nesta. He takes her to school, and he is at the gate waiting for her when she comes out.'

'If he had married again,' Mairo persisted, 'it would have meant he could have given her a proper home.'

'What do you mean by that?' Susan Greenford looked annoyed.

'Nothing, really. I know you've done all you could for her. She's been well fed and more than well clothed. It's just that . . . well . . . John and I were only saying the other night . . . you are a bit old to be looking after a young child. It's not really much of a life for her . . . that's why she's so quiet and so wrapped up in herself, I suppose.'

Mairo's words rankled. Susan knew there was just a grain of truth in what she said, so she began asking Gwen to bring her two youngest, Idris and Bronwen, for the day. These visits rarely turned out for the best, however. Idris was nearly seven years older than Nesta and found her much too meek and mild and he teased her unmercifully.

Myfanwy and Nesta still played happily together but

only if she came on her own. When Glyn came as well, the three of them quarrelled continuously until Susan finally, unable to stand the noise any longer, would put on her hat and coat and take them back home again.

'I'm getting too old for that sort of carry-on,' she told Nesta severely, when they were on their own once more.

'It's not my fault, Grandma,' Nesta would tell her contritely. 'I don't know why you ask them here in the first place.'

'So that you won't be lonely,' Susan told her tartly.

'I am happy enough on my own. As long as I have a book to read, I don't need anyone to play with.'

'Better not let your Da hear you say that or he might not come to see you again,' Susan told her jokingly.

'Oh Grandma, you know I didn't mean him!' She gave a deep sigh. 'He's different, he's special. When will he be home again?'

It was a question Nesta seemed to ask daily. Her enormous brown eyes, that dominated her elfin face, would stare solemnly up at her grandmother, demanding an answer.

When Rhys wrote telling them the date of his next leave, her grandfather helped her to make a special calendar so that they could mark off each passing day. As the number lessened, Nesta grew pale and tense with excitement.

'If you don't eat your dinner up you will have wasted away before your father gets here,' James Greenford would warn her when she refused her food.

'Or else your Da will think I starve you!' her grandmother added.

But it was no good. For at least a week before Rhys was due to dock Nesta would be on edge, starting at the slightest sound, listening for his arrival long after she had been put to bed, unable to concentrate on her lessons at school or on anything she did at home.

And each time Rhys came home they seemed to grow

closer to each other. He had changed over the years. He had grown thinner, quieter, more withdrawn. His dark grey eyes were more piercing and his bearded face had a haunted look.

The resemblance between him and his daughter seemed to increase as Nesta grew tall and leggy. They had the same thick dark hair and, though her eyes were brown whereas his were slate grey, they had the same intense expression, just as they both had the same curved, sensitive mouth and determined chin.

Although he no longer read to her at night, he still sat by her bedside, until her lids grew so heavy that she slipped into sleep while he was still talking to her.

When he met her from school each afternoon he would take her somewhere special, as if desperately trying to make up in the few short weeks he was at home for all the time they were apart.

Her favourite outing was to the museum. The elegant, gleaming, white stone building in Cathays Park, with its imposing statues in marble and bronze, and rooms full of pictures and relics from the past, never failed to impress her.

Hand in hand they would wander, reading the printed descriptions under each exhibit, exchanging glances of amusement, amazement, or understanding, before passing on to the next.

Sometimes, but only very occasionally, he would take her to the docks. Tiger Bay was no place for a young girl but as long as she was with him he felt she was safe and he knew it delighted her to share something of his background.

Once in a while they would visit Alice at The Hope and Anchor. In the privacy of the back parlour, Rhys would enjoy a pint of beer and Nesta a glass of fizzy lemonade and some crisps.

Each time Rhys came home Nesta begged him to take

her to North Wales, to meet her other grandparents. Above all, she wanted to see the mysterious, cloud-topped, heaven-kissing mountains that he talked about so much. Always he promised they would go the next time he came ashore, but he never actually got round to making the visit. There was always so much for them to see and do in Cardiff and their time together was so brief.

'Promise you'll take me there on your next leave,' she begged as he kissed her goodbye.

'All right. But that won't be for quite a while. This time I shall be away for a year. It's going to be my last trip though,' he told her quickly as he saw her face cloud.

'You're going to get a shore job and we can live together always,' she smiled eagerly.

'Something like that.'

'Can't you do it right away . . . not go away again, I mean?' she begged.

'No, princess, that's not possible. I need this extra long trip to make enough money to stay on shore. It may not be easy to find work right away so I will need some money to live on until I do.'

'Why do you call me "princess" . . . is it something to do with my name?'

'How did you know that?' he asked, looking down at her in surprise.

'At school we have been doing history about Wales in the olden days,' she told him. 'There used to be a princess called Nest whose father was called Rhys.'

'That's right! And she lived near Snowdon, not far from where my home was.'

'And you'll take me there?' she begged, her eyes pleading.

'I will. The very next time I come home,' he assured her.

9

The flu epidemic of the winter of 1932 was particularly virulent. It rushed through Britain like an avenging angel. No one was safe. In Wales, where almost one third of the people were out of work and struggling to make ends meet, it claimed countless lives. The elderly and the very young seemed to fall victims to it almost overnight.

While out shopping, Susan Greenford had complained of feeling shivery. By the time her husband James arrived home from work she had taken to her bed. Before morning she was dead and he was lying prone with exactly the same symptoms.

Their double funeral took place a week later.

Nesta was shocked beyond belief. As she cried herself to sleep in the makeshift bed in Myfanwy's room, everyone assumed she was grieving over the loss of her grandparents.

If anyone had taken the trouble to ask her they would have found that the real reason for her hysteria and copious tears was that she wanted her father.

Since he had sailed away, more than nine months earlier, she had lived on hope and promises. The hope that this would be his very last sea trip and his promise that once he did come ashore for good he would take her to North Wales.

He had told her so much about the countryside where he had grown up. She could picture the towering, craggy mountains with their hidden lakes, pine forests and deep sun-dappled cwms. She wanted to see them for herself, to breathe the clear, sharp air, dabble her feet in streams and pools. She wanted to see the wild horses, hear the sheep calling to each other and watch the eagles soar. And she wanted to do all these things with him.

The history and mystery of Snowdon and Beddgelert filled her mind to the exclusion of everything else. She longed to see with her own eyes the cave where Owain Glyndwr had hidden, to see the quarries where they tunnelled deep into the heart of the mountains to mine slate. And, above all, she wanted to visit her father's home in Blaenau Ffestiniog.

Now that both her grandparents were dead, she felt desolate.

The only home she had ever known was gone, everything divided between John, Gwen and Betty, or sold off to a dealer. Her own clothes were in a brown-fibre suitcase and the rest of her belongings, her books and toys, in a tea-chest stored in Uncle John's garden shed.

'Leave it there packed and ready until we decide where you will be living,' he told her when she asked if she could have some of her books.

She knew he had been to the shipping office and asked them to send a message to let her father know what had happened because she had overheard him telling Mairo.

'They said they couldn't do anything until *The Magpie* put into port and the next scheduled stop was Bombay in three weeks' time.'

'Three weeks! And how long will it take him to get home from there?' Mairo snapped.

'Heaven knows!' They didn't hold out much hope of him getting back before the end of his trip, anyway.'

'And when is that?' Mairo persisted.

'Sometime in May, providing all goes well.'

'May! That's three months away. We're not going to have Nesta here until then, are we?'

'I don't mind her staying on,' John prevaricated. 'She's company for Myfanwy . . .'

'Well I do! Just think of all the extra cooking and washing . . .'

80

'One more can't make that much difference,' John protested mildly.

'That's all you know,' Mairo flared. 'Nesta and Myfanwy gang up against our Glyn. They spend their time giggling and shutting him out, it's not fair on the boy.'

'Glyn and Myfanwy don't get on all that well together at the best of times,' John defended. 'In fact, I would have thought he would be happier if he didn't have Myfanwy pestering him to play with her all the time. He wants to get out with other boys in the street, not be playing with our Myfanwy and her dolls.'

'That's as it may be,' Mairo said tightly, 'but what I said still stands. I don't want Nesta here.'

'Where else can she go?' John asked, stroking his moustache absently.

'Let one of your sisters have her.'

'We'll see.' John was never one to argue. A heavily-built man, he found most people were ready to agree with him. Only Mairo, quick, sharp, and self-assured, was his match. He wasn't surprised by her attitude. Mairo disliked the domestic side of married life and felt that increasing the number she had to look after was adding to her daily drudgery.

Before she had married, she had been First Sales in Ladies Wear at David Morgan's, in Queen Street Arcade. Handling fine fabrics, soft furs, rich silks and delicate lace was much more to her liking than washing pots and pans.

She had ambitions. Not for her rooms at the back of John's bakery. Regardless of the fact that it meant a long journey for John at half-past four each morning, winter and summer, she had insisted they should move to a smart little house near Roath Park.

'Train the boy to light the fires for the ovens before you get in,' she told John sharply when he complained about having so far to travel when winter came and the mornings were icy. 'That way you could stay in bed another hour.'

'Four-thirty, five-thirty, what difference does it make? It is still cold and dark,' he grumbled.

His first batch of bread had to be ready by seven each morning, yet he was often still baking buns, cakes, and the special orders that seemed to be increasing all the time, late into the afternoon. It was a good business, but to hire another skilled baker would eat into his profits. So he struggled on, helped by a young apprentice and a delivery boy while Mairo stayed at home, bringing up Glyn and Myfanwy.

'I tell you what, Mairo. Let Nesta stay here until we get a message back from her father,' he compromised.

'That might take weeks ... months even.' Her black eyes flashed angrily.

'No it won't. I'll be back down to the shipping office again next week to see what is happening. Leave things as they are until then.'

'Until next week, then ... no longer.'

When John went back to enquire if they had managed to contact Rhys the situation proved baffling. Their agent in Bombay had reported that Rhys Evans was not on board *The Magpie*. He had left the boat at Calcutta.

'Told you he'd get out of coming back to look after his kid,' Mairo exclaimed triumphantly, her thin lips curved in a sneer.

'Don't talk so daft,' John exclaimed angrily. 'How was he to know what had happened?'

'He'll never come back now,' she persisted spitefully. 'That's the last we'll see of him, you mark my words. Once he knows it is up to him to look after Nesta you won't see sight nor sound of him.'

'He dotes on the child.'

'Really? Why doesn't he send money for her keep, then?'

'What?'

'Yes you hadn't thought of that, had you?' Mairo said triumphantly. 'Whoever looks after Nesta has to pay for her food and clothes.'

'Mother never said anything about that . . . do you mean she and Dad . . .?'

'She used to say he left money with her each time he came home,' Mairo admitted. 'But where was it?' she added triumphantly. 'None lying around the house, was there?'

'I don't know, I never thought to look.' John passed a hand worriedly through his thick brown hair.

'Anyway, it is not the money, I just don't want her here, so you had better have a word with your sisters.'

'Yes, all right,' John agreed wearily. 'I'll try and find time to go and see our Gwen tomorrow.'

'No,' Mairo swung round, 'not your Gwen. I think she'd be better with Betty and her lot.'

'In Pontypridd! Rubbish. She's used to living in Cardiff.'

'What difference does it make where she lives?' Mairo retorted angrily. 'She isn't old enough to go out and about on her own.'

'Then why send her to Pontypridd? If she is in Grange-town, then at least we can keep an eye on things. She can even come and stay for the weekend occasionally and give our Gwen a break.'

'It's not fair on your Gwen,' Mairo murmured per-suasively. 'Nesta and Bronwen don't get on all that well. It would be far better for her to go to Betty's. Her three are older than Nesta so they won't resent her so much.'

Betty Jenkins was an angular woman with hard blue eyes. She welcomed Nesta grudgingly. After the spacious atmos-phere at Mairo's, Nesta found the small terraced house in Pontypridd claustrophobic.

The bedroom she had to share with her cousin Dilys had been crowded when there was only one bed in it. Now, with a bed for Nesta as well, it was almost impossible to move. And, because Dilys resented the intrusion, she grumbled inces-santly about the space Nesta's clothes took up in the wardrobe and the fact that she had to share the room with her at all.

Betty's husband Dai was a thin strained-looking man with dark brown eyes, a narrow tight mouth, and sparse brown hair. His skin was pitted with ingrained coal dust, even though he stripped off and sat in the tin bath in the kitchen each night when he arrived home from the pit.

At first Nesta thought he disliked her because he hardly ever spoke to her, but she soon came to realize that he seldom talked to anyone. He spent most of his time either crouched in his armchair at the side of the fire, sucking noisily on a blackened clay pipe, or in the shed at the far end of the narrow strip of garden at the back of the house, where he kept his pigeons.

The most offensive thing about Dai Jenkins was his cough. The years he had worked underground had left their stamp. He coughed incessantly, spitting great globules of phlegm into the fire where they sizzled on the hot coals or dripped from the bars, leaving ugly, scaly, brown scars.

None of the others seemed to notice, or they were so used to it that it didn't bother them. Nesta felt her stomach churning each time he did it, especially if they were having a meal.

The first week Nesta was there, Aunt Betty kept her at home, taking her with her when she went shopping in the town or to visit any of her friends. On the Thursday, she took her into the hairdressers, where Dilys worked as an apprentice, to have her hair cut.

'We'll have it done properly the first time and then after that our Dilys can keep it trimmed. Too much trouble bothering with that long hair,' her aunt told her.

'But I like it long,' Nesta protested.

'Well, you can grow it again when you are older. You need it short for school, get nits in it otherwise.'

'Grandma liked me to have it long.'

'Yes, well that's as maybe but she's not here to look after it for you now. On the way back we'll call at the school to tell them you'll be starting on Monday morning.'

'Is it a Catholic school?'

'No. It's the same school as our Chris goes to.'

'But I want to go to a Catholic school. I ought to go to Mass on Sundays, too.

'No one goes to church in our house,' Betty told her. 'Your Uncle Dai isn't a Catholic. Just say your prayers. God will understand.'

'I can't. Dilys makes fun of me.'

'Take no notice,' Betty Jenkins sighed. Having Nesta living with them was not going to be easy, she reflected. Already Dai was grumbling about the cost and Dilys resented having to share her room. She hadn't realized that Dilys was picking on Nesta, though. She would have a word with her about that. If Nesta was to make her home with them then the others would have to accept her.

Chris seemed to be the only one who got on with Nesta, but then, Betty thought fondly, he was so good-natured. He took after her own side of the family with his fair, curly hair, and blue eyes. Like Nesta, he always seemed to have his nose in a book, which was probably why he had to wear glasses.

Betty felt a pang of guilt as they left the hairdresser's. Nesta looked like a shorn lamb. With her close-bobbed hair, her thin neck resembled a long stalk and her enormous dark eyes seemed too big for her pinched little face.

She stood meekly at Betty's side when they reached the school, almost as if taking away her long hair had in some way robbed her of spirit.

'Now make sure you know where you have to go on Monday morning,' Betty told her as they left the grim redbrick building, with its tall narrow windows, and crossed the asphalt playground. 'You come in this gate, it's marked "Girls" and you go through that door over there.'

'Does Chris come to this school as well?'

'Yes, but don't count on him walking with you, or waiting for you when you come out at night. He'll want to be with the rest of the boys.'

In that Betty was wrong.

Chris left the house before Nesta each morning but she would find him waiting for her at the corner of the road. When the school came in sight, he would give her a little push, telling her to run along, he had some friends to meet. She understood that he didn't want the other boys to see them together and went the last few hundred yards alone cheerfully enough.

It was the same at night. He left the school with a gang of his own pals, then waited for her at the corner of the road. When they reached their own street he would hang back, giving her time to go indoors ahead of him.

Chris was the only one she confided in, the only one who understood how unhappy she was because her father had never come to take her away.

On the few occasions when Uncle John came to see how she was getting on, she had pleaded with him to try again to get news of her father.

'I have left a message with the shipping agents,' John told her. 'It seems he jumped ship in Calcutta though, so it is unlikely he will ever get in touch with them again.'

'Then how will he find me?'

'I don't know.'

'Couldn't you ask the people who have moved into Grandma's house to tell him where I am living, so that if he went there they could tell him where to find me?' she pleaded.

'That's a good idea.'

'Have you told Alice Roberts where I am?' she persisted. 'He's bound to go there to see her and she could tell him.'

'Next time I'm down the docks I'll do that,' he promised, stroking his moustache. But Nesta sensed he didn't mean it.

Nesta gradually resigned herself to the fact that no one was going to help her find her father. Every night though, before she went to sleep, she took out the framed photograph of him that had belonged to her mother, and the smudged photograph of the two of them taken together, and studied them. Then she would lie there in the dark, thinking about him, weaving dreams about what they would do when they were together again.

Once she tried to persuade Chris to go with her to Cardiff to see Alice Roberts.

'We would need money for our fares,' he told her.

'I've got nearly a pound saved up,' she told him.

'Cost more than that, I expect.'

'Once we get there Alice will give us the money to come home,' she said confidently.

'Our Mam would kill me,' he said, shaking his head. 'And don't you go trying it on either. All sorts of things can happen to girls in Tiger Bay. The white slave traders might kidnap you!'

'I don't believe you.'

'It's true! I've read about it in *The Echo*. They steal young girls, smuggle them out on the boats to Africa and the East and sell them as slaves.'

'You're making it all up!'

'No, I'm not. I suppose they don't talk about such things at that posh grammar school you go to now,' he grinned.

There was a note of derision in his voice but she knew that deep down Chris envied her. He had told her so when he first heard she had passed the scholarship.

'Wish I had,' he sighed. 'If I went to the grammar school then I wouldn't have to go down the pit when I leave school next month.'

At first the rest of the family had been against Nesta going to the grammar school.

'She's uppity enough as it is,' Dilys jibed. 'There will be no living with her if she goes there.'

'It's out of the question,' Dai coughed. He spat ferociously at the glowing fire. 'We couldn't afford it, for one thing.'

Then, when they found that her scholarship entitled her not only to free uniform but a season ticket for the bus and free meals, they changed their minds.

As Nesta listened to them arguing about her future she fumed inwardly. She desperately wanted to go to the grammar school and waited anxiously for their decision. When they finally decided it was beneficial to them to let her go, she refused to show any reaction, but secretly she was jubilant.

Nesta had been living with the Jenkins in Pontypridd for almost four years when disaster struck.

The first she knew about the explosion at the Tregarw Pit, where her Uncle Dai worked, was when she came home from school. The street was full of women, some with babies wrapped in shawls, huddled in groups, grey-faced and grimly silent as they waited for news.

Dai Jenkins was not amongst the seventy-eight men who were stretchered out. He had been working at the coal face when the explosion occurred and, as the roof caved in, he had been buried alive under the falling debris. Rescue workers had struggled valiantly for several hours to try to reach him and the six other men buried alongside him, but they had been forced back by poisonous fumes.

That night, curled up in the hard, narrow bed that had been wedged into one corner of Dilys's bedroom, Nesta wept copiously. She was not crying because she was saddened by her uncle's death but because she knew she was wicked beyond forgiveness. Her first thoughts on hearing the terrible news had been relief that never again would she have to listen to him coughing, hawking and spitting.

Three days after his funeral, Betty received an official visit from the mine-owner. As his big black car drew up outside her door a knot of women gathered, curious to know what has happening.

Ten minutes later, when the man left, they were almost

88

as distraught as Betty to learn that she must vacate her terraced house before the end of the month. It belonged to the pit-owners and, now that her husband was no longer one of their workers, they were demanding it back.

Long after she had been sent up to bed, Nesta crouched shivering on the stairs, listening to her aunt and cousins making plans, waiting to hear what her own fate was to be.

The announcement was not long in coming.

'You won't be going to school in Pontypridd anymore,' Aunt Betty told her next morning at breakfast. 'You are going to live with our Gwen. I'm moving into the flat over the hairdresser's where our Dilys works. Lucky we are to get somewhere like that. There's only two bedrooms though. Our Richard and Chris will have one and Dilys and me will share the other. There's no room for you.'

'I could sleep in the living room,' Nesta said hopefully.

'No, it wouldn't be right. You go to our Gwen's. Be nice for you there, back in Cardiff again. If you can find that woman you used to know at the pub down on the docks, she may be able to tell you where your Da is.'

The mention of her father upset Nesta far more than the fact that she would be leaving the Jenkinses.

'If none of you can find her, or my Da, then I don't stand much chance, now do I?' she retorted balefully.

'Don't be cheeky,' her aunt snapped. 'Your Uncle John tried and tried. It would have suited all of us to find him so that his folks could have helped look after you. Kept well out of it they have and no mistake. I don't know where you would have ended up if it hadn't been for us, and that's a fact!'

Nesta bit her lip to keep from crying. She wanted to fling herself into her aunt's arms, hug her and thank her, but she knew Aunt Betty didn't really like her and would only push her away and tell her not to be so silly.

10

At first sight Gwen Lewis looked like an overweight and older version of Betty Jenkins but Nesta soon found that living with the Lewises was a completely different experience from her four years with the Jenkins family.

Aunt Gwen was flabby and slatternly in her habits as well as in her appearance. Aunt Betty might have been sharp-tongued and shrewish but she had run her home efficiently. Although she had not shown Nesta very much affection, she had always made sure she had clean clothes and a clean bed.

After the good wholesome stews and casseroles and mouth-watering, home-baked puddings and tarts that she had grown used to, Nesta found the greasy, fried foods that Aunt Gwen dished up gave her indigestion and brought her out in spots. A meal of fish and chips from the shop around the corner, or a plate of doughnuts or iced cakes from the baker's, was Aunt Gwen's idea of a treat.

Elwyn, the eldest son, had already left home but the house was still overcrowded. Aunt Gwen and Uncle Lloyd used the big front bedroom that looked out on to Corporation Road, and Idris, who was twenty, had the small single bedroom also at the front of the house. Bronwen had the tiny bedroom down three steps at the back of the house.

The middle bedroom was used by Gwladys and her husband Dylan Hughes. They had only been married a few months and they also used the middle room downstairs as their living room. Gwladys, however, since she had to share the stove and sink in the scullery, seemed to spend most of her time in with her mother. The arguments between the two of them were noisy and frequent. At first their shouting had alarmed Nesta but after a few weeks she was able to lose herself in a book and shut her ears to the commotion.

The sleeping arrangements irritated Nesta the most. Since there was no room for an extra bed in Bronwen's room, she had to sleep on the put-you-up sofa in the front room downstairs. This meant she had to open up the bed each night and fold it away every morning before she went off to school.

What she found even more annoying was that if any of the family were using the room in the evening she couldn't go to bed until they did, no matter how tired she might be.

Bronwen, who was sixteen, seemed to take a perverse delight in bringing friends home and sitting in the front room as late as she dared.

Aunt Gwen would yell and shout, 'Time those girls were off to their own homes,' but it made no difference, since Bronwen usually ignored her.

Nesta would sit out in the gloomy kitchen, trying to read or do her homework. Finding space to spread out her papers was almost impossible. The kitchen table was always cluttered with newspapers, old letters, bills, dirty dishes, and the remains of the day's meals. Her Uncle Lloyd would sit in his armchair by the side of the fireplace, his feet in the ashes that spilled out from the black range, listening to the wireless, which he always turned up as loud as possible, and filling the room with clouds of acrid smoke from his pipe.

Nesta found she disliked her Uncle Lloyd Lewis even more than Uncle Dai Jenkins. A heavy, corpulent man with red cheeks, a bulbous nose and watery blue eyes, his wide loose mouth seemed to be continually open. His voice was loud and his speech dominated by swear words. Nesta was physically frightened of him, especially after she had seen him raise one of his enormous red hands and slap Idris smartly around the ears for contradicting him.

He was the most selfish man she had ever met, demanding

91

attention from the moment he came downstairs in the morning until he went to bed at night. He had a voracious appetite and every night came home with an enormous parcel of chops, sausages, liver, bacon, and pieces of steak from the butcher's stall in Cardiff Market where he worked. Anything that could be tossed into a frying pan for a quick and easy meal was acceptable to Gwen. Nesta longed for one of the tasty stews that had been Aunt Betty's standby. When she tentatively suggested it to her Aunt Gwen, Lloyd Lewis had taken offence.

'Uppity little chit, aren't you?' he sneered. 'If our food's not good enough for you then you know what you can do. No one asked you to come here in the first place.'

Although she hid her tears, Nesta found his remarks hurtful and she became even more withdrawn, seldom speaking when he was at home. Her greatest solace was to fantasize about her father coming back to Cardiff and finding her.

She didn't know how this could happen since she had long ago given up pestering any of them to try and get in touch with him. Although they resented having to look after her, none of them seemed willing to do anything to try and find him. They wouldn't even let her go to see Alice Roberts.

Aunt Gwen tried to be kind, Nesta had to admit, but she did it in such a strange way that it only alienated Nesta from the rest of the family. She was constantly praising her for setting a good example and openly admired her short hair style and neat school uniform.

'You want to try and be a bit more like Nesta,' she would scold when Bronwen appeared for breakfast, unwashed, her hair still rolled up in pipe-cleaners.

'She's just a kid, still at school,' Bronwen would snap. 'She doesn't have to get up and go to work. The streets are aired before she sets out.'

'Not on Sundays, they're not,' her mother would argue, 'and you are still the same then. You only manage to get to late Mass by the skin of your teeth.'

'I wouldn't bother going at all except that Father Ryan won't let me go to the dances in the church hall if I have missed Mass,' Bronwen said sulkily.

'And I shall stop you going unless you take Nesta along with you,' her mother said promptly.

Bronwen's lip curled and she flashed an angry look at Nesta but she knew better than to enter into an argument with her mother.

Bronwen might laugh behind her mother's back but she knew she had to toe the line. Even though she had left school, her mother still kept her under strict control.

She was only allowed to go to the pictures if her mother went as well or, occasionally, if accompanied by one of her brothers or sisters. Bronwen could fret and fume all she liked but in this respect her mother's word was law. Bronwen put it down to the fact that her elder sister, Gwladys, had got into trouble when she was only sixteen. The baby had died but the stigma had remained. Gwladys had been twenty-six before she had managed to find herself a husband.

'And Dylan's not much of a catch,' Bronwen told Nesta. 'Foxy little bugger, you want to watch him. All he thinks about is touching girls up.'

Nesta shared her cousin's dislike of Dylan Hughes. He was a thin wiry man with a long sharp nose, shifty black eyes and dark hair that he wore greased back so that it hugged his skull like a cap. Nesta felt a shiver go through her every time he gave her one of his leering smiles.

Whenever she came within reach his thin bony hands would touch or stroke. Several times, when she had opened the door of the front room in the morning, she had found him standing outside in the passageway. He would pretend to be taking his coat down from the peg in the hallway but she suspected that he had been watching her through the crack of the door jamb.

She was so positive that he spied on her while she was

getting dressed that she took to hanging a dress over the crack in the door to stop him peeping through. Far from discouraging Dylan this only made him more persistent than ever.

His job as a barman in one of the pubs in town meant that he didn't usually get home until about midnight. Everyone, including Gwladys, had usually gone to bed. Nesta would sometimes hear the click of the front-door lock as he entered the house and would wait with bated breath for the sound of his footsteps on the stairs. More often than not she would hear him pause outside her door. Then, in the light from the street lamp outside, she would see her door slowly open and she would stuff the sheet into her mouth to keep from screaming.

She didn't know why she was so scared since all he ever did was to stand at the side of her bed staring down at her. He would rub his thin, bony hands together and breathe noisily, while she watched from beneath half-closed lids, praying he would think she was asleep.

By the time he turned and went upstairs she was usually shaking and too petrified to sleep in case he came back again.

Finally, when she could stand it no longer, she decided the only way to keep him out was to wedge a chair against the door so that it was impossible for him to open it.

Gwen discovered this by accident when she tried to come into the room to get some glasses from the corner cupboard after Nesta was in bed one night. Furiously she banged on the door.

'Whose house do you think this is?' she hollered at the top of her voice. 'How dare you shut me out of my own front room when I've been kind enough to put a roof over your head. Get out of bed and open the door this very minute.'

When Nesta, bleary-eyed and frightened, opened the door, her Aunt Gwen seized her by the shoulders, shaking her until her teeth chattered as she scolded and upbraided her. When she heard the reason she seemed to be even more incensed and went away to bang on Gwladys's door to demand an explanation.

Gwladys could be just as noisy and argumentative as her mother and the row that ensued was still going strong when Dylan Hughes arrived home over an hour later. He was immediately drawn into the dispute and, although he hotly denied ever spying on Nesta, Gwladys sulked for days.

Nesta went in fear and trembling in case Dylan decided on some sort of reprisal. His sharp foxy sneer haunted her and she felt his small black eyes following her whenever he was in the house. In some ways, though, the confrontation had been a blessing in disguise.

'Bet he leaves you alone in future,' Bronwen sniggered. 'You've been lucky. He thinks he's God's gift to women. He's always stroking my hair and trying to kiss me. Just being brotherly, he calls it, but I'm not that daft. I know his type. I meet them every day in the factory.'

'Why do you go on working there if it is like that?'

'The money's good. And I get to meet a lot of boys. Have a good time really. If I didn't work there then I'd have to go into a shop, or something, and I wouldn't see as many fellas. And our Mam is determined she's not going to let me go out on my own at night. Just because our Gwladys got herself knocked up she thinks I might do the same. Stupid cow!' Her blue eyes gleamed cynically. 'I know how to look after myself. No man's going to poke me until I'm ready.'

Nesta was shocked by her cousin's outpourings. She knew Bronwen regarded her as a little innocent but in some ways she felt sorry for her. Pushy, sexy, cheeky, with her bright blue eyes and permed gingery hair, she was pretty in a brash sort of way. All she seemed to think about was getting out of the house to go dancing or to the pictures.

Nesta quite enjoyed going to the pictures, even if Aunt

Gwen came along as well. When she did, Bronwen always manoeuvred it so that Nesta sat in the middle. At first Nesta didn't understand the reason for this. Then it gradually dawned on her that once they were in their seats a young chap always came and sat on the other side of Bronwen. And from the giggling and fumbling that went on, she soon realized that it was all part of a pre-arranged plan on Bronwen's part.

Aunt Gwen also insisted that Nesta went with Bronwen to the dances at the church hall.

'See you at ten o'clock out here in the cloakroom. If you bump into me inside the hall I don't know you ... understand?' Bronwen would tell her the moment they had hung up their coats.

'Yes.' Nesta would agree. She didn't want to be introduced to any of Bronwen's boyfriends. She couldn't dance and had no interest in learning.

During the winter she was happy enough sitting in a corner, watching what was going on around her, or reading a book.

As the evenings grew lighter, however, she found more pleasant ways of passing the time. Once Bronwen was in the clutches of one of her numerous boyfriends Nesta would slip away from the dance-hall.

One of her favourite ways of spending a warm summer evening was to visit the Italian ice-cream shop on the corner of James Street bridge, buy one of their enormous creamy cornets, then wander slowly along the canal towpath as far as the Royal Hamadryad Seamen's Hospital, enjoying her ice-cream and watching the small cargo boats being loaded and unloaded.

Or she would walk down to the Pier Head and watch the boats lying at anchor, and then wander through the maze of dockland streets that made up Tiger Bay, searching for Alice Roberts. The Hope and Anchor pub was still there but the name of the landlord had changed. It was no longer Roberts and she didn't dare go inside to ask if they knew where Alice Roberts had gone. Instead she wandered the streets, checking the name over the door of every pub she passed, hoping that one day she would find her.

But she never did.

When she reached her sixteenth birthday, Aunt Gwen told her that when she left school in two weeks' time she would have to find a job.

'It costs money to keep you, we can't go on doing it forever,' her aunt pointed out when Nesta begged to be allowed to stay on at school for another year.

'But the School Certificate results aren't out yet. If I get good marks I can sit for my Higher School Certificate and when I pass I will be able to go to university,' she added hopefully.

'Go to university! You can get that nonsense out of your head right away,' Uncle Lloyd thundered. 'I'm not working my fingers to the bone paying for that sort of daft education. I didn't do it for any of my own, so I am quite sure I am not going to do it for you!'

'I'm not asking you to pay. I shall get a scholarship.'

'You've got one of those now, but I still have to provide you with food and pocket money, as well as clothes to wear when you go to the pictures or go dancing with our Bronwen,' he argued.

'Please,' Nesta begged. 'I won't go out anywhere, I'll be too busy studying. Just let me stay on at school.'

'No!' His huge fist came crashing down on to the table. 'And that is final, and that's an end of the matter.'

It was then that Nesta made up her mind to go along to the seamen's mission in Bute Street and see if anyone there could help her to find her father.

A thin elderly man in the janitor's office peered at her from over the top of a pair of steel-rimmed glasses and told her he would 'see the guv'nor'.

As she waited in the dingy hallway it took all her courage

not to turn and run away. She remembered Chris Jenkins's warnings that it wasn't safe to go anywhere in Tiger Bay on her own because she might be kidnapped by white slavers. And, as seamen of all ages and nationalities stared at her, grinning or even giving her a lewd greeting, her heart thudded with fear at the thought that he could well be right.

The janitor took her up a wide stone staircase to the offices above, where a middle-aged man in a dark suit and white winged collar listened to her request for news of her father with an unblinking stare.

'You say it is seven years since you last heard from him?' he asked making notes on a pad in front of him.

'About that. I was nine when my grandparents died.'

'And he was on *The Magpie*. Have you tried the shipping agents?'

Nesta shook her head. 'I don't know where to find them.'

The official rose from behind his desk and consulted a filing cabinet. After a few minutes he drew out a sheaf of papers and took them back to his desk. He scribbled an address down on the pad in front of him, tore off the page and handed it to Nesta.

'Does your guardian know you are here?' the man asked as she reached the door.

'No.' Nesta bit her lower lip uneasily. 'I . . . I just came on my own.'

'I don't think you should wander around these streets alone,' the man warned in a kindly tone. 'You are a very pretty young lady, you know, and there are some strange characters around Tiger Bay. I should get someone to go with you to the shipping agents. Good luck.'

Blushing furiously, Nesta scurried down the stairs. She looked at the address the man had given her. The offices were only a few streets away so, regardless of his warning, she set off.

'I would like to be able to help you,' the bearded man there told her, 'but there is nothing at all in our records about Rhys Evans after he left *The Magpie* in Calcutta.' He shuffled his papers. 'According to our records, he never even came to collect the monies that were due to him. He may have met with an accident of some kind. Have you thought of that?' He hesitated. 'He might even be dead, you know.'

'No, he's not dead,' Nesta said confidently. 'I would know if he was dead. He's alive, I can feel it.' She reddened, aware that the man was looking at her in an amused way. 'Thank you, anyway,' she mumbled as she turned and left the office.

It had become dusk while she had been making enquiries and now, as she hurried along the lamplit streets, she felt quite scared. Tiger Bay had such a bad reputation and she was in the the heart of it. Sikhs, coloureds, Arabs, mulattoes and Lascars pushed and jostled her as she made her way back to the Pier Head. Several spoke to her, but she took no notice. She wanted to run but she was afraid to do so in case it attracted attention and someone tried to stop her.

By the time she boarded a tram at the Pier Head her heart was racing and she was almost too breathless to ask for her ticket to Grangetown.

11

When she heard the results of her School Certificate exam, Nesta was in seventh heaven.

She deliberately walked home from school just for the sheer pleasure of having time to think about what her future could have been. Her head was so full of daydreams that even the colourful shop windows in St Mary Street failed to attract her attention.

Normally if she had to walk it was because she had spent her tram fare on sweets, and looking at the pretty dresses and elegant outfits in shop windows gave her something pleasant to think about as she trudged the rest of the way along the Taff Embankment to Corporation Road. Today, though, she hardly noticed the drab stretch of the Taff, with its grey cracked mud-flats, or noticed the acrid smoke that hung in a haze above Curran's factory where Bronwen worked.

Her mind was too full of the exam results. She had passed in every subject and was qualified to sit for her Higher School Certificate.

As she turned down Aber Street she was surprised to see Bronwen walking just ahead of her. Eager to tell someone her news she called out to her.

'You're late home,' Bronwen chided. 'Missed your bus did you?'

'No, I just wanted to walk. It's nice to be out in the sunshine after being cooped up in school all day.'

'It was absolutely sweltering in our factory,' Bronwen grumbled. 'We asked the foreman if we could take our overalls off but he wouldn't let us. Said it might turn the men on. He might just as well have said yes though, because most of us went to the cloakroom and took our dresses off instead.' She lifted the edge of her brown overall to display a flash of bare leg.

'You mean you got nothing at all on under that?'

'Only french knickers,' Bronwen laughed. 'Are you shocked?'

'Your affair, isn't it?' Nesta shrugged. 'I wouldn't want to go round like that.'

'Well, we're all different about what we do and don't do, aren't we?' her cousin said archly. 'I wouldn't like to go roaming round Tiger Bay on my own, especially late at night, but some people don't mind doing that.'

'Who told you?' Nesta asked, feeling nettled.

'I have my spies. Better not let my Mam find out,' she warned. 'She'd half kill you. What were you doing there, anyway?'

'Just walking.'

'Looking for that Dad of yours more likely,' Bronwen said scornfully. 'Why don't you forget him? It's so long since you saw him you probably wouldn't recognize him, anyway. Was that why you walked home?' she went on, when Nesta merely shrugged her shoulders. 'Hoping you might bump into him?'

'I walked because I wanted to think ... I heard the results of my exams today,' she added quickly, eager to share her good news, her dark eyes shining.

'You passed, then?'

'Yes. In all the subjects. That means I can sit my Higher School Certificate and then ...' she paused and sighed dreamily, 'if I pass three of them I could go to university.'

'I wouldn't count on it,' Bronwen said cuttingly. 'While you've had your nose buried in a book the rest of us have been getting ready for war.'

'What are you talking about?'

'Yes, little Miss Know-It-All, that's news for you, isn't it? Well, I know because our factory is going to stop making pots and pans and start making munitions ready for the war. I know because I'm going to be made a charge-hand.'

'You've got it all wrong, Bronwen. You must have,' Nesta exclaimed. She looked up at the crystal-clear blue sky, felt the heat of the late afternoon sun on her head and shoulders and refused to believe what she was hearing. 'There isn't going to be a war.'

For once, the rest of the Lewis family agreed with Nesta. They laughed at Bronwen's story almost as much as they ridiculed Nesta's hopes of staying on at school and eventually going to university.

'You can forget that right away,' her Uncle Lloyd boomed. 'I told you before when you brought the matter up!'

'It's out of the question, Nesta,' her Aunt Gwen agreed. 'It's work for you. The best thing you can do is get down to Curran's with our Bronwen. There might even be an opening for you in the office if you don't fancy factory work.'

'No thank you!'

'Well, you've got to work, my girl. If you don't want to go to Curran's then you had better find yourself some other job *before* you leave school next week. If you don't, then I'll march you down there myself,' Lloyd Lewis threatened.

Nesta knew he meant it. She was equally determined not to work in a factory, so next day she asked for time off from school so that she could go looking for a job.'

'Why do you need to be in such a rush, Nesta?' Miss Parker, her form-mistress, asked in dismay.

When she heard Nesta's account of what had happened when she had told her family about her future plans, her mouth tightened angrily.

'Well, we can't have you working in a factory,' she agreed. 'Leave this with me. I'll have a word with the Head.'

Mr Perks, the formidable headmaster, sent for Nesta first

thing after assembly the next morning. Five minutes later she emerged from his office, collected her blazer from the cloakroom, and hurried off to keep an appointment at the City Hall.

The interview was a mere formality. Within the hour it was agreed that she would start the following Monday morning in the Treasurer's department.

Landing a job at the City Hall was quite an achievement, Nesta decided as she walked along the thickly carpeted corridors and down the elegant staircase lined with marble statues.

In the busy main hall, she tried to see past the grille windows to the area beyond and wondered just where she would be working.

'Can I help you?' A man behind one of the grilles looked at her quizzically.

'No, no, it's all right,' she blushed furiously. 'I . . . I was just looking around.' She felt her colour rising again. 'I'm starting work here on Monday . . . I just wanted to see what it was like.'

'A new colleague! I shall look forward to seeing you,' he told her gravely.

Nesta was tempted not to tell the Lewises about her job. Then the realization that she really had nothing suitable to wear, apart from her school uniform, forced her into doing so.

'You can borrow something of our Bronwen's until you get your first week's wages,' Aunt Gwen offered.

'I was hoping you might be able to lend me some money to buy a dress, or a skirt and blouse,' Nesta pleaded. The thought of wearing any of Bronwen's cheap, tarty-looking clothes appalled her.

'Borrowing even before you begin work! I don't know about that,' Aunt Gwen pursed her mouth. Then, as she saw disappointment shadow Nesta's eyes, she relented. 'Oh, all right. Only don't make a habit of it, understand? How much will you be getting, anyway?'

'Twelve and sixpence a week.'

'Is that all? Our Bronwen gets over a pound. She gives me ten shillings a week. You ought to do the same.'

'Ten shillings! I'll only have half a crown left for fares and clothes and everything else,' Nesta exclaimed in dismay.

'Better ask for more money, then, or get yourself a job where they pay better wages.'

'Couldn't I give you seven and sixpence a week . . . just for a while, until I get a rise?'

'Well, don't let your Uncle Lloyd know. Here,' she held out a pound note 'take this and get yourself something to wear. It will be your birthday in a few days so you can have that as a present. Only don't tell the others.'

Nesta spent Saturday looking round the shops. They were full of wonderful clothes she would have liked to buy if only she could have afforded them.

Eventually, she chose a pleated skirt in red and grey check which she thought would look smart with her school blouses. If she wore her red school blazer and her red cardigans with it, she decided, it would look like a complete outfit.

It seemed strange to think that she would never be going back to school again. She wondered if any of the girls she had known there would ever come into the City Hall, or whether she would see them when she was out shopping. She had never had any close friends because she would never accept invitations to their homes. Most of the girls in her class lived in the better part of Cathays, and she would have been ashamed for them to see where she lived.

Although she hotly denied Bronwen's accusation that she was a snob and ashamed of them all, she knew in her heart it was true. She had never forgotten the day when the entire class had been taken on a visit to Cardiff Market as part of a study group. As they were passing her Uncle Lloyd's stall she caught sight of him, a striped boater on his head, his large hands red with the blood dripping from the lump of raw beef he was holding up in the air, shouting out the price of it to the crowd. She had turned away quickly, praying he hadn't seen her, afraid that if he had he might call out to her and shame her in front of the other girls.

Nesta found her working days much longer and more tiring than school. The work itself was exacting and not terribly interesting. As the most junior member of the rates department she was expected to act as messenger, taking trays of letters and documents to the other departments. She also had to seal up the countless rate-demand bills and make sure they were sent out at the end of each afternoon.

In the hot stuffy hall, her white blouses were grubby by the end of the day and she needed a clean one for every day of the week. Aunt Gwen grumbled incessantly about 'all this washing', especially when it was raining and Nesta had to hang them on the ceiling-rack in the poky bathroom to dry.

Bronwen would push them to one end, or take them off altogether and drop them into the corner of the room, because she said they were in her way when she was having a bath. The men were just as inconsiderate. Idris would clean his razor on them and her Uncle Lloyd wiped his hands on them.

Nesta sometimes wondered if they did it deliberately. She knew none of them approved of her working in the City Hall. Bronwen was now earning twice as much as she was and they all kept telling her that she ought to change her job and go and work in a factory.

'When are you going to start earning some real money, we can't keep you forever?' her uncle would boom, eyeing her plate with a frown whenever they all sat down for a meal together.

'I'm only here for one meal a day,' Nesta would protest.

'You have breakfast before you go out in the morning, don't you?'

'One slice of toast and a cup of tea, nothing else.'

'There's always plenty cooking, but you always turn your nose up at it,' her aunt bristled. It never failed to annoy her that Nesta refused the morning fry-up of sausage, streaky bacon, black-pudding and thick wedges of fried bread that she always cooked for the rest of them. 'That's why you look half-starved. Thin as a rake, you are, not bonny like our Bronwen.'

Fat was a more apt description, Nesta thought as she looked across the table at her cousin. Bronwen was at least a stone heavier than her, even though she was about three inches shorter. And her figure was as round and plump as her face and she overflowed out of her low-necked dresses and blouses.

Nesta was secretly glad that Bronwen was fatter than her, otherwise, knowing Bronwen as she did, she would have been constantly borrowing her clothes. Not that my clothes would appeal to her, Nesta thought with amusement.

Bronwen liked vivid shades and garish patterns. With her gingery hair there were lots of colours she should have avoided but Bronwen seemed to delight in flaunting convention. Clashing reds, strident purples, mauves, greens, and blues as bright as her eyes were her favourites. Even without her frizzily permed ginger hair it was possible to recognize Bronwen a mile off. She was as pushy and noisy as she was outrageous, and Nesta often wondered what sort of a charge-hand she could possibly be.

Aunt Gwen still insisted that if Bronwen wanted to go dancing then she must take Nesta along as well. Once she started work, however, Nesta rebelled.

'I am going to sign on for a secretarial course at the Technical College, even if it does mean no more dances for you,' she told Bronwen.

'You do what you like,' Bronwen told her. 'I'm eighteen now and I don't give a fig about what Mam thinks. If she doesn't like it, I'll leave home. Anyway, once this war gets started she won't have any hold over me anymore. If she starts making a fuss, I shall join up. I'll go in the ATS and live my own life.'

Everyone was talking about the war. By September, it was no longer idle chatter but established fact. The Prime Minister, Neville Chamberlain, had failed in his attempt to make peace with Adolf Hitler. Germany had invaded Poland on the first of September and two days later Britain and France declared war on Germany.

Everything seemed to change overnight. Gas masks were issued, there was talk of rationing, and everyone was asked to help in the war effort.

The atmosphere at Corporation Road became even more gloomy and uncomfortable when Idris and Elwyn were both called up for the army. Dylan also received his calling up papers. And Bronwen openly announced her intention of going into the ATS.

'What about Miss High-and-Mighty?' Gwladys asked spitefully. 'Safe and sound in her cushy little job at the City Hall, is she?'

'I'll probably have to go into the ATS when I am eighteen, if the war is still on,' Nesta told her.

'I don't see why you can't go into a munitions factory now,' Gwladys retorted.

'Because it's shift work and I want to go to college,' Nesta informed her. 'My Da would have wanted me to go to university, so this is the next best thing.'

'Huh!' Gwladys stood with her hands on her hips, staring at her young cousin. 'It's time you forgot all about that Dad of yours the same as he's forgotten about you!' she said derisively. 'If he's still at sea then he's probably dead by now, the way the Jerries are sinking our boats.'

12

Unlike Bronwen, who found the war, with its blackouts and constant threat of bombing raids, an endless source of excitement, the early months hardly affected Nesta at all.

When the sirens went she followed the others into the Anderson shelter in the backgarden or, if it was during the daytime and she was at work, into the underground shelters at the City Hall. She carried her identity card wherever she went and, like everyone else, occasionally grumbled about the shortages, in particular about the lack of clothing coupons.

When the air-raids started, Aunt Gwen decided it was too risky for them to go the pictures in town, and encouraged Bronwen to bring her friends home. As a result, there was soon a constant succession of soldiers, sailors or airmen visiting the house. Americans, with their lavish gifts of nylons, cigarettes and chocolate bars, were the most popular.

Now that she no longer had to go to dances with Bronwen, Nesta found she had more time for reading and studying. Most evenings she stopped at the public library on her way home, sometimes to change her library books but mostly to scan the newspapers and magazines in the reading room or browse in the reference section.

Since working at the City Hall she had become fascinated by Welsh culture, and as soon as she finished her secretarial course at the Technical College she intended to enrol as a student of Welsh history.

Her appetite had been whetted by the stories her father had told her when she had been a very small child. He had told her she had been named after Princess Nest, the daughter of Rhys ap Tewdwr and wife of Gerald of Windsor who had lived in the twelfth century, and this had always fired her imagination.

It was on one of her evening visits to the library that she fell into conversation with Tecwyn Phillips.

She already knew him by sight. He worked in the rates department and he had spoken to her the day she had gone to the City Hall for her interview. Since then, whenever their paths crossed, they had exchanged smiles. He was so very much her senior that she was a little in awe of him. This was the first time they had met on neutral ground.

'Are you here for the meeting?' he asked, his deep-set eyes behind the dark-rimmed glasses fixing her with a piercing stare.

'Meeting . . . what meeting?' She frowned, not fully understanding what he was talking about.

'Plaid Cymru, of course. There's a meeting here this evening, to outline their aims. Once this war ends, there's bound to be a general election. Then it will be up to us Welsh to make sure the right sort of person is returned to represent Cardiff in Parliament. You do agree with that, I hope.'

'You mean Wales for the Welsh!'

'A convert!' His black eyes shone excitedly. 'You'll come to the meeting then?'

'Well . . . I don't know . . .'

'Come on!' He took her firmly by the arm and guided her towards a small ante-room which was already filling up. He found two seats near the front and left her to see his chair wasn't taken by anyone while he went to have a few words with one of the organizers. When he returned he handed her a leaflet.

'That should tell you all you need to know about Plaid Cymru. Their aims are all written down there. And there's a form on the other side if you want to join. We need new members, so give it some thought.'

Before she could answer they were hushed into silence

by the chairman rapping on the table and introducing the main speaker for the evening.

Nesta listened to the lecture on Welsh Nationalism with increasing interest. It was coupled with a plea that they should all unite in the fight to ensure that the identity of Wales, its culture and civilization, was retained.

Afterwards she found herself glowing with enthusiasm. When Tecwyn invited her to go for a coffee with him she accepted, eager to pour out her own views on the subject to a receptive ear.

He encouraged her interest with a compelling fervour, expounding his own theories in a frenetic voice that carried with it a burning conviction.

He tried to draw her out about her own political background, assuring her that as a second generation born in Cardiff and with a father who came from North Wales, she could indeed claim to be more Welsh than English. He disconcerted her, however, by telling her that there were considerable differences, both in language and culture, between the Welsh of North Wales and those who lived in South Wales.

'Here in Cardiff, very few people speak Welsh,' he pointed out. 'In the Rhondda valley only two per cent of the children speak their mother-tongue and in Merthyr Tydfil less than one per cent! In North Wales, now, almost fifty per cent speak Welsh. An even greater number in some of the more isolated rural areas. There, they even conduct their parish meetings and church services in Welsh.'

'Does it matter?'

'Unless you have the tongue, you will always be considered a foreigner in North Wales,' he warned her.

'Do you speak Welsh yourself?' Nesta asked.

'No.' Tecwyn shook his head sadly. 'I've tried to learn several times but I never could master it. Now, if you are good at languages, since you have only just finished your schooling, you should be able to pick it up easy enough.'

'I would certainly like to try.'

'Mind you,' he warned, 'don't forget there are two distinct dialects. In fact, even the grammar is different here in the South from that in the North.'

'I'm thinking of taking a course in Welsh History at the Tech next year, after I've finished my secretarial course,' Nesta told him.

'Then, in that case you couldn't do better than to come to our next meeting. It will be held a fortnight today, and admission will be by ticket only because the speaker will be Saunders Lewis.'

He could tell from her blank expression that she had never even heard the name. With pride he explained that Saunders Lewis was perhaps the greatest living Welshman fighting for the cause of Plaid Cymru.

'Will you come as my guest?' he invited. 'If you are at all interested in the Welsh mind, Welsh culture and the Welsh language there is no finer speaker.'

Nesta went home in a daze. It seemed as if a whole new world had opened up. She was tingling with excitement and she had a strong conviction that she was doing something of which her father would approve wholeheartedly.

Even though Aunt Gwen and the rest of the Lewis family told her she should stop thinking about her father, since he was probably dead, the feeling that this was not so grew increasingly stronger. It was as if an invisible thread linked them together and she felt convinced that not only was he still alive but that someday they would meet again.

The only person who had ever believed her had been Chris Jenkins. It was a long time since she had seen him and, for a fleeting moment, she wondered whether, like her cousins, Idris and Elwyn, he, too, had been called up for National Service.

The departure of the two boys had certainly changed her lifestyle for the better. After Idris had finished his training he had been sent to Italy. And, since it seemed unlikely that he would be home again until the war ended, Aunt Gwen had told her she could have his room.

'Be better than sleeping on the put-you-up. Give you a bit more privacy.'

Nesta had accepted with alacrity and moved her belongings upstairs right away. The opportunity to have a bedroom, where she could lock the door and no one would have any excuse for barging in, was like a dream come true.

'Our Bronwen needs the front room for her courting,' Aunt Gwen went on. 'Serious she is this time. There will be wedding bells before the year's out, mark my words. They want to get married before Hank is sent overseas. The wives of American soldiers get a marvellous separation allowance, you know. She will be able to save enough for them to set up home at the end of the war,' she added gleefully.

'Or pay her fare back to America,' Nesta smiled.

'America! Our Bronwen go to America? Don't talk so daft, girl. She would never leave Cardiff.'

'But Hank may want to go back to his own country.'

'Well he will have to go on his own then, won't he?' Aunt Gwen snapped. 'My Bronwen won't leave me.'

'Then there is not much point in them getting married, is there?' Nesta asked bewildered.

'She may as well have her separation allowance,' her aunt sniffed.

Nesta didn't bother arguing any more. She knew it was pointless. She had never understood Bronwen's interest in men to the exclusion of everything else. Maybe, as Bronwen was always saying, she was the odd one. She was far happier studying or reading about Wales than going dancing or to the pictures.

Two weeks later, when she attended a Plaid Cymru meeting to hear Saunders Lewis speak, this fascination was strengthened even more.

An aesthetic, craggy-faced man with a receding hairline, he inspired patriotism. The words that flowed from his thin lips held the packed room spellbound. He spoke from the heart. And, as his words conjured up an inspiring picture of a Wales of the future, when a national conscience would be reflected in actions as well as music and literature, he carried his whole audience with him.

Nesta listened enthralled, leaning forward in her chair so as not to miss a single syllable of his exhortation.

Tecwyn had already told her a great deal about Saunders Lewis. He was not just a man of words but a fine scholar and a lecturer at University College, Swansea.

A few years earlier, when the War Office had built a bombing-site at a beauty spot on the Llyn Peninsula in Caernarvonshire, he had instigated and taken part in an arson attack, as a form of protest against the way the government were desecrating the Welsh countryside. The outcome of his fire-raising had been that he had spent nine months in Wormwood Scrubs prison.

Now, listening to this fiery, erudite Welshman, Nesta was convinced that to be a member of Plaid Cymru would fulfil her deep longing to really belong. '*Hiraeth*', that's it, she thought with a smile. She knew that the nearest translation of the word was 'nostalgia' or 'longing' and she felt that described her own feelings perfectly.

When the meeting ended, her brain was buzzing with all she had heard and she felt bubbling over with enthusiasm.

A few days later she was jolted back to reality.

'What are you getting all dolled up for then? Going out with that bloke from the City Hall again?' Bronwen smirked as she stood in the doorway of the small front bedroom watching Nesta combing her hair.

'I'm going to a meeting at the library. Tecwyn will probably be there,' Nesta answered, frowning at her reflection in the mirror as she carefully blotted the lipstick she had just applied.

'Our Mam will half kill you if she finds out,' Bronwen warned her. 'You are only seventeen and he looked old enough to be your Da. I bet he's married.'

'What if he is? I only went to a meeting with him.'

'Oh, yes!' Bronwen grinned knowingly.

'It's the truth,' Nesta retorted heatedly.

'Well, don't lose your rag,' Bronwen taunted. 'A sure sign you're guilty if you blow your top. I must say he wouldn't be my choice but then you always were a queer one.'

'It's got nothing to do with you, anyway,' Nesta told her. 'I don't interfere in what you do or who you go out with.'

'No, but I am over eighteen. And even now our Mam carries on something alarming if I want to go to a dance. I tell you what,' she offered slyly, 'I won't mention to our Mam that you are going out with a married man if you'll come to St Mellons with me next Saturday night.'

'St Mellons? Do you mean the RAF base? You must be mad. Why would I want to go there?'

'There's a dance on that I want to go to,' Bronwen told her. 'I've promised to meet someone there.'

'I thought you were supposed to be engaged . . . to Hank the Yank,' Nesta said in surprise.

'He's not around to take me out though, is he? And I'm not sitting at home until he gets back.'

'Aunt Gwen would be furious if she ever found out.'

'She will think I'm going with you.'

'Don't be ridiculous, Bronwen! She knows I would never have a date with an airman.'

'That doesn't matter,' Bronwen snapped impatiently. 'We'll tell her there's a dance and she won't mind as long as we both go.' She paused, 'If you don't, I shall tell on you and she will stop you going out at nights altogether.'

'I only go to Tech or to the library,' Nesta argued.

'That's what you tell my Mam . . . and she believes you.

If I told her that I'd seen you out with a married man, though . . .'

Bronwen left the rest of the sentence unsaid but her bright blue eyes spoke volumes as they met Nesta's.

'Tell her what you like,' Nesta shrugged.

'She will stop you going out.'

Nesta stared defiantly at her cousin. Then the thought of being late for the Plaid Cymru meeting, which Tecwyn had assured her promised to be even better than the last one, made her change her mind.

'All right. I'll come with you to St Mellons. But not because you are blackmailing me! If I stay and argue with you I shall miss the opening of my meeting,' she added as she stood up and slipped on her jacket.

Three hours later, as she sat drinking coffee with Tecwyn, she knew her decision earlier in the evening had been the right one.

The speaker had been a fine orator and reporter. His talk on what was happening in other parts of the country, in North Wales in particular, had been both informative and stirring.

Tecwyn was bubbling with enthusiasm when the meeting ended, the lilt in his voice rising and falling as he went over the various points the speaker had discussed.

'Who is the Dragon he kept mentioning?' Nesta asked.

'I don't know who he is exactly,' Tecwyn assured her, 'but he is of considerable importance. That's why he calls himself the Dragon. Symbolic, see?'

'He certainly sounds fiery,' Nesta laughed. 'That is if all the things he is reputed to have done are true.'

'Oh they're true all right,' Tecwyn assured her. 'The Dragon has been active for some considerable time now. He started coming to the fore just before the war started. He rarely speaks at any meetings, but he does a tremendous amount of work behind the scenes.'

'How do you know?'

'Always leaves a signature, doesn't he? Never fails. The Dragon is his trademark, if you like. Saunders Lewis, and one or two others, know who he is, but they respect his wish to remain anonymous. Bit like a spy. And his actions prove to be much more effective if people don't know for sure who is behind them.'

Just as she was dropping off to sleep that night, her mind full of all that she had heard that evening, Nesta heard a faint tapping on her bedroom door.

'It's only me,' Bronwen announced in a whisper. 'Just come to remind you about Saturday night.'

'Go away,' Nesta told her sleepily. 'I've said I'll come and I never go back on my word, you should know that by now.'

13

The promise to go to a dance with Bronwen niggled Nesta for the rest of the week. She had so many other things on her mind that the thought of spending an evening in the claustrophobic atmosphere of an RAF camp was like a dark cloud hanging over her. She didn't enjoy dancing and she would have far rather spent the evening at the library, seeing if she could dig up more information about the Dragon.

'I think you two girls should think again about going to that RAF dance at St Mellons,' Aunt Gwen told them anxiously as she put down the paper she was reading. 'It says here that there was a bombing raid in Liverpool last night and they say that next time Jerry will come south and that Bristol and Cardiff will be the targets.'

'Load of rubbish! They can't be sure,' Bronwen protested.

'It's the docks they're after, see,' Aunt Gwen said worriedly. 'If they can blow them up it stops the boats bringing in supplies of food. They want to starve us out, that's what they are trying to do.'

'Well, there's no docks at St Mellons, so that's all right then,' Bronwen said quickly.

'There's the docks at Barry and Newport, though,' her mother reminded her. 'And St Mellons is not all that far outside Cardiff. If the docks here are one of their targets, then like as not some of the bombs will fall that way.'

'It was a full moon last night. That will be gone by Saturday night,' Bronwen snapped irritably.

'What's that got to do with it?' her mother asked frowning.

'Jerry only bombs places when there is a full moon and they can see their target. That is why they have just bombed Liverpool,' Bronwen added in exasperated tones. 'They won't be back again for weeks.'

'I don't know about that. I think you'd better see what your Da thinks about you going.'

'Oh, stop fussing, our Mam. Tell you what,' she went on quickly, as she saw her mother's chin jut for an argument. 'If we have any bombing raids between now and Saturday then we won't go.'

Nesta found herself praying there would be at least one raid somewhere, to make it impossible for them to go to the dance. The next three nights were overcast and cloudy, however, and no German bombers ventured across the Channel with their death loads.

The RAF had arranged for special coaches to collect girls from various points in Cardiff and take them out to the camp. As Nesta and Bronwen made their way to a pick-up point Nesta secretly hoped it might have gone without them.

The evening went much as she expected. As soon as they reached the camp, a handsome blond sergeant claimed Bronwen. From his enthusiastic greeting it was obvious he knew her.

The moment she was on her own, Nesta found herself surrounded by young airmen. Even when she told them she didn't dance, several were eager to try to teach her. Against her will, she found herself on the dance floor getting hotter and more fed up by the minute and wishing she had never come.

It would have been much better to have let Bronwen tell Aunt Gwen about the meetings with Tecwyn at the library. They had, after all, been perfectly harmless, even if he was a married man. And he had mentioned that he would be bringing his wife to the next meeting, so it wasn't as though they were doing anything underhand.

After an hour on the dance floor, Nesta felt so exhausted that she insisted on stopping for a drink. She was half-way through her glass of lemonade when the sirens sounded. She looked round for Bronwen but there was no sign of her.

Before she could decide what to do for the best, the lights flickered and dimmed and she found herself caught up in the general mêlée. Senior officers barked out orders and the airmen shepherded everybody off the dance floor and towards the air-raid shelters. Overhead the drone of approaching heavy bombers brought their own dire warning.

Even before they reached safety there was the high-pitched scream of bombs as they whistled earthwards, followed by the dull thud as they reached their target. Simultaneously, ear-shattering explosions shook the ground. The night sky was lit up as flames followed, and as tongues of fire licked at the nearby buildings the air became a cacophony of crackling and crashing as masonry crumbled.

Concern for Bronwen's safety uppermost in her mind, Nesta pushed her way through the mass of men and girls huddled in the shelter searching for the sergeant who had claimed Bronwen.

'They went off to the Three Stars Hotel. It's just down the road,' a corpulent warrant officer told her. 'They'll be tucked up in bed now so they'll never even hear this lot,' he grinned, his pale eyes narrowing.

'Could you take me along there ... please ... right away,' she asked.

'Turns you on, does it?' He let out a long low whistle. His arm slid round her waist, his podgy fingers fondling her breast.

'Come on then, let's go before you change your mind,' he said sharply, as angrily she pushed him away.

Grabbing her hand, he elbowed a path through the milling bodies towards the door. The cold night air was like a slap in the face and she shivered.

'Hang on, I'll have you between the sheets in no time,' he muttered hoarsely. His groping hand went round her waist again. This time it slid down to encompass her buttocks and suddenly he was pulling her against him, his mouth hot and wet devouring hers.

As she wrestled to free herself there was a thunderous roar, the ground shook, and she found herself lifted into the air by the force of the explosion. Screaming with fright she clung to her companion and felt a jarring thud as they both hit the ground. She tried to get up but found herself trapped beneath him by debris that had showered down on top of them.

Panic-stricken, Nesta struggled to separate herself from the embrace which locked them together. She managed to free one hand and push his face away from her own. As she did so she was conscious that something warm, wet and sticky was oozing from his mouth.

In the light from the fires raging all around she could see that her hands were covered with something dark and sticky. Her horror intensified as she realized it was blood. As her eyes focused on the face that had been pressed against her own she saw the eyes were wide and staring.

Sweat rivered down the nape of her neck.

As she pushed him away, more blood gushed from the gaping mouth and sagging lips. A horrendous scream filled the air. It seemed to be coming from somewhere far away but she knew instinctively that she was the one who was making the chilling sound and desperately tried to stop.

She lost all count of time as terror engulfed her. She felt as limp as a rag doll. Hands dragged her from under the rubble and carried her back inside the shelter. Her cuts and grazes were bathed, and she was given a drink of water. Gradually the thundering of her heart slowed and the thumping at her temples eased. The waves of sickness subsided. The nightmare was over.

For a while, though, she couldn't even remember where

she was or what she had been doing when the raid started. All she wanted to do was lie with her eyes closed, trying to shut out the memory of what had happened. By breathing slowly and very deeply she could momentarily drift into a state of unconsciousness, until the noise that was going on all around her in the shelter dragged her back to reality.

Much later, after the raid ended and the girls who had come out from Cardiff were being escorted on to the coaches, she remembered about Bronwen. Panic-stricken she ran from coach to coach, asking if anyone had seen her or knew where she was.

'You'd better get on one of these yourself,' the camp commandant told her. 'If she turns up we'll see she gets home safely.'

'Someone told me she had gone to the Three Stars Hotel.'

'I've never heard of it,' he said blankly.

'One of the warrant officers promised to take me there,' Nesta insisted. 'We were on our way when the air-raid started.'

'Well, even if there is such a place he won't take you there now,' the camp commandant told her brusquely. 'He's dead!'

Her mind was in a turmoil as she sat huddled in the coach on the journey back to Cardiff. She dreaded having to tell Aunt Gwen that Bronwen was missing. How would she ever explain how they came to be separated. She certainly couldn't tell her aunt that Bronwen had last been seen going off to a hotel with one of the sergeants.

As she walked towards the house after she left the coach, her heart sank when she saw there were lights on downstairs. She felt so shaken by all that had happened that she had hoped it might be possible to sneak up to her room undetected and leave explanations until the next morning. By then, with any luck, Bronwen might even be home.

The tirade broke even before she could close the front

door. Aunt Gwen was in the hallway, her fat face puce with anger. Seizing Nesta by the arm she shook her furiously, calling her every vile name she could lay her tongue to. Nesta stood dazed, her back to the wall, protesting feebly at the onslaught.

'Rotten little bitch,' her aunt screamed, 'going off like that and leaving our Bronwen. Lucky for you she wasn't killed or you'd have that on your conscience as well as everything else. No wonder you stopped going to church. Couldn't face confession. I know it all now. Not satisfied with carrying on with a married man behind our backs, you sleep around as well. If it wasn't for upsetting our Bronwen even more I'd make you pack you bags and get out right now, this very minute. Your Uncle Lloyd threatens to take a strap to you so you'd best keep out of his way.'

Over her aunt's shoulder she saw Bronwen was standing on the stairs, a finger pressed to her lips, signalling her to say nothing.

She had no idea how Bronwen had got home before her but indignation that she was having to take the rap for Bronwen's misdeeds surged through her. While she had been churned up with worry, Bronwen had been at home, safe and sound.

At that moment she hated them all.

An awful pessimism descended slowly into her mind. If only she knew where to find her father, she thought bitterly, so that she could go to him.

Choked by unshed tears, she pushed past Bronwen and made her way up to her room. Her aching head and the soreness of the bruises and lacerations on her face and hands were as nothing to the hurt she felt deep inside her.

Next day Aunt Gwen and Bronwen seemed to spend the entire Sunday talking about the previous night's air-raid at the RAF camp.

'The moment the sirens sounded, I knew you would be

worried out your mind, Mam, so I got on the first coach I could back to Cardiff.'

'You did the right thing,' her mother agreed.

'I asked everyone if they had seen Nesta. No one seemed to know where she was, only that she had left the dance hall with someone early in the evening,' she added slyly.

Nesta listened but said nothing. She didn't even bother to explain or correct Bronwen's version of the story, knowing that her aunt was unlikely to believe her even if she did. She was quite certain that Bronwen hadn't been on the first coach that had left the dance, or on any of the others either, but suspected she had returned by car or taxi.

As soon as they had eaten Sunday lunch and she had helped to wash up, Nesta went up to her bedroom. The shock of what had happened the night before had left her feeling drained. She was lying on her bed reading when Bronwen burst into the room.

'Chris Jenkins is downstairs. He's been called up and has come to say goodbye.'

Nesta was delighted to see him, though sorry to hear the reason for his visit. She had always been particularly fond of her cousin Chris and had pleasant memories of the way he had walked her to school when she had lived with his family in Pontypridd.

'I wanted to bring you these, Nesta,' he said holding out a bundle of papers. 'Mam told our Dilys to give them to you when you were leaving our place but she didn't bother. I've been looking after them ever since. I thought they might be something you'd want.'

'It was nice of you to take the trouble,' she smiled warmly, touched by this thoughtfulness.

'To be honest, I put them away in my cupboard and forgot about them until I was packing my things ready to go in the army. That framed photograph of your father is there, the one our Dilys broke and for which I promised to get the glass mended for you. Taken a long time but it's done now,' he grinned.

After Chris had left and she had promised to write to him as soon as he sent her his army address, Nesta took the bundle of letters and photographs up to her bedroom.

She unwrapped the photograph and studied the lean handsome face of the man who was her father. His grey eyes looked almost black as they stared back at her above the well-shaped nose. The firm clean-cut mouth, the square chin, and the thick, dark hair brushed back from the wide forehead were just as she remembered.

The picture gave no indication of his height or the broadness of his chest. She could vaguely recall how he had towered over her and how she had felt higher than the rooftops when he had carried her on his shoulders.

His unforgettable voice with its mellifluous lilt rang in her ears. The last time he had been on shore leave their very last outing had been to the museum and then, because it was a lovely sunny day, to Roath Park. She remembered how they had stood hand in hand, watching some boys sail a boat on the lake, so very happy in each other's company.

As she put down the photograph and picked up the bundle of letters, once again she had the strong premonition that her father was still alive and that someday she would find him.

The letters were all very old. Ones which her mother had tied up with ribbon and saved. Aunt Betty must have collected them from the house in Coburn Street after her grandparents had died. They dated from when her parents had first married until a few weeks before her own birth.

At the bottom of the pile, wrapped up in brown paper, was a thin book. She looked at it dumbfounded. It was a Post Office Savings book in her name. With trembling fingers she turned the pages, then drew in her breath sharply as she saw that the total sum entered was two hundred and fifteen pounds!

It was a small fortune.

Excitedly she looked back at the entries and slowly it dawned on her that the dates all related to times when her father had been home on leave. Instead of spending the money her father had handed over to pay for looking after her, her grandmother had banked it all in her name.

Nesta sat for a long time mesmerized by her discovery. Then she turned back to the letters and began to read the very last one in the pile. It was full of assurances that he would be home on leave well before the baby was born and promises of the future they would all have together.

If only it could have come true, she thought sadly, her eyes misting over with tears. As she read to the bottom of the last page she gasped in astonishment.

At first she couldn't believe her eyes.

Quickly she sorted through the rest of the pile, turning to the last page of each letter. In all of them the final line was the same.

He hadn't signed any of them 'Rhys' or 'Your loving husband' as she would have expected. In every one, the final signature remained the same. They all ended:

> 'With fondest love,
> Ever yours,
> The Dragon.'

14

Nesta's dark eyes were shining with enthusiasm as she looked up from the pamphlet Tecwyn had given her to read.

'Great stuff, isn't it?' he enthused.

She nodded. The flowing phrases and vivid descriptions the writer had used to expound his theories were indeed stirring but to her they were more than that. The phrases and eulogies were uncannily familiar because she had read many of them within the last few days in an entirely different context. In many of the paragraphs, the turn of phrase, the way of expressing things, was identical to passages in the letters her father had written to her mother. Now, as she read through the pamphlet yet again, she was more than ever convinced that the Dragon and Rhys Evans were one and the same.

The idea had steadily grown ever since she had seen the way her father had signed his letters all those years ago. At first she had told herself that it was sheer coincidence. Remembering how proud he had been of his Welsh ancestry, she toyed with the idea that he had used the symbolism as some kind of joke. Or, perhaps it was the way he had seen himself, as a fiery creature who had escaped from the mountains to explore the world, returning only occasionally to the safety of his lair.

If that were so, then the Dragon of those letters and the Dragon who made such impassioned speeches about the need for Wales to have Home Rule must be one and the same.

She had thought of every possible argument why it should not be so, but none of them had stood up to scrutiny. The more she had studied the speeches, the writings, and every other scrap of information she could find about the Dragon and his association with Plaid Cymru, the more convinced she became that she was right.

Tecwyn had been a useful source of information. He was an ardent admirer of the Dragon and supported most things the Dragon said or did. He regarded the Dragon as an orator who was as impassioned in his championship of Wales as Lloyd George had ever been.

'We are fortunate that we have the Dragon in North Wales, Aneurin Bevan in South Wales and Saunders Lewis in mid-Wales linking them together,' he exclaimed with satisfaction.

Knowing Nesta was more interested in the Dragon than in either of the others, however, he had gone to great lengths to find out more about him.

'He's a very elusive character, and there's countless stories circulating about him,' he told her. 'Whenever he addresses a meeting, people come away so dazzled by his words that they talk of nothing else for weeks. At the end of the meeting, though, he just slips away, refusing to be interviewed or photographed, so for the most part it is hearsay. The best description I can get is that he is a tall, thin chap, of around forty, with a shock of dark hair, a beard and compelling eyes. Rumour has it that at one time he went to sea,' he added as an afterthought.

The news left Nesta even more convinced that the Dragon was her father. She could think of nothing else and daydreamed about the day when she could actually meet him. Even so she was determined to find positive proof, such as a picture of the Dragon, before she confided her secret to anyone, including Tecwyn.

She spent every moment she could at the library, searching through back issues of newspapers and magazines, digging out every scrap of information she could about the Plaid Cymru movement, hoping to find a picture of the Dragon.

She was so absorbed in her project that she was taken by surprise when her Aunt Gwen stormed into her bedroom one evening and began upbraiding her, blaming her for the fact that Bronwen seemed depressed.

'You never go out with her or even talk to her these days,' Aunt Gwen complained. She began to weep, great racking sobs that shook her plump body. Her face became swollen and blotched as she rubbed at her eyes, trying to stem the tears.

'I don't understand,' Nesta exclaimed, bewildered and distressed by her aunt's outburst.

'Our Bronwen . . . gone and fallen for an air force sergeant. Silly little fool. Can't put him out of her mind.' A sob tore at her throat. 'And he's missing . . . not returned from a raid over Germany.'

'Oh no! Poor Bronwen.'

She tried to feel sorry for her cousin but, knowing what a flirt Bronwen could be, Nesta was not altogether surprised.

'Yes, poor Bronwen,' her aunt repeated bitterly.

'So she will be marrying Hank after all?'

'Hank . . . Hank!' Her aunt spat the name at her. 'He took himself off months ago.'

'But they were engaged . . . she never told me . . .'

'You wouldn't have listened even if she had,' her aunt stormed. 'Your head is too full of your own carry-on to give a damn about anyone else.'

Nesta went out of her way to talk to Bronwen but her cousin turned on her angrily.

'What did you have to go and remind my Mam about that Yank for?' she snapped, her blue eyes blazing. 'She's been nagging me ever since about how I've lost a good meal ticket. I've a good mind to go and jump in the canal and put an end to it all,' she snivelled, pushing her frizzy ginger hair back from her face. 'You don't know what it's like having to work in a munitions factory. Men pawing you, pinching your bottom and trying to get you into a corner all the time.'

'I don't believe you!' Nesta exclaimed, shocked. 'If it is like that, when why stay there? You could always go and work somewhere else.'

'And get nabbed for the ATS? No thank you!'

'The war is bound to be over soon, they won't be calling anyone else up.'

In that Nesta was proved wrong.

Three days after her eighteenth birthday, an official-looking brown envelope arrived for her, and Bronwen was quick to taunt her by repeating her earlier words.

'They won't be calling anyone else up,' she mimicked Nesta's voice. 'Fancy that, Miss Know-It-All. Serve you right. Now you'll find out what life is all about.'

'I'll manage,' Nesta told her confidently.

'I can see you living in barracks, up at seven o'clock every morning, scrubbing floors or, better still, out on the square drilling.'

Nesta said nothing. Inwardly she felt excited by the enforced change in her lifestyle. She had been wanting to leave Corporation Road for some time but she hadn't known how to go about it. Now the problem had been solved for her. And, since it was a government order, there was nothing her aunt could do to stop her, Nesta thought jubilantly.

It was a warm, drizzly day in mid-July when Nesta went for her medical. She passed AW1 and was told to report for training in two weeks.

The prospect filled her with a mixture of excitement and apprehension. On her way home, she had a flash of inspiration. She had some holiday due to her so why not go to North Wales and see for herself the mountains she'd dreamed about all her life.

She hoped Aunt Gwen wouldn't raise any objections. When she told her, however, she found that her aunt was too full of her own problems to pay very much attention.

'Go to North Wales, go anywhere you like,' Aunt Gwen stormed. 'I never want to set eyes on you again. Brought nothing but trouble to our family and that's a fact.'

'What have I done wrong now?' Nesta asked with a touch of irritation.

'Our Bronwen's pregnant and you're as much to blame as she is,' Aunt Gwen stormed. 'Don't you try to tell me you didn't know what was going on,' her aunt went on bitterly. 'None of this would have happened if I hadn't let her go with you to St Mellons.'

Memory of that hateful evening flooded over Nesta as she stared at her aunt's furious face.

'What do you mean?'

'Too busy having your own fun, weren't you? Never a thought about Bronwen. And I only let her go because of you.'

'That's not true . . .'

'No point in going over it all again,' her aunt said bitterly. 'Our Bronwen's pregnant and the father's missing, presumed dead. Having you saddled on us all our life has been bad enough! Now this is another one we'll have to bring up.'

Nesta stared at her aunt speechless, shattered by the venom in the older woman's voice. She was stunned to find her aunt resented her so much and that she had been such a burden to them.

Tears of self-pity prickled behind her eyes. She had always tried so hard to fit in, even done Bronwen's share of the chores as well as her own. Ever since she had started work she had handed over most of her wages to Aunt Gwen.

She'd had enough.

Determinedly she went up to her bedroom and took down the brown-fibre suitcase from the top of the wardrobe. Hidden inside it was the Post Office Savings book. She had never been tempted to spend any of it. Now she would use it to go to North Wales. If she could trace her grandparents they might even be able to tell her where she could find her father, she thought excitedly.

In a burst of confidence and because she felt she must share her secret with someone, when she arrived at the City Hall next morning she told Tecwyn of her plans. She also told him about the bundle of letters and the signature on them.

Tecwyn heard her out in silence, tapping his lower lip thoughtfully with his fountain pen.

'Well . . . what do you think?'

'I don't know what to say. You could possibly be right,' he admitted cautiously.

'Everything else seems to fit. His background, age . . .' her voice trailed off, as her dark eyes met his hopefully.

'Nesta,' his own eyes were pleading behind his heavy-framed glasses as he reached out and took her hand, 'Let me come to North Wales with you.'

'No!' She pulled back in alarm, flinching from his amorous gaze. 'You can't do that . . . it wouldn't be right.'

'Why not?' His eyes became wistful and unfathomable.

'You . . . you're married!' Her aunt's recriminations about her association with a married man filled her head. She had always thought of Tecwyn as just a friend who shared her political interests, nothing more. Now the gleam in his eyes and the emotion in his voice disturbed her.

'My marriage has been one of habit for along time now,' he said with a sad little smile. 'Sylvia won't raise any fuss . . . even if I never come back. It's you I'm in love with, Nesta,' he said softly, taking her hand again. 'If you go away there will be nothing left in life for me.'

Her heart racing with panic Nesta drew back, staring at Tecwyn wide-eyed as Bronwen's words, 'old enough to be your father', rang in her head.

Tecwyn's impassioned declaration frightened her. She didn't know how to handle the situation. She didn't want to hurt Tecwyn's feelings but the thought of him even kissing her was repugnant. She saw him as though through Bronwen's eyes. A nondescript, bespectacled middle-aged man with a receding hairline and she had to fight back a hysterical giggle.

'I know I am older than you, Nesta,' he pleaded, 'but I would be good to you, we could be happy together. I will give up my job here and we'll go and live in North Wales, if that is what you want.'

'No . . . no!' she heard herself shouting. Then as she saw the stricken look on Tecwyn's face she turned and ran out of the office, racing down the wide corridors towards the outside world as though a devil was after her. She heard Tecwyn running after her, calling her name as she fled down the wide steps outside the City Hall. She bolted blindly into the mêlée of traffic as she raced across Park Place, into Queen Street and on through the Arcade.

When finally she stopped for breath she was outside the railway station. It was as if fate was helping her to reach a decision, she thought, as she sat in the station buffet drinking a cup of tea and trying to convince herself that she was doing the right thing. In her heart she knew she could not go on living with the Lewises at Corporation Road. And, because of Tecwyn, she would have to leave the City Hall. The thought saddened her. She had enjoyed working there. Built in glittering white Portland stone, a massive Welsh dragon on the very pinnacle of the great dome high above the council-chamber, and an imposing clock-tower at one corner, it was a magnificent landmark, and she had grown fond of its lofty marble hallways and larger-than-life statues of Welsh folk heroes.

She would also miss her lunchtime strolls in Cathays Park or in the grounds of Cardiff Castle, and her visits to the nearby museum, that always brought back poignant childhood memories of outings with her father.

It was no good dwelling on the past, Nesta told herself. She had two weeks before she went into the ATS and she intended to enjoy them.

She would start by doing something she had dreamed about all her life. She would find her other grandparents, if they were still alive, and see if they could help her trace her father. If it didn't work out, well at least she would have visited North Wales and seen some of the places her father had told her about.

She looked at her watch and then at the list of train times. She had exactly an hour in which to collect her suitcase from Corporation Road and be back at the station in time for the next train.

It was too late now to change her mind, she resolved as she counted out her money and bought a ticket to Blaenau Ffestiniog. In one hour she would be leaving Cardiff, and the Lewises, behind her.

It would be like starting a new life.

Slowly it dawned on her that she was free and in charge of her own destiny. For the first time in her life she was going to be able to do whatever she wanted. Never again would she have to go to dances with Bronwen or listen to her aunt grumbling at her because she was reading a book.

Ever since she could remember she had been forced to fit in with other people's plans and live her life as they chose. Now there would be no one to dictate to her, no one to resent her presence, no one at all that she was answerable to ... not until she went into the ATS.

Even that would be preferable to living with people who didn't want you, she told herself. There would be rules and discipline but they would be the same for everyone. There would be no favouritism or petty jealousies or constant friction, like there had been between her and Bronwen.

As she hurried along the Taff Embankment with its wide

grey mud-flats on each side of the river, she felt light-headed at the prospect of what might be in store.

The scrap of pasteboard in her hand was her passport to the future, she thought with growing excitement.

15

By the time she reached Chester, Nesta was impatient to see the mountain ranges she had dreamed about for so many years. As they passed Abergavenny she had caught a glimpse of the Sugar Loaf, but that had soon disappeared into the distance, and, since then, the train had skirted the border between England and Wales and the view had been mostly of lush green fields, lakes, rivers and woods.

The stations had carried no names, because of wartime security, so except when they actually stopped at a station, and the name of the place was called out, she had only been able to guess which towns they were passing through.

All the way from Cardiff the train had been packed with servicemen carrying tin hats, gas packs and cumbersome kitbags that wouldn't fit on to the luggage rack. And even though the window had been down as far as it would go, it had been unbearably stuffy.

Now that she had an entire compartment to herself, she stretched out her long slim legs, enjoying the chance to cool off, and settled back in her corner seat to enjoy the scenery as they travelled along the edge of the coast.

The sea glittered like blue glass under the hot July sun. In a very short time the track swung inwards, and, away in the distance, she could see dark hazy smudges on the horizon. Was it possible that they were the outlines of mountains, she wondered, her attention rivetted on them.

The craggy peaks seemed to scrape against the sky. Their sheer majesty took her breath away. They made the Sugar Loaf and the ranges near Caerphilly and Pontypridd seem like mere hillocks.

Once they reached the heart of the mountains, she

glimpsed the sparkle of water in many of the hollows. And around these lakes, sheep were grazing, black and white blobs on the undulating scrub and grass.

A ticket inspector boarded the train at Colwyn Bay and in a lilting voice told her the best way to get to Blaenau Ffestiniog.

Her mind buzzing with the Welsh placenames, Nesta anxiously checked where they were each time the train stopped. She felt overwhelmed by the grandeur of the scenery. It was so much more magnificent than her wildest imaginings. Bewitched by it all, she could hardly wait to reach her destination.

There was a mirror on the wall above the seat opposite so, balancing as well as she could in the swaying carriage, she peered into it, studying her reflection critically.

As she combed her thick dark hair and put on some fresh lipstick, anxious to look her best, she wondered if her grandparents would know who she was when they met her.

Everyone said she was like her father and Nesta supposed they must be right, since in the one photograph she had of her mother she was round-faced and pretty with fair, wavy hair.

Blaenau Ffestiniog came as a shock.

After the enchantment of the changing scenery ever since she had left Chester, Nesta was unprepared for the sombre bluish-grey atmosphere of the town. Not even the brightness of the afternoon sun seemed to be able to add colour to the drabness.

Nesta felt a shiver of dismay run through her as she stood outside the railway station holding her brown-fibre suitcase and wondering which way she should go.

The tier upon tier of grey terraced houses looked so much alike that her spirits sank. Finding her grandparents, when the only thing she knew about them was that they must be in their sixties and that their name was Evans, suddenly seemed an impossible task.

She turned to go back to the station, intending to ask

the ticket collector's help, when she saw a policeman watching her.

'Are you lost?' he asked, walking towards her.

'Not exactly. I've come to visit my grandparents but I haven't their address,' Nesta explained, feeling her cheeks colouring up with embarrassment.

'And who are they?'

'Their name is Evans . . . I'm afraid that's all I can tell you.'

'Evans, is it!' He pushed his helmet back from his brow and shook his head, his dark eyes crinkling with laughter. 'Have you any idea just how many people there are in Blaenau Ffestiniog with that name? No,' he mopped his forehead, 'that's a daft question. You wouldn't have just said "Evans" like that if you had.' His face grew more serious. 'Can you tell me a bit more about them?'

'Not really. I've never met them,' she said awkwardly.

'I see!' He regarded her shrewdly. 'Whose parents are they then, your father's or your mother's?'

'My father's.'

'Do you know their first names . . . or your father's Christian name? That might help.'

'I'm not sure what their Christian names are but his is Rhys. His father and his brothers all work in the slate quarries,' she added hopefully.

'So do most families around here!'

'Yes,' she sighed, with a pang of disappointment. 'I suppose they must do,' she added, looking round at the blue-greyness on every side.

'Evans . . . Rhys Evans,' the policeman repeated, rubbing his chin thoughtfully. 'There used to be a chap of that name but he never worked in the quarries. He left home when he finished at school . . . I haven't seen anything of him for a long time . . . several years in fact.'

'My father went to sea as soon as he left school,' Nesta said quickly.

'He did? Then I think you must be looking for Caradoc Evans,' he told her, the eagerness in her voice bringing the grin back to his face.

'Come on, I'll walk you. They live in Moel Road. It's not far, first turning on the right.' He bent and picked up her suitcase. 'There's heavy this is! I'd better carry it. Can't have a pretty girl like you huffing and puffing. Do they know you are coming?'

'No . . . we . . . we don't keep in touch.'

'Going to be something of a shock for them then, isn't it?' He stared at her curiously. 'Is your Dad meeting you there?'

'No. I . . . I'm not sure where he is . . .' she hesitated, biting her lip. Aware that the policeman was probing she decided it might be unwise to say any more.

'I can manage from here,' she said, taking her case from him as they turned into Moel Road. 'Thank you very much for helping me.'

Nesta waited at the low gate that separated the tiny strip of front garden from the pavement until the policeman had disappeared from sight before walking up to the front door.

Her heart was hammering painfully as she waited for her knock to be answered. Out of the corner of her eye she saw the net curtains twitch as if someone was peeping out to see who it was.

The door was opened by a plump elderly woman wearing a starched, lace-edged white apron over a blue cotton dress. Her abundant grey hair was drawn back into a bun, emphasizing the pointed chin and aquiline nose. Her shrewd blue eyes regarded Nesta enquiringly.

'Mrs Evans? I . . . I'm your granddaughter,' Nesta gulped, her carefully rehearsed speech forgotten.

'Have you come to the right house?' The woman looked her up and down suspiciously.

'My father was Rhys Evans . . . your son.'

Nesta felt her courage evaporating as a look of disbelief appeared on the older woman's face.

'I'm Nesta ... he must have told you about me!' She indicated the case at her feet. 'I've just got off the train from Cardiff. You are my grandmother, aren't you?'

Gwyneth Evans stared at the slim, dark-haired girl standing on her doorstep as if she was seeing a ghost. She often thought about the child her son had fathered, the grandchild she had never seen, and wondered what had happened to her.

Lying in bed at night, listening to her husband's steady snores, she had searched her heart, wishing she hadn't turned Rhys away when he came to her for help. She tried to tell herself that it would have been better to have had the baby adopted and severed all connections with it. That way the child would have had a good home. As it was, he had lost the child anyway.

Rhys had always seemed to be unlucky, she thought sadly. Right from childhood he had been at loggerheads with his father. Refusing to work in the slate quarries had been the start of it all, and then running away to sea had been the last straw. Caradoc had rejected him from that point onwards. Yet he was still her son and she couldn't put him out of her mind or her heart.

Now this dark-haired young girl, with her determined chin and sensitive mouth, reminded her so vividly of Rhys. The set of the girl's shoulders, her tentative smile, brought memories rushing into Gwyneth Evans's mind. It was like spinning backwards in time and she found it confusing.

'How do I know you are who you say you are, when I have never set eyes on you in my life before?' she prevaricated.

'I ... I'm sorry about that ... it's not my fault,' Nesta answered defensively. Suddenly she wondered what she was doing in this strange town, standing on a doorstep arguing about who she was. It wasn't turning out at all like she had imagined. She had dreamed so many times of her first encounter with her grandmother, how they would rush into each other's arms and there would be kisses and tears of joy.

'You had better step inside,' Mrs Evans invited reluctantly. 'I don't want the entire street to know our business. Leave your case in the hall.'

She led the way down the narrow passage towards the living room at the back of the house.

'Sit down then.' Mrs Evans indicated a straight-backed wooden chair by the table, then sat down opposite her. 'Now, what is this all about? You say you are my granddaughter, Rhys's girl!' She studied Nesta carefully. 'You are not much like your mother, leastways, not as I recall.'

'I am supposed to be like my father.'

'You're built like him, I'll give you that. Thin as a cane. You have his chin and dark hair . . .'

'I haven't seen him since my grandmother died,' Nesta rushed on, trying desperately to establish a rapport between them. 'Can you help me find him?'

Before Mrs Evan could reply they were interrupted by the sound of someone coming into the house.

'Hello. Visitors is it?'

Nesta found herself looking up into the face of an elderly, craggy man with piercing dark eyes. His shabby corduroy trousers were speckled with grey dust and there was even a film of grey over the wrinkled skin of his neck where his striped grey-and-blue shirt was unbuttoned.

'Real scorcher today,' he puffed, mopping his forehead.

'You had better sit down, Caradoc. Bit of a surprise, like.' Mrs Evans said nervously, her mouth pursed as she prepared him for the news.

'Oh?' He looked enquiringly at her.

'It seems that this is our Rhys's girl.'

'Oh?' This time his voice had changed, hardened. His dark eyes blazed as he turned to stare at Nesta, impaling her with their intensity.

'She has come on the train from Cardiff.'

'What for?'

His clipped assertive voice chilled Nesta. She looked help-lessly at her grandmother, the tightness in her throat making it impossible for her to speak.

'She's looking for our Rhys.'

'You won't find him here, girl,' he barked. 'Best be on your way.'

'We can't just turn her out into the street, Caradoc!' Mrs Evans protested in a shocked voice.

'Where are you staying, girl?'

'I . . . I don't know. I haven't made any plans. I . . . I thought perhaps I might stay with you . . . just for a few days,' she added hastily.

'That's your case is it, out in the hall? Turn up without warning and expect us to provide hospitality. Just like your mother. She and Rhys arrived without warning, expecting to stay here. It doesn't do to take people for granted.'

'But that was twenty years ago,' Nesta exclaimed in astonishment.

'What has time got to do with it? The answer is still no!'

'Are you asking me to go?' she said in dismay.

'Telling, not asking!' His tone was clipped, implacable.

Nesta stared back at the scrawny work-stained figure in front of her, aware of the hostility in his dark eyes and in the thin hard line of his mouth, wondering if it was really happening or if it was just a bad dream.

'Let the girl have a bit of a rest and a cup of tea first, Caradoc,' Gwyneth Evans said placatingly.

Although the temperature was well into the seventies, there was a fire burning in the polished black range. Mrs Evans bustled forward to move the kettle that was balanced on a trivet in front of it over the glowing coals.

She spread a starched white cloth on the table and reached down cups and saucers from the dresser.

Caradoc Evans moved over to the leather armchair on

the far side of the fireplace. Keeping his back half-turned as if to avoid looking at Nesta, he sat with his work-grimed hands outstretched to the fire.

She watched him, her heart heavy with sadness, knowing he was brooding about the past. There were so many questions she wanted to ask about her father but she respected his silence.

No one spoke until the tea was brewed.

'Help yourself to sugar,' Gwyneth Evans murmured as she placed a cup in front of Nesta.

'Thank you, Grandma . . .'

'There's no reason to call her that,' Caradoc Evans growled, setting his cup down on the fender and looking up angrily.

'But she is my grandmother, just as you are my grandfather,' Nesta said defensively.

'Drink your tea and then be on your way,' he said harshly, his voice like a whiplash.

'Very well!' She stared back at Caradoc Evans defiantly. 'Tell me where I can find my father and I'll go to him.'

'We can't help you, he's not visited us for a good many years,' Gwyneth Evans intervened quickly.

'But you must have some idea where I can find him,' Nesta persisted, more gently.

Before Mrs Evans could answer, two men, both in their thirties and obviously brothers, came into the room through the back door. Like Caradoc Evans they wore dust-stained working clothes. Both were thin and the elder of the two had a slight stoop.

'Visitors, is it?' one of them exclaimed in surprise.

'This is our Rhys's girl,' their mother told them.

'Hallo. I'm Hwyel,' the younger of the two nodded briefly. Nesta noticed that his hair was thick and dark just like her father's had been, but he was smaller and thinner, his face pale and tired-looking.

Tudor, the elder brother, was a younger edition of

Caradoc Evans. A scrawny man with a thin hard mouth and greasy hair that shone in the sunlight.

'Drink your tea and then go and get cleaned up while I get your meal ready,' Mrs Evans told them, filling two large cups.

'Visiting, are you?' Tudor asked, wiping the back of his dust-grimed hand across his mouth as he finished his tea.

'I . . . I'm looking for my father.'

The silence that followed her remark became unbearable. She noticed her two uncles exchange looks and saw Tudor shake his head as if warning his brother to say nothing. Her senses quickened. They knew something, she was sure of that.

Caradoc Evans drained his cup and set it down with a clatter on the steel fender. As he raised his head his eyes glittered angrily.

'If you've finished your tea, then be on your way, girl. We don't want you here, stirring up the past. Your mother came here uninvited and caused trouble. Took our Rhys from us.'

'That's rubbish,' Nesta exclaimed, outraged. 'She didn't take him from you at all. He had already left home and gone to sea when my mother met him.'

'My other two boys have worked alongside me at the quarry ever since the day they finished at school,' Caradoc went on, impervious to her outburst. 'Obedient, they've been, not headstrong like your father. We live quietly, happy enough in our own way. Good God-fearing boys both of them. Chapel every Sunday. None of this popery business for us.'

'My father didn't change his religion. He never became a Catholic,' Nesta said quietly.

'She changed him! Your mother corrupted my son,' Caradoc Evans repeated vehemently. 'Warm-hearted, peace-loving boy. Happy enough and carefree until he met up with her. Given time he could have come back to work alongside his brothers at the quarry. Only she changed him. Look at him now, a man full of hate and bitterness towards the world.'

'How do you know, if you never see him?'

Nesta heard her grandmother's quick intake of breath and glimpsed the fear flickering in the older woman's eyes. There were startled expressions too on the faces of her uncles, and somewhere in the back of her own mind there was a vague foreboding.

'You are their daughter, there's no denying that,' Caradoc Evans roared. He rose from his chair and his thin stooped figure loomed over her menacingly. 'Born in sin and stained with it. Get out!' He pointed a calloused forefinger at the door. 'Never come here again.'

Nesta's spine crawled with fear. She felt both alarmed and crushed by her grandfather's rejection, but she was determined not to let him see how much he scared her.

'Just tell me where I can find my father,' she repeated stubbornly.

'Out! Out of my house,' Caradoc Evans raged, hatred in his dark eyes, his wrath rising, his whole body trembling with anger.

'Come, you'd best be on your way,' her grandmother urged. Placing her hand protectively on Nesta's shoulder, she propelled her towards the front door.

'Do you know where my father is?' Nesta pleaded.

'Ssh!' Gwyneth Evans laid a finger on her lips and looked quickly over her shoulder, almost as if she was afraid Caradoc Evans might attack with his fists as well as with words. 'Our Wynne knows. He goes to her place sometimes.' She twisted the edge of her apron nervously. 'I . . . I've seen him there.'

'Where does she live?'

'Just start walking down the road. I'll send our Hwyel after you. He'll take you to her place.'

As Nesta bent to pick up her suitcase, Gwyneth Evans

pecked at her cheek. Nesta hesitated for a brief second, then flung her arms round the older woman and hugged her warmly.

Her grandmother's tears still damp on her cheeks, Nesta straightened up and walked out of the front door.

16

Nesta liked her Aunt Wynne on sight and was eager to know her better.

The warmth of her aunt's welcome reduced Nesta to tears. It was the first spontaneous friendliness she had encountered since she had left Cardiff, and she had felt quite startled when her aunt hugged and kissed her and seemed so delighted to see her.

Wynne Morgan's homely face, with its blunt nose and round full chin, was transformed by her wide smile. Nesta sensed an immediate feeling of understanding between them.

As she and Hwyel had walked from Blaenau Ffestiniog to the huddle of neat stone cottages under the shadow of the Moelwyn Mawr mountain, where Wynne and her husband Huw Morgan lived, he had tried to reason with her and warn her against trying to find her father.

'It's a madcap scheme, girl,' he protested. 'Best leave things alone. You've managed without him all these years, so why bother now? You are practically a woman, well able to stand on your own feet. Go back to Cardiff, pick up your life, not mope around here.'

'I intend to find him,' Nesta protested stubbornly. 'Anyway, that's not my only reason for coming here. I wanted to meet you all before I went into the ATS. Not that it's proved worthwhile,' she added bitterly.

'That's what I'm trying to tell you. You're not our sort. We are hard-working chapel folk. The slate quarries are our life. If our Rhys had gone to work alongside Dad when he left school, like the rest of us did, then this would never have happened. Upsetting it is. Never seen our Dad so enraged . . . not for a long time, anyway.'

'Not since my father brought my mother to your house,' Nesta jibed.

'What do you mean ... what else do you know?' He threw her a sideways glance and Nesta was quick to seize the opportunity.

'Sent them away too, didn't he?' she accused.

'Don't approve of politics, see,' Hwyel said in a worried tone. 'Politics and religion don't mix.'

'You mean Plaid Cymru!'

It was a long-shot but it seemed to strike a nerve. Hwyel's face darkened.

'Some of the reasoning behind Plaid Cymru is right-thinking but not the means they use to achieve it,' he pronounced.

'What do you mean by that?' Nesta probed.

'Don't get me started, it riles me so much that I say things I shouldn't,' Hwyel muttered.

Nesta shot him a sideways glance. His thin face had tightened, his mouth was a hard line as if he was deliberately silencing himself. She wondered whether she should ask Hwyel outright whether or not the Dragon was his brother.

Some inner caution stopped her. Instead she began questioning him about the mountain ranges that surrounded them, asking him to point out Moel Hebog and Snowdon, Moelwyn and Cnicht.

He did so grudgingly, as if reluctant to share his knowledge. His audible sigh of relief when Wynne's cottage came in sight made Nesta smile to herself.

'There's like our Rhys you are in looks with your dark hair,' Wynne exclaimed. 'Same-shape face, too, and his determined chin,' she added laughingly. 'Pity young Trevor has gone into the army. He's a year older than you, it would have been nice for the two of you to have met. Still, there's always next time. This old war can't last forever.'

'You are sure it is all right, then, for me to stay here for a few days?' Nesta asked anxiously when they were left together.

'For as long as you like, cariad.'

'I have had my calling up papers for the ATS. That's why I thought I would take a holiday,' Nesta explained.

'If I'd known how to get in touch with you I would have asked you to come and see us long before this,' Wynne told her as she led the way upstairs to a small bedroom with whitewashed walls and a sloping ceiling.

'I hope you will be comfortable here,' she murmured, smoothing the crocheted bedspread and twitching the flowered curtains into place. 'Let me know if there's anything at all you want, now won't you, Nesta?' She smiled warmly, her blue eyes brimming with kindness. 'Make yourself comfortable and then come on down and have some tea. I've just made a fresh batch of bakestones.'

Nesta washed her face and hands and changed her dress, which was creased by travelling, before going back downstairs. The warm savoury smell coming from the kitchen reminded her she had eaten only a sandwich since breakfast time.

'It's such a lovely day I thought we could sit outside. Cooler there than in here. Come on, we can have a cosy little chat before Huw gets home.'

Carrying a loaded tray, Wynne Morgan led the way to the back garden. It was bright with summer flowers. Marigolds, pansies, blue alyssum and bright red geraniums fought for space in the border that separated the lawn from the vegetable patch.

While her aunt poured out the tea, Nesta sensed the immense power of the mountains that rose like monstrous silent sentinels all around them. Wispy clouds floated over the peaks, casting irregular shadow patches on the green scrub. Excitement surged in her veins. She wanted to climb up those steep, craggy sides, high above the sunlit valleys and cwms to the rocky peaks and view the world spread out at her feet.

'I often asked Rhys to bring you up here to see us, you know. After your mother's parents died and he couldn't find you, he was sorry then that he'd never bothered,' Wynne Morgan sighed. 'What did happen to you?'

She listened with rapt interest as Nesta told her about living in Pontypridd and then having to move back to Cardiff to live with the Lewises after her Uncle Dai Jenkins had been killed.

'I remember reading about that pit disaster,' Aunt Wynne remarked. 'Terrible thing these mining explosions. It's much the same in the slate quarries. You can never foretell when it will happen or how many will be injured. Lucky we've always been as a family. Neither Dad, or my two brothers, have ever been in any trouble.'

'Does Uncle Huw work in the quarries?'

'Oh yes, but he's a surface worker so there's not the same risk. Dad, Hwyel and Tudor work underground as a team. They are always watching out for each other. It is very dangerous, though. And hard. Dad has a terrible stoop. It comes from having to crouch all day working the slate. Tudor is not so bad but our Hwyel is almost as hunched as my Dad.'

'I remember my father telling me what it was like and how the grey dust was everywhere; in your hair, your clothes and even in your food. Somehow it sounded worse than coal dust.'

'Ever since he was old enough to understand, our Rhys vowed he would never work in the quarries,' Wynne murmured, her face crinkling into an understanding smile. 'Broke Dad's heart, though, when he ran away to sea.'

'And is he still at sea?'

'Oh no!'

'He's here . . . in North Wales . . . isn't he?' Nesta said softly.

'Why do you say that?' Wynne's face had a shuttered look.

'Come on, Aunt Wynne . . . give. Uncle Hwyel wouldn't tell me anything. I'm sure Grandmother knew something but she was too frightened to speak out. That was why she sent me here.'

'You are right . . . it is difficult to know where to start, though.'

'Is he the Dragon?'

'You know!' Her aunt's face was a mixture of relief and consternation as she fought to keep her voice steady.

'I guessed it when I was given some letters he had written to my mother. It wasn't just that he had signed them "the Dragon" but some of the phrases in them were the same as those the Plaid Cymru "Dragon" uses in his speeches.'

'So what else is there to tell?'

'Where I can find him?' Nesta leaned forward eagerly, her eyes searching her aunt's face anxiously. Now the moment she had waited for had arrived she was afraid that the information she wanted so badly might be withheld.

'I'm not sure.' Aunt Wynne reached out and took Nesta's hand in hers. 'He moves like a shadow. We never know when he will come. He roams the country, working for the cause he believes in. When he has the time he visits us. He knows there will always be a welcome here for him. Huw believes in what Rhys is doing but he isn't fanatical about it. There's a fervour about our Rhys that sometimes frightens me by its intensity.'

'Why did he stop going to sea?'

'You don't know! There's silly of me, how could you, when you've not seen him since your grandparents died. How old were you then?'

'Nine.'

'Poor little love! Suffering a loss like that and no one to comfort you. Wondering day after day when your Da would come for you. Heartbreaking it must have been.'

'Why didn't he come for me?'

'Oh he did,' Aunt Wynne assured her. 'He scoured Cardiff

looking for you. He was distraught when no one could tell him where you were.'

'Didn't he go to Coburn Street . . . where I used to live?' Nesta asked, her dark eyes puzzled.

'He went there and he tried to find that friend Alice Roberts from the pub in Tiger Bay. Oh, it's the truth, cariad,' she avowed as she saw disbelief shadow Nesta's eyes.

'Then why didn't he find me?'

'He was too late. You'd all gone months before. What you don't understand, cariad, is your father was very ill. He didn't jump ship in Calcutta, he was left behind when the boat sailed because he was ill. For months and months he was stranded out in India. When he recovered and tried to get home he couldn't get on a ship because someone had stolen all his papers!'

'So what happened?'

'When he eventually did get back to Cardiff, your grandparents had been dead for almost eighteen months. None of the neighbours in Coburn Street knew where you'd gone to live. Some of them even thought he had collected you and taken you away.'

'So he just went back to sea?'

'Oh no. His illness had made that impossible. They wouldn't take him on again. He came home to recuperate. When he was better, our Dad got him a job in the quarries. He even promised Rhys he could work above the ground.

'Dad's always been a rockman. He searches out the seam of slate below ground, finds the right place to bore into it and places the explosives,' Wynne explained as she saw Nesta frowning. 'Wonderful at the job he is too. When he blasts, the block comes out perfect, never smashed up and unusable like some of them. Our Tudor works alongside him. He splits the block along the grain with hammer and chisel and then loads it on a truck so that it can be brought to the surface for the rest of the team to work on.'

'He always said he'd have no part of quarrying,' Nesta said quietly.

'All very well for Rhys to say that when he was a lad and had no responsibilities. Bit different when you are a grown man,' Wynne affirmed.

'He would still feel the same,' Nesta murmured.

'It made our Dad wild when he refused even to give it a try,' Wynne Morgan sighed. 'He couldn't believe Rhys could be so stubborn. Because of the depression, blokes from around here were walking all the way to London to try and get work. And he was offering a plum job and Rhys was turning it down!'

'So what happened?'

'There was a terrible row. They are as pig-headed as each other and once they got their horns locked neither of them would give an inch. In the end Dad told Rhys to go and warned him never to come back again. Our Mam comes here to see him from time to time. Hwyel knows but he'd never let on. Too scared of what our Dad might do if he ever found out.'

'So how does he make a living?' Nesta questioned.

'He helps out with lambing and haymaking from time to time on the hill farms, but I don't know what else he does. It puzzles me how he manages and worries my mother,' her aunt frowned.

'He works for Plaid Cymru, though, doesn't he?'

'Oh yes! He gets involved with politics. He is always talking about righting all the wrongs the English have wreaked on the countryside. He goes about making impassioned speeches about freeing Wales from the English and so on. Like a modern day Owain Glyndwr, he is. Calls himself "the Dragon" . . . but then you know all about that.' She sighed, shaking her head disconsolately. 'Most people seem to know who he is but they never let on.'

'Why does it matter? I would have thought they would be proud of what he was doing. It is only right that Wales should have Home Rule.'

'A convert before you've even met up with him, are you?' her aunt said wryly. 'There's proud he'll be of you.'

'I do believe in what he and the rest of Plaid Cymru are trying to do,' Nesta affirmed. 'I've been to meetings in Cardiff. I've even heard Saunders Lewis speak.'

'He's a fine orator,' Aunt Wynne agreed. 'Not just politics with him, either. He is a fine dramatist and a great supporter of the Eisteddfod. Do you speak Welsh, Nesta?'

'No. But I want to learn,' she added eagerly.

'Odd isn't it. Cardiff is the capital of Wales yet they speak less Welsh there than they do up her.'

'Perhaps my Dad will teach me Welsh when I find him.'

'I doubt that,' Aunt Wynne smiled sadly. 'Lost the tongue has our Rhys. Comes with leaving home as young as he did, I suppose. Perhaps that is why he is so fanatical about everything Welsh these days.'

'Don't you believe in what he is trying to do, Aunt Wynne?'

'Well, yes, I suppose I do. It's just the way he goes about it. Leastways, not so much him as the people he works alongside.'

'What do you mean by that?' Nesta frowned. 'Hwyel said the same thing.'

'Well, take this Saunders Lewis,' Aunt Wynne argued. 'Clever man but a fanatic. It was sheer madness to cause all that damage on the Llyn Peninsula. He only ended up in prison, and so did many of those who helped him. No sense to it.'

'I don't know anything about that . . .'

'The British government commandeered the land intending to use it as somewhere to practise bombing. Getting ready for the war, see. All the people round about here were up in arms about it.'

'So what did Saunders Lewis do?'

'He incited a body of men to burn the army school down! Well, the outcome was that Saunders Lewis and two of his supporters from Caernarvon went on trial at the Old Bailey down in London and they were imprisoned in Wormwood Scrubs for nine months. Scandal it was.'

'What do you think they should have done?'

'I'll tell you some other time.' Aunt Wynne stood up and picked up the tray. 'Your uncle will be home any minute and I've done nothing about his meal. We don't want him to come home hungry and catch the pair of us sitting out here gossiping, now do we, cariad?'

Nesta took to her Uncle Huw at first sight. He was a large pleasant-faced man. His thick brown hair receded in front and his face and forehead were tanned and roughened by exposure to the elements. His small brown eyes twinkled merrily under bushy brows and he had a quick wide smile.

Even before they sat down to a hearty evening meal, Nesta could see from his rotund shape that he was a man who enjoyed his food.

The meal over and the dishes washed, they sat talking. It was the first time she could ever recall anyone actually listening to what she had to say. In the past, she had either been ignored or expected to accept other people's opinions whether she agreed with them or not.

It had been a wonderful evening and long after she went to bed Nesta lay awake thinking over the things the Morgans had told her. She made up her mind she would go along to the political meeting in Dolgellau that her uncle had spoken about. Perhaps someone would be able to tell her where she could find her father, or let him know she wanted to see him. It was certainly worth a try, she decided.

Before she fell asleep, half-forgotten fantasies that she had built around her father floated into her mind. Perhaps one day they would be together again, just the two of them in a long, low cottage like Aunt Wynne's, tucked away in the shelter of one of the mountains.

17

Aunt Wynne walked as far as the bus stop with Nesta but refused to go with her to the meeting in Dolgellau.

'That sort of thing is not for me,' she said firmly. 'It's a pity young Trevor isn't here, though, he would have gone with you. Take care now. If it was winter I wouldn't want you to go all that way on your own but it's safe enough on a light night. Anyway, Huw will walk down to the bus stop to meet you.'

'Don't worry. I'll be fine,' Nesta assured her.

'Are you sure that you are going to be able to find your way to the market hall and everything now?' Aunt Wynne asked in a worried voice, as the bus came in sight. 'It's in Eldon Square, can you remember that? The assembly room is upstairs.'

'I've got a tongue in my head, I can always ask some-one.'

'Well, do be careful, Nesta.' She stood in the roadway waving until the bus turned a corner.

Nesta settled back in her seat, content to enjoy the scenery. As the bus crossed the moorland, Nesta had her first glimpse of Trawsfynydd Lake, its blue water sparkling and shimmering in the July heat.

Once they reached the mountains that made up the Cader Idris ranges, Nesta felt her spirits soar as high as their craggy peaks. Someday, she vowed, she would come back there with her father and spend a whole day walking and exploring. They would follow the Dysynni River through the valley and find the narrow road he had told her about that led up to where Tal-y-llyn Lake lay hidden under the beetling crags of Cader Idris.

She arrived in Dolgellau too early for the meeting. It was a picturesque little market town so she wandered round the narrow streets, fascinated by the way they led from one small square to another.

By the time she got back to Eldon Square again, Nesta found that the assembly room was packed. She finally found a seat at the back of the hall and looked round with interest, wondering if her father was somewhere amongst the crowd.

The audience seemed to be made up of local townspeople, the men wearing respectable dark suits and hill farmers in tweed jackets. When the speakers assembled on the platform, and the chairman banged on the table with his gavel to start the meeting, Nesta felt there was no one present who remotely resembled her father.

Even though it was nine years since she had last seen him, and Aunt Wynne had said he had altered a lot and that he was now thin and bearded, she was sure that with his height and thick dark hair he would stand out and that she would recognize him.

The first speeches were mainly about the aims of the Plaid Cymru movement, things she had heard said from the platform at the meetings she had attended in Cardiff.

The final speaker, however, stressed the need for homes in the area after the war ended.

'Many who have gone into the forces as mere boys will come back as men,' he proclaimed. 'They will have married and want to settle down and raise families. And where will they live?'

His impassioned question hung on the air. For a moment there was an electric silence. Then Nesta felt her concern begin to turn to consternation as the atmosphere in the hall changed. A dozen voices began shouting answers and it seemed to inflame the rest of the audience.

'The war has given the wealthy English from Liverpool, Manchester and Birmingham a legitimate excuse to buy up land and cottages.' The speaker paused, his burning gaze raking the crowd, bringing growls of agreement and support. 'Local families have been turned out of their homes because their menfolk have had to go to war. Women with small children have been forced to move in with their parents because they can't afford to pay the rent and feed their young families on a soldier's pittance!

'Money-grabbing landlords then sell these same cottages to the English on the pretext that they are helping people to find a safe retreat from the bombings,' he declared cynically.

'And what happens once the bombing stops?' he challenged, looking round the hall. 'I'll tell you what happens . . . the English keep them! They don't really need these cottages that rightly belong to the Welsh because they still have their fine mansions back in England. But they hang on to them just the same! And for what purpose . . . why, to use as weekend retreats and holiday homes!

'Think about it!' he exhorted them, pausing dramatically.

Gritting her teeth, Nesta tried to contain her anger as murmurs of discontent again rumbled through the gathering.

'Local people, whose rightful homes they are, crowd in with their parents,' the speaker repeated. 'And everyday they will walk past what was once their own home and see it shuttered and empty!'

Cries of 'Kick them out!' 'Burn the places down!' began to resound through the hall.

Nesta could stand it no longer.

'Stop it all of you!' she yelled, jumping to her feet.

There was an astonished silence. A sea of faces turned in her direction and she found herself flushing furiously. Her rage and revulsion at their attitude gave her the courage to go on.

'Burning down cottages and behaving towards their

owners as you suggest is criminal,' she told the crowd. 'You gain no sympathy from anyone by doing that. You only turn people against the Welsh and bring ridicule on the Plaid Cymru movement. And you destroy all the work people like Saunders Lewis have fought so hard to achieve. There are so many other ways you could support the cause . . .'

The attention with which the entire meeting had listened to her denouncement of their tactics suddenly erupted into an outcry of fury. Pandemonium broke out. People from all sides began shouting and waving their fists threateningly in her direction.

Cries of 'Spy', 'Talebearer', 'Tory', 'What about the Hunger Marches?', 'Kick her out of here for a start', rose on the air as people jostled her angrily.

Her eyes blazing, although her lips were trembling, Nesta stood her ground. She wanted to yell back at them that not only was she a supporter of Plaid Cymru but that the Dragon was her father, but she knew none of them would believe her.

She was pinned in by a seething mass of irate people and knew she must get away before something terrible happened. As tempers flared higher, the language changed to Welsh and she found the enraged babble being directed at her was all the more frightening because it was unintelligible.

Frustration and outrage mingled when the crook of a stick caught her under the chin. As she thrust it to one side she felt the warm trickle of blood as a finger nail seared her cheek.

Somebody caught her by the arm and dragged her towards the centre aisle. She fought to free herself but it was useless. Rough hands pushed and pulled, clutching at her as if they would tear the clothes from her back. She pulled away, trying to see who was grasping her arm and found herself looking up into a pair of vivid green eyes under a shock of fair wavy hair.

'Use your elbows, heels, anything . . . but keep going,' he whispered sharply.' They'll lynch you otherwise!'

The animosity all around her was at fever pitch. Men were shouting at each other as they took sides in futile arguments that had nothing to do with the main issue. It was as if once their anger was unleashed there was no restraint.

Deftly the young man guided Nesta along a small dark passage and out into the cool of the late July evening. Even then he didn't pause but hurried her round to the far side of the building and unceremoniously bundled her into a small car.

As they drove past the front of the market hall, the crowd were spilling out into Eldon Square. Spasmodic fighting was still going on and Nesta found herself trembling as she thought of what might have happened.

'Here,' the young man whipped a clean white handerchief from his pocket and dropped it into her lap. 'Blow your nose, dry your eyes and mop up the spilled blood. Then tell me where you want me to take you.'

'It's all right, don't waste your petrol ration on me. I can catch a bus.'

'That would be the same as throwing you to the lions,' he grinned. 'You might be a fighter but, believe me, you are no match for them. Not that you didn't put up a good show,' he added quickly before she could speak.

Her rescuer, she saw to her surprise, was in his early twenties. He was broad-shouldered and rather handsome, with a firm chin and sensitive mouth. She liked the way his thick, fair hair waved back from his forehead and the brilliance of his green eyes under well-defined brows. He was dressed in dark grey trousers and a tweed sports coat over a plain white shirt, but he didn't look like a farmer or a business man.

'Well?' he asked as they reached the outskirts of the town, 'where do you live?'

'I'm here on holiday and I'm staying at a cottage just outside Blaenau Ffestiniog. It must be at least eighteen miles,' she said worriedly. 'Perhaps if you dropped me at a bus stop, far enough outside Dolgellau to be safe . . .'

'I'd never rest in my bed knowing I'd left you to the mercies of that lot,' he told her. 'Anyway, it will make a wonderful story.'

'What do you mean?' She shot him a puzzled look.

'I'm a reporter on the *Liverpool Echo*,' he told her. 'My name is Gwilym Vaughan, by the way.'

'You are a long way from home!'

'Not really. Our circulation covers North Wales. Anyway, Plaid Cymru is always news and it was rumoured that the Dragon was going to be at the meeting tonight.'

'The Dragon!' Her interest quickened. 'Have you ever met him?'

'I've been lucky enough to hear him speak once or twice. I've tried several times to get an interview with him but he is very elusive. Once a meeting is over he just seems to vanish.'

'Tell me what else you know about him,' she begged eagerly.

'Why are you so interested?' he asked, giving her a sideways glance.

'I . . . I've heard a lot about him but no one ever seems to actually meet him,' Nesta replied, colouring slightly.

'He's tall, thin and bearded, and he has strange, piercing, grey eyes. There's a sort of haunted look about him, almost as if his thoughts are miles away . . .'

'I know what he looks like . . . he . . . he's my father,' Nesta interrupted.

'What!' Gwilym shot her a startled look. 'Did I hear you aright . . . did you say that the Dragon is your *father*?'

'Yes. I am Nesta Evans.'

Now that she had actually uttered the words aloud, and heard the wonder and astonishment in Gwilym Vaughan's voice, she felt an inward glow.

She felt inordinately proud of her father because he was making such a positive stand against what seemed to be overwhelming odds and, more than ever, she longed to meet up with him again.

She stared out at the darkening countryside flashing past them as they left Dolgellau and headed north towards Blaenau Ffestiniog. The journey earlier in the evening had been through an ever-changing kaleidoscope of colour. Now the mountains were gigantic shadows etched against the night sky, their tips spattered with twinkling stars. Was the Dragon out there, seeking solace in the heart of them, just as Owain Glyndwr had done over five hundred years ago, she wondered.

'It seems incredible to think that despite the passage of time men are still fighting to preserve Wales for the Welsh,' Gwilym remarked, as if reading her thoughts.

'From the time of the Norman Conquest until Llewelyn ap Gruffudd lost out to Edward I, it was the Welsh Princes. Five centuries ago it was Owain Glyndwr,' he went on. 'After the Dragon . . .' he paused and looked at her speculatively, his green eyes glinting, 'will it be Nesta Evans?'

'You are laughing at me!' she said, feeling piqued.

'Not really. But you were very spirited tonight.'

'I can't believe I actually stood up and said all those things,' she admitted. 'I've never done anything like that in my life before.'

'Been taking lessons from the Dragon?'

'I wish I had. I haven't seen my father for over ten years,' she said ruefully.

'Really! This is even more of a scoop than I had thought,' Gwilym enthused.

'You are not going to print that!' Nesta exclaimed in alarm.

'Why not?'

She sat silent, not knowing what to say. It seemed childish to tell Gwilym that if her father read something like

161

that and it was attributed to her, he might feel betrayed. Anyway, she felt she owed it to Gwilym that he should have the chance of turning in a good story. It was one way she could thank him for saving her from the hostile crowd, as well as for driving her home.

'I wouldn't do anything to jeopardize what the Dragon is trying to do for Wales,' he said quietly. 'I would like to do an in-depth profile though. And you could probably help with some background details. Look,' he glanced at her quickly, 'why don't I just file a routine report about tonight's meeting and then we can meet again and you can tell me what you know. It might help you to find him.'

'All right.'

She gave the reply eagerly, without hesitation, delighted at the prospect of seeing Gwilym Vaughan again as well as at the possibility of tracing her father.

'It will have to be soon,' she warned him. 'I'm only staying with my aunt for a few days. I . . . I'm going into the ATS in two weeks' time.'

'Oh!'

The disappointment in his voice set her heart racing. She was glad that in the darkness of the car he couldn't see that she was blushing furiously.

They pulled up outside the Morgans' cottage, just as Huw was setting off to meet Nesta.

He was most concerned when he saw the grazes on Nesta's face and heard what had happened at the meeting. He insisted that Gwilym should come in.

'I knew it was daft letting you go off like that on your own,' Aunt Wynne exclaimed. 'I've been sitting her worrying about it all evening. Madness speaking your mind like that, girl, in a roomful of strangers,' she admonished.

'He's a nice enough young man but I hope you can trust him,' Huw Morgan said worriedly after Gwilym left. 'If he prints a lot of nonsense about you and your father it might lead to trouble. The *Liverpool Echo* is like the Bible to some of the folks round about here. They believe every word they read in it.'

'Gwilym has promised not to mention my name in his report about tonight's meeting,' Nesta assured him. 'He wants to do an in-depth story about my Da, though, and I've agreed to tell him what I can. I felt I owed it to him for all his help,' she added lamely as she saw the consternation on her aunt's face.

Gwilym returned next day bringing a pile of newspaper cuttings with him. As Nesta went through them, and read the colourful extracts from the many speeches the Dragon had made, her excitement mounted.

'Who is Blodwyn Thomas?' she asked, frowning as she put down the last one.

'One of the hill farmers around here, I think,' Gwilym told her. 'Perhaps Mrs Morgan can tell you.'

'Blodwyn Thomas! Why she lives at Gwyndy Farm not far from Pen-y-Gwryd. She's one of the local magistrates,' Wynne told them. 'Her husband, Major Powell Thomas, was on the reserve list and he was called up the moment the war started.'

'It says in a couple of these articles that the Dragon sometimes helps out on her farm,' Nesta murmured.

'How do you get to Gwyndy Farm from here?' Gwilym asked.

'It's quite a distance, the other side of Glyder Fach.'

'That's over three thousand feet high,' Nesta exclaimed.

'Well there are easy ways of getting round it,' her aunt laughed. 'The Llanberis Pass would be the best route if you are going by car.'

'Why don't we all go?' Nesta said eagerly.

'Not me, cariad,' Aunt Wynne laughed. 'The mountains are all right to look at from a distance. Too steep those sort of drives for me, makes me feel giddy. Nice views, mind you. There's some pretty lakes hidden away in the cwms but I'm not much of a one for exploring. You two go. Make a nice day out. I'll pack you up a picnic to take with you and I'll have a cooked meal waiting when you get back.'

The scenery held Nesta entranced. It was a day of sunshine and shadows. Banks of bubbling white clouds swirled over the twin summits of Glyder Fawr and Glyder Fach.

The view up the valley from the hollow of Cwm Dyli, with the high peaks of Snowdon grouped around it, stretched to infinity. The mountain air was clean, tangy and invigorating.

Gwilym was an interesting companion and never tired of pointing out landmarks or answering her many questions.

By the time they reached Gwyndy Farm, the day had proved so memorable that Nesta was loath to spoil everything by returning to reality.

'It's what we came for,' Gwilym insisted as Nesta paused uncertainly at the gate. 'No harm in just asking if he is here or whether she has seen him recently, now is there?'

Nesta still held back.

The mental image she had built up of her father was a satisfying one and she was fearful of destroying it. In her mind she knew exactly what he was like. She often held imaginary conversations with him and knew what he would say or do in any situation.

She had placed him on a pedestal and she was afraid that turning her dream into reality might ruin it forever.

18

Nesta and Gwilym had already started to walk away from Gwyndy Farm when a woman's voice hailed them. Turning round, Nesta saw a tall, heavy-hipped woman dressed in a dark-blue Welsh tweed skirt and light-blue short-sleeved blouse striding towards them. Her dark-blonde hair was drawn back in a thick pleat giving her strong bony face, with its determined mouth, a hard look. Her blue eyes regarded them with a suspicious gleam as if she thought they were intruders.

'This is not a right of way, you know,' she snapped, staring first at Gwilym in his grey flannels and cream shirt and then at Nesta in her pale-green cotton frock. 'Trippers, are you?'

'No!' Nesta flared. 'There's no law that says you can't enjoy a stroll in the sunshine, is there?' She bit her lip quickly. She knew she sounded childish but the woman's brusque manner had stirred her to anger.

Blodwyn Thomas ignored her, letting her gaze linger on Gwilym. 'On leave are you?'

'No.' His tone was polite but cool.

'Why aren't you in the forces, then? You look fit enough.'

'I will be . . . soon,' Gwilym told her calmly.

Their eyes locked. When Blodwyn Thomas found he was not going to tell her any more about himself she turned her hard blue scrutiny on Nesta.

'You don't live around here, so why are you snooping around my farm?' she asked sharply.

'As a matter of fact we were looking for my father.'

'Well, you're not likely to find him here. There isn't an

able-bodied man around the place, they've all been called up. When I saw you by the gate, I thought you were the Land Girl I'd ordered. Getting hold of workers is like finding a pot of gold. The only help I've had since my husband was called back into the army is from a doddering old fool of eighty and a friend who drops by occasionally. Not that I can count on him being around when I need him,' she complained.

'Is the friend you mention "the Dragon", by any chance?' Nesta asked.

'So I'm right, you are spying!' Blodwyn Thomas's eyes narrowed suspiciously.

'Not really. I half expected to find him here, though.'

'And what do you want with him? Trying to steal him from me to work somewhere else?' She laughed thickly. 'You won't succeed. He is not for hire.'

The silence hung on the warm air like a banner. Nesta glared balefully, surprised that her father should befriend such a woman. She remembered the stories he had told her about the witch Blodwyn the Malign and thought how easily this hateful woman could be one of her descendants.

'But he does come here?'

'If you've come here looking for him, then you must think so,' the woman parried. 'What do you want with him, anyway?'

'I'm his daughter, Nesta.'

In the silence that followed, the plaintive bleating of sheep out on the mountainside was the only sound to be heard. Blodwyn Thomas stood transfixed, her icy blue eyes raking over Nesta, scrutinizing her as minutely as if she was a painting in which she was about to invest her life savings.

'Rhys Evans is not here. He comes and goes, I can't rely on him,' she grumbled. 'This war makes everything so difficult. Not only is feed in short supply but, when it comes to selling, the government has brought in all sorts of restrictions and form-filling . . .'

'Would you tell my father that I'm staying with my Aunt Wynne,' Nesta cut in. 'He knows where to come.' She had taken such a dislike to Blodwyn Thomas that she wanted to leave as quickly as possible. She wished she had not listened to Gwilym; coming to Gwyndy Farm had ruined their outing.

'He might not be back for weeks.'

'Then I shall miss him,' Nesta said wistfully. 'I'm going into the ATS in a few days' time.'

Blodwyn Thomas placed her hands on her hips, threw back her head and howled with laughter.

'What's so funny about that?' Nesta asked, her voice edged with irritation.

'The Dragon's daughter joining the English army!' Blodwyn guffawed. 'He *will* be proud of you,' she added sarcastically.

'When it comes to the war, surely the Welsh are as anxious as the English, Scots and Irish to unite against a common enemy,' Nesta said with spirit.

'Perhaps you are right,' Blodwyn shrugged. 'My old man claimed it was his duty to defend his country against the enemy when he packed his kitbag and left. What he really meant was that it gave him an excuse to get away from this prison.'

'Prison?' Nesta looked quizzically at the rambling double-fronted white farmhouse with its grey slate roof and cluster of adjoining barns and stables grouped round the large yard.

'That's what he thought Gwyndy Farm was. It belonged to my father,' Blodwyn explained. 'When he was alive all my husband could talk about was the day when it would be ours and he could leave the army and take over here. When he did he found it was damn hard work. And he hated the wildness of the place.' She smiled enigmatically as she glanced up at the mountains that ringed them. 'To him those peaks were threatening.' Blodwyn paused and stared intently at Nesta. 'Do you think they are?' she demanded.

'No.' Nesta let her gaze take in the rolling green sides dotted with sheep before looking upwards towards the towering peaks. 'Awe-inspiring but not intimidating.'

'You are seeing them in summer sun, remember,' Blodwyn told her. 'They look different when there's rain storms brewing or the tops are shrouded in mist.'

'Majestic, perhaps, overpowering even, but still not threatening,' Nesta told her decisively.

'You sound just like your father!' Blodwyn sneered as she turned away and began to walk towards one of the barns. 'I've work to do,' she called over her shoulder.

'Can we come back again, perhaps in a few days?' Gwilym shouted after her.

'Please yourself.' Blodwyn Thomas didn't turn round, merely lifted her broad shoulders in a shrug.

'Come on, we won't waste the journey, I'll take you sightseeing,' Gwilym suggested. 'Let's start with Beddgelert, it's not far from here.'

'To see Gelert's grave?'

'You know the legend, do you?'

'It was one of my favourite stories,' Nesta smiled. 'I could never hear it often enough, even though I used to have nightmares about it afterwards!'

The war, rationing and even the life she had known in Cardiff all seemed light years away as they wandered round Beddgelert and then sat sunning themselves on the picturesque stone bridge that spanned the River Colwyn. Moel Hebog rose up against the sky, a more kindly bastion than Snowdon but imposing nevertheless.

Their promise to Aunt Wynne that they would be back in time for an evening meal prevented them from exploring further. Reluctantly they walked back to where the car was parked.

'I wanted to take you to Cwm Croesor, the valley that

lies between the Moelwyn and Cnicht mountains, and so many other places,' Gwilym told her.

'What about the top of Snowdon?' Nesta teased.

'That too, if there was time. It's an easy walk up, providing you choose the right path. You have to be sure of the weather, though. Once the mist comes down, the top of Snowdon and the other peaks alongside it can be covered within minutes.'

As they pulled up outside the Morgans' cottage, Gwilym asked, 'Will you come back to Gwyndy Farm with me in a couple of days' time?'

'I suppose I should. It may be the last chance I have to find my father before I go into the ATS.' She gave a long sigh. 'Wouldn't it be wonderful to be in the Land Army and work here instead of going into the ATS.'

'Why don't you?'

Nesta looked at him, startled.

'I'm sure it could be arranged,' Gwilym told her. 'Blodwyn Thomas said she wanted a Land Army girl, so why not ask her to take you on?'

'Work for Blodwyn Thomas!' A shiver rippled through her. Then, as the idea took hold, she gave a small smile. 'At least I would get a chance of meeting my father,' she said thoughtfully.

'Think about it. You'd have your aunt living nearby, so you would have someone to visit. That's if Blodwyn ever let you have any time off.'

Nesta thought about Gwilym's suggestion during their evening meal, trying to balance her intoxication with the mountain scenery against the harsh practicalities of working on a farm. Several times she was tempted to air the idea and see what reaction it brought from her aunt and uncle, but Gwilym and Huw Morgan were so engrossed in a discussion about the war, however, that she never found the right moment.

'Keep the day after tomorrow free,' Gwilym told her as

she walked out to the car with him when he was leaving. 'I'll take you back to Gwyndy Farm so that you can have another look at the place. If you decide you fancy staying on, you could ask Blodwyn Thomas then.'

'She might turn me down. I have no experience of farm work,' Nesta demurred. 'And what about my call-up for the ATS?'

'I think she would be glad of any help she can get,' Gwilym assured her. 'And since Blodwyn Thomas is a local magistrate, she would know how to persuade the authorities to let you switch. It's all service to your country.'

'I will think about it,' Nesta promised.

'I want you to stay here,' Gwilym told her. His tone was insistent and she saw a look in his green eyes that sent her pulse racing.

'You'll be going in the army yourself, soon,' she protested.

'Not for about six months. I've been deferred because of my job. Who knows, by then the war might be over, I might never have to go,' he murmured as he drew her into the circle of his arms.

Her own response was timid. She had always found the way Bronwen's friends kissed and mauled each other repulsive. But this was different. His mouth was warm and gentle as it met hers, his kiss light and sensitive.

When Nesta finally drew away from Gwilym's embrace her eyes were starry. She felt pleasantly flustered. She half hoped he might pull her back into his arms. Instead he opened the car door and slid behind the wheel.

'I'll see you the day after tomorrow, then,' he called above the noise of the engine as he drove away.

When Nesta eventually mentioned the idea of going to work at Gwyndy Farm as a Land Girl to her aunt and uncle it met with a mixed reception.

'Be wonderful! You could make your home with us . . .

that is when you are not working,' Aunt Wynne enthused, her round face beaming. 'There's plenty of room, even if our Trevor comes home on leave.

'Hold it,' Huw Morgan cautioned. 'We don't know yet if Nesta will get the job. Blodwyn Thomas might be in agreement about having her there, but we don't know whether she can pull enough strings to get Nesta off her ATS call-up. And another thing,' he waved his pipe in the air to emphasize what he was saying, 'working at Gwyndy Farm won't be any picnic.'

'No one said it would be,' Wynne countered.

'Blodwyn Thomas will be a stern task-master. She's a hard woman, and will want her pound of flesh and no mistake. Ask anyone who has been up before her when she is on the Bench.'

'It stands to reason she's got to be firm when she's punishing wrong-doers,' Wynne protested. 'But working for her would be different.'

Nesta was so confused and full of doubts that she was tempted to forget the idea altogether.

'Let fate decide,' Gwilym suggested, as they drove to Gwyndy Farm.

'What do you mean?'

'Tell Blodwyn Thomas that you would like to come and work for her as a Land Army girl. If she agrees and can get you out of the ATS, then that's it.'

Blodwyn recognized their car as they pulled up and this time her welcome was a shade more cordial. She invited them into the huge, stone-flagged kitchen. Reaching three large glass mugs down from the dresser, she filled them from a barrel standing in one corner of the room.

'You do drink cider?' she asked as she handed one of them to Nesta.

'I . . . I don't know. I've never had any,' Nesta said hesitantly.

Blodwyn gave a half sneer as she lifted her own drink to

her lips and took a draught of the clear golden liquid that emptied nearly a quarter of the contents in her mug.

Nesta took a gulp and shuddered as the sharp dryness hit the back of the throat. From a corner of her eye she saw Gwilym was still drinking, and when he set down his mug he had managed to drink just a little more than Blodwyn.

'Rhys Evans has not been here since you called the other day,' Blodwyn told them. 'Wasting your time and mine to keep coming here,' she added ungraciously.

'We didn't come looking for him, not this time,' Nesta told her.

'Why have you come then?' The blue eyes were suddenly sharp and suspicious as Blodwyn looked from Gwilym to Nesta and back again. 'Are you after some sort of story?' she asked in an accusing tone.

'I wanted to know whether you would take me on as a Land Army girl?'

'What!' Derision and amazement mingled on Blodwyn's face. Her big frame in its corduroy breeches and short-sleeved red-flannel shirt shook with laughter. 'What good would you be to me?' she asked contemptuously.

'You said you needed help on the farm,' Nesta reminded her stubbornly.

'I need a man around the place. Someone to harness up a horse, help with lambing, do the milking. Someone strong enough to swing a churn up into the cart and toss a bale of hay down from the loft. I don't want a mincing town girl in white sandals and a flowered frock, who thinks it would be a picnic and an excuse to get out of going into the services.'

'I can always get the right clothes and I'm willing to learn. I don't mind hard work . . .'

'Hard work! You don't know the meaning of it,' Blodwyn scoffed.

'Well, that's it then.' Tears of disappointment stinging behind her eyes, Nesta stood up to leave.

'I'll give you a try.'

Nesta was already stepping out into the sun-dappled yard when Blodwyn's voice cut like a whiplash. For a moment she couldn't believe she was hearing aright.

'Start next Monday. Bring your army papers with you and I'll get them to change your call-up to "Land Army". You will have to live in, I suppose you know that. And no followers. Is that understood?'

'You mean I can't visit Nesta!' Gwilym exclaimed in astonishment.

'She's here to work.' She glared at Nesta. 'Those are my terms.'

19

Nesta found the work at Gwyndy Farm far more gruelling than anything she had ever done in her life before. Her day started out on the yard at six sharp each morning. After mucking out and feeding, there was milking to be done before breakfast. And then the milk had to be taken to the collection point on the main road before the rest of the day's chores were started.

By the end of the week Nesta felt as if every muscle in her body was sore. Even her bones ached. Her hands were blistered and her finger-nails broken.

'Do you still want me to try and get you transferred to the Land Army or have you had enough?' Blodwyn asked with a taunting smile as she saw Nesta flexing her shoulders and wincing uncomfortably.

'As long as you are satisfied with my work, I'll stay,' Nesta replied grimly.

'I suppose it's better than no help at all,' Blodwyn conceded grudgingly.

Next day Blodwyn drove to Bangor to see if she could make the necessary arrangements for Nesta to work on the land instead of going into the ATS.

'There's some working clothes for you,' she announced when she returned, tossing a parcel on to the table.

'I . . . I haven't any coupons,' Nesta said apologetically as she opened it up to find two pairs of dungarees. 'I spent them all when I knew I was going in the ATS.'

'Don't worry about it. Once your Land Army papers come through you'll get clothing vouchers for dungarees and for your uniform breeches and green jumper to wear when you go out. You won't have much time for that though,' she warned ominously.

On that score Nesta found Blodwyn was right. Her day not only began early but was long and arduous. Yet, to her surprise, she found she was enjoying every moment.

The countryside had cast its spell over her and, even when sunshine gave way to wet dismal days, and the mountains crowded in from under glowering skies making Gwyndy Farm seem the most isolated place in the world, she had no misgivings.

Her only disappointment was that she hadn't been able to make contact with her father. She began each morning full of hope that perhaps he would arrive. But as the days wore on and there was not even any news of him, she became despondent.

A fortnight after Nesta moved into Gwyndy Farm, Gwilym, ignoring Blodwyn's warning to stay away, called to make sure Nesta was settled in all right.

'You can have a couple of hours off if you want to,' Blodwyn told her grudgingly. 'Mind you are back in time to pen up the chickens, I'll see to the rest.'

Gwilym took Nesta to Beddgelert again and, as they wandered hand in hand along the riverside paths, Nesta had never felt happier. The ripeness of late August was evident all around them. Bracken growing on the lower slopes of the mountains was beginning to change colour, the fronds were now yellow and gold, and the grass, though it had lost its lush greenness of early summer, was tall and dense and peppered with red poppies and white marguerites.

Almost the first question Nesta asked was whether Gwilym had any news about her father.

'No,' he told her, 'there has been a lull in the meetings and activities of Plaid Cymru. Everyone is hanging on the Prime Minister's words wondering just how Churchill is going to deal with the war situation.'

'Food shortages seem to be uppermost in most people's minds at the moment,' she agreed. 'Blodwyn says even animal feed will be in short supply this coming winter.'

'My editor still wants a story about the sale of cottages in North Wales as "safe havens" for wealthy English people,' Gwilym told her, changing the subject abruptly. 'If you hear any rumours on that score, let me know.'

'Of course, but it is not very likely. I don't see many people,' Nesta told him ruefully.

'What about the other farms round about? Doesn't Blodwyn ever invite any of her neighbours in for a meal or a drink?'

'The only one I've met is Cara Pugh. She has called once or twice . . . usually to borrow something.'

'Is her father Aneurin Pugh?'

'That's right. He's a Member of Parliament. Do you want me to ask Cara if she knows anything? She seems quite friendly.'

'That might be jumping the gun,' Gwilym warned. 'Just keep your ears open and see if you hear her, or anyone else, discussing the cottages.'

'That sounds rather sneaky!'

'So is selling off Welsh cottages to the English,' he parried. 'Someone is making a lot of money out of these deals.'

'If people are only buying them as safe retreats while the bombing is on they will sell them back afterwards, surely?'

'Some may, but the prices they will be asking will be astronomical. Far more than ex-servicemen will be able to afford. And, if they can't get their asking price, then most of them will simply use them as holiday homes.'

'That's right! Before the war started, just like they said at the meeting in Dolgellau, a great number of the cotton tycoons and shipping magnates from Liverpool had weekend cottages out round Mold and Mostyn and along the coast as far as Rhyl and Prestatyn. That was the start of the unrest, and it's growing stronger all the time. But it should be easy enough to discover who owned the cottages in the first place,' Nesta frowned.

'No,' Gwilym shook his head. 'The transactions are all handled by a London property dealer. Half the time the cottages change hands without anyone even coming to look at them. The first thing local people know is when a place that has stood empty for a couple of months is suddenly occupied!'

'Someone locally must know what is happening,' Nesta persisted.

'You would think so, but there seems to be a conspiracy of silence. Even when farm cottages are sold, the farmer will claim that he was only renting them for his workmen from some property dealer in London.'

'Hasn't anyone approached these London agents?'

'Of course they have. The answer is always the same. They are acting on behalf of clients and refuse to name them. It's all part of the changing face of Wales, I suppose, like planting conifers everywhere.'

'I thought there had always been fir trees here.'

'At one time the forests were mostly of oak, beech and other broad-leaved trees. Now Sitka spruce is the favourite because it grows so rapidly. Bit by bit they are replanting with conifers. Acres and acres that shut out light and air and rob the soil. Once the fir trees are harvested nothing else will grow there. They even change the appearance of the countryside.'

'In what way?'

'Take a look round you.' He waved an arm towards the mountains that stood stacked like wave after wave of an incoming tide. 'Look at the colours, the way the lush green grass on the lower slopes gradually becomes overtaken by bracken. At this time of the year you have a vista of colour, every shade from green and fiery red to golden amber as it rises up the sides of the mountain. Then it's brown scrub, or heather, until finally you get the rocks where nothing grows. Those colours are changing constantly during the year, according to the season.'

'And when the mountainside is planted with conifers, it is green the entire year round,' Nesta observed thoughtfully.

'That's right! So far, it is only the government who plant conifers to any great extent. Someday, though, unless Plaid Cymru comes to power and can stop them, the hill farmers will sell off their land to speculators for forestry development. Then the landscape will be changed forever.'

Gwilym's doom-laden prophecy haunted Nesta. She began to understand even more clearly her father's allegiance to the movement, and her longing to meet him, and talk with him, increased daily.

Nesta had been at Gwyndy Farm for almost a month before Blodwyn gave her a day off. Feeling self-conscious in her Land Army outfit of cord jodhpurs and a green sweater, she went to visit the Morgans.

'There's smart you look, Nesta. The uniform suits you a treat,' Aunt Wynne told her. 'And you've fattened out. They're feeding you well, then?'

'Yes, I am eating twice what I used to when I lived in Cardiff,' Nesta laughed. 'I'm working twice as hard as well.'

'Nice, though, to be out in the open rather than in a stuffy office all day.'

'Better ask her that after she's weathered the winter up at Gwyndy Farm,' Huw Morgan warned. 'Bitter cold it can be. And if there's snow, then like as not you'll be cut off. No time for huddling over the fire, either. You'll be out in it, digging the sheep out of snowdrifts, helping with early lambs as well as coping with all the other work around the farm.'

'There, there,' Aunt Wynne interceded, 'stop it Huw, you'll be putting the girl off.'

'Only preparing her for what's in store. Anyway, that's a couple of months away. Enjoy the good weather while it lasts. And make the most of your time with that Gwilym. He'll be the next one to be called up. You are still seeing each other?'

'Whenever he can manage to get this far,' Nesta said, blushing. 'Petrol's the problem. It seems to be harder to get hold of than ever.'

'He gets an extra allowance working on the *Liverpool Echo*, doesn't he?'

'Yes, but he has to account for how he uses it. He only comes out this way if there is something special to report.'

'Our Rhys has never turned up,' Wynne said, shaking her head. 'Funny that. At one time he was always dropping in. He knew I was always pleased to see him.'

'When he could stop for a few days, I used to go and fetch Wynne's mother back here to see him,' Huw told her.

'We had to be careful, mind. I'm damn sure my Da would have stopped her had he known,' Wynne added. 'So silly, the row between him and Rhys. Pig-headed pair!' She sighed. 'No changing either of them.'

'Does she know I'm still here?' Nesta asked.

'Yes. Huw will try and fetch her next time we know you are coming to see us. She has a heart of gold, but she has to be careful because of my Da. Don't want to start any trouble.'

'He didn't like me, I'm afraid,' Nesta said ruefully.

'His bark is worse than his bite. He has never got over the fact that our Rhys wouldn't work in the quarries. Hard man, my Da. Likes people to look up to him and obey him. Tudor and Hwyel learnt that a long time ago. It doesn't worry them now. They know that if they want to go on living at home then our Da's the boss and they accept that.'

'Haven't either of them ever thought of getting married?'

'Not them! Mam makes them too comfortable. She's ruined them for any wives. Waits on them hand and foot, cooks and washes and irons for them. Treats them as though they were small boys still. And so they are in a way. With chapel twice on Sundays and a couple of nights down the week there has never been much time for them to do any courting. Your Da and me were the only ones to break free. And, of course, our Bowen, in a way. He was killed in the last war when he was only eighteen.'

'I didn't know that!' Nesta exclaimed in surprise.

'Dad was heartbroken. That is when he turned to religion. Always been strong chapel, mind you, but he became fanatical. He has been a lay preacher ever since. You might not think it to look at him but he is a wonderful exponent of the "*hwyl*".'

'The what?'

'The "*hwyl*". It is a bit like the chanting that goes on in your Roman Catholic service but it has more feeling. My Da can carry the entire congregation into a state of religious ecstasy. Listening to his voice rising and falling is a very moving experience.'

'Enough of that.' Huw said firmly. 'Nesta's only got a couple of hours, don't let's waste it dwelling on the past.'

As the autumn became winter, Nesta understood what Huw Morgan meant. The cold was intense. Icy winds swept down from the mountains and, from early November onwards, their snow-clad tips were shrouded in grey swirling mist for days at a time. The plaintive bleating of stranded sheep, coming from out of the mist, sounded like the persistent wailing of a ghostly banshee.

Blodwyn seemed to know from their cry whether they had merely lost their direction or whether they were in serious trouble. Nesta began to dread the summons to go searching for them. The dense vapour seemed to freeze her bones as they trudged up the slippery slopes. If the sheep had wandered higher, to where the grass became patchy scrub, then the chances were that it had slipped into a crevice. By the time they had hauled it out and set it on the downward path back to the farm, her own hands and knees would be raw and sore.

In December there was a heavy snow fall, whipped into drifts by the searing winds. For days they were utterly isolated at Gwyndy Farm. Not even the postman managed to get through. The milk was not collected and in the end, because they had no more churns to put it in, they were forced to feed it to the pigs.

Unable to go and see Aunt Wynne, Nesta accepted an invitation to walk over to Dyli Farm and spend an afternoon with Cara Pugh.

Cara was about her own age. She was short and curvy with small features that made her wide-spaced blue eyes seem enormous. Her hair was dark and framed her high cheekbones in a cascade of curls. She dressed outrageously in vivid colours. Nesta often wondered where she managed to get the clothing coupons to buy so many outfits. Even her jodhpurs were of the finest cloth and so beautifully tailored that it was obvious they had been specially made for her.

'I hate everything to do with farming except riding,' Cara confided, as she handed Nesta a port and lemon. They were sitting in front of a huge log fire in the oak-beamed sitting room of Dyli Farm. Outside the wind was howling and Glyder Fawr and Glyder Fach rose like majestic sentinels, their steep craggy sides draped in mantles of unsullied snow, their peaks icy white fingers stabbing the pale blue sky.

'Whatever made you come and work for Blodwyn?' she asked curiously.

'I thought I would like it better than the ATS,' Nesta told her after a moment's hesitation.

'You too!' Cara pulled a face. 'You know,' she went on,

taking a contemplative sip from her glass, 'I'm not sure that life in the ATS wouldn't have been better. You'd meet people, travel, do something different.' She sighed. 'It isn't at all what I had in mind when I told my father I'd work for him. I meant in London, in the House of Commons.' Her eyes grew dreamy. 'Now *that* would have been fun.'

'And wouldn't he agree?'

'Heavens no! Afraid I might get corrupted, or bombed!'

'Well, he might have a point,' Nesta admitted. 'You are safe here. I was in Cardiff when it was bombed and it wasn't funny, I can tell you.'

'But you didn't get hurt!'

'I was one of the lucky ones. Lots of people did and a great many more lost their homes.'

'I know, but so much is happening and I feel I'm not part of it. Being safe isn't very exciting,' Cara pouted.

'You could be in worse places,' Nesta murmured. 'Look at it this way, lots of people from Liverpool, Manchester and the Midlands must think so, or they wouldn't be buying cottages so that they can come and live here.'

'I know, and isn't it causing a stir,' Cara giggled. 'Some of the local people are furious. I think it's rather fun having new people around. Most of them are filthy rich and you never know who you might meet.'

'That's true. Blodwyn was saying the other day that the people who are moving into Morfa Cottage own a shipping line. I wonder if it is true.'

'Well, your Blodwyn should know. After all, she sold them the cottage,' Cara sniggered.

'Blodwyn did!'

'Oh dear, didn't you know? Perhaps I shouldn't have let the cat out of the bag,' Cara tittered. 'Blodwyn has been selling off cottages right, left and centre since the Major was called back into the army. He'll have a fit when he comes home.'

'But surely she can't do that if they are his?' Nesta said, shocked.

'Oh yes she can. I heard my father say that she made sure that the Major gave her power of attorney before he went away. She has probably decided to feather her nest in his absence. He's years older than her, you know,' Cara prattled on. 'I wouldn't be surprised if she didn't clear out before he got back. Rumour has it that she has a fancy man.' Cara's voice dropped almost to a whisper. 'I have never actually met him but I have seen him around the place. Tall, good-looking and in his forties. He has a beard and looks *very* romantic! Has he visited her since you've been at the farm?'

Nesta shook her head, not trusting herself to speak, knowing the description fitted her father. She still found it hard to accept that he could be attracted to someone like Blodwyn.

At the moment, though, what was uppermost in her mind was the news that Blodwyn was the one who was selling off the cottages. That had come as a complete shock.

20

The spirit of Christmas seemed to die once Nesta knew that Blodwyn Thomas was responsible for selling off cottages to the English.

They had spent the day at Aunt Wynne's. Gwilym had wanted her to visit his family in Liverpool over the holiday but Blodwyn had vetoed the idea. Christmas or not, the animals still had to be looked after and, although the weather had turned mild, it was unpredictable.

'If we have a sudden change and another heavy downfall of snow, then you might not be able to get back here, and I would be left to cope on my own,' Blodwyn pointed out.

Nesta had been bitterly disappointed.

Her friendship with Gwilym had deepened since the night he had rescued her from the angry crowd in Dolgellau. She often found her thoughts straying to him, remembering the way his green eyes could one minute be gleaming with silent enjoyment yet be diamond-hard and unfathomable the next. He was so handsome with his firm chin, sensitive mouth and wide-set clear eyes and he was always so well-spoken and charming to Huw and Aunt Wynne as well as towards her.

He didn't look like a journalist, he was much too smartly dressed. She had always imagined a reporter to be older, smaller, with a sharp, prying face, not a fresh, open countenance and a shock of wavy fair hair.

His analytical mind sometimes disconcerted her. He asked such incisive questions that she often wondered if her answers would become copy for his next deadline.

Despite this she enjoyed his company and felt quite upset at the thought of not seeing him at all over Christmas.

'Why don't you both come here for your Christmas dinner?' Aunt Wynne invited. 'It will be our first Christmas without Trevor at home and we are going to find it very quiet.'

Gwilym had accepted the compromise with alacrity. He had driven over early Christmas Day and they had agreed to have a midday feast so that Nesta could be back at the farm again by four o'clock to see to the animals.

The Morgans had risen to the occasion and there was more than enough to go round. Blodwyn Thomas had sent over a plump chicken, so Wynne had bought a joint of roasting pork with her meat coupons.

'I shouldn't have eaten so much Christmas pudding,' Nesta exclaimed as they sat round the fire afterwards. 'I feel too full to go back to work. I wish I could stay here all afternoon,' she sighed, as she stretched lazily.

She and Gwilym were sitting on a settle drawn up to the blazing log fire, Wynne and Huw in armchairs on either side. The tongues of flame licked around the apple logs Huw had saved specially for the Christmas fire, sending a shower of sparks on to the soot-black back of the chimney and a sweet pungent odour into the room.

'At least you won't have to walk back,' Huw commented, as Nesta and Gwilym prepared to leave.

'It's only a ten-minute drive from here back to Gwyndy Farm,' Nesta laughed, as she got into Gwilym's car and he insisted on wrapping a rug round her legs.

'Not the way I'm going!'

It was a bright clear day with white clouds scudding across the sky. The lower slopes of the windswept mountains were dotted with sheep, the tops, iced with snow, looked like the peaks of a meringue. The setting sun, suspended like a huge ball of fire, spread a rosy glow over the entire sky.

'I am taking you to the Aberglaslyn Pass first,' Gwilym told her as they drove away from the Morgans.

Nesta found the view breathtaking.

In places the sides of the narrow roadway were still quite icy, and patches of snow patterned the deep gorge as it dropped to where a tumbling swollen stream split the valley. Deepening shadows, as the sun dipped behind the mountain ranges that stretched tier upon tier as far as the eye could see, lent an awesome splendour to the scene.

Gwilym pulled in to the side of the deserted road and switched off the engine.

'This is one of my favourite spots,' he told her as they sat there warm and contented, satiated by the view. 'I used to make a point of coming here whenever I had to cover a story in this part of North Wales.'

Gently but firmly he pulled Nesta round so that she was facing him. With his thumb he tenderly outlined the curves of her face, then holding her chin between thumb and forefinger cupped her mouth to his.

She strained towards him, her mouth soft and ready for his kiss. As he slipped his hand inside her coat, fumbling beneath the layers of scarves and woollies, she unfastened the buttons, making it easier for him to reach the pulsating warmth of her body.

The feel of his fingers caressing her breast, gently teasing the nipple until it became a small hard button, was unbearably exciting. Trembling with her own desire, she moved against Gwilym's hand, hungry for closer contact.

As their kisses deepened she was enmeshed in the throes of a delirious ecstasy. His touch sent ripples down her spine, her heart was filled with tenderness towards him. She felt breathless with the sheer wonder and joy of it all.

When they eventually pulled apart it was as if they were suspended in time with the world spread out at their feet.

Beyond the fir trees and rushing stream, naked brown precipices, like a curtain wall, shut them off from the rest of the world. She wanted to stay there, cocooned in his arms, until the pale yellow morning sun brought a new day.

The bleating of unseen sheep brought her back to reality. Struggling to look at her watch she knew she was already late. Unwilling to lose the close contact that had been established between them she sat with her arm linked through Gwilym's as they drove towards Gwyndy Farm.

The grandeur of the surrounding countryside seemed like an extension of her own exhilaration. The magnetism of the mountain ranges held her enthralled.

'I can understand why my father, and the rest of the Plaid Cymru supporters, are so adamant that Wales should be kept for the Welsh and left unspoiled,' she murmured.

'There is no news at all about him, I'm afraid,' Gwilym told her. He lifted one hand from the steering wheel to squeeze her hand consolingly. 'You've not heard anything?'

'Not about my father, but I do have some news about the cottages. I meant to tell you as soon as we met but it went right out of my head,' she added guiltily.

'What have you heard?'

'Cara Pugh says it is Blodwyn who is selling them.'

'Blodwyn Thomas!' He gave her a quick startled look.

'That's right. It seems the Major gave her power of attorney before he went away . . .'

'Which is why everything is being handled by a London agent,' Gwilym exclaimed. 'We can soon check that out . . .'

'Even if it is true it still doesn't help me find my father,' Nesta interrupted.

'Don't be too sure. There's a grapevine system. The news will probably filter through to him.'

'I suppose it's worth a try.'

'Let's hope your father does surface,' Gwilym said, frowning. 'He ought to be warned about Blodwyn's activities.'

Gwilym's quick-fire questioning broke the spell between them. When he kissed her goodbye outside Gwyndy Farm, Nesta could tell that his mind was on the property deals, not her, and she wished she had kept the news for some other time.

Blodwyn had already started the milking. As she hauled bales of hay up on to the slopes for the sheep and penned up the chickens, Nesta found herself wondering if Gwilym's feelings for her were as deep as she believed or whether he simply fostered their friendship hoping for a scoop.

Her pessimism left her dispirited for days. She even made a New Year resolution not to meet Gwilym again since it wasn't worth the heartache.

Her determination was undermined early in the New Year when he wrote asking her if she could take the following Saturday off. He wanted her to come to Liverpool to meet a special friend. The words 'special friend' were underlined and Nesta felt her cheeks burning with excitement as she read and re-read them.

By the time the weekend arrived she felt so jittery that she almost wished Blodwyn would say she couldn't go.

After the quiet isolation of Gwyndy Farm, Lime Street Station at Liverpool was an inferno of noise and uniforms. Soldiers, sailors, airmen and naval personnel of all ranks milled about, hurrying to board trains or making for the main exit.

Heads turned to look at the tall slim girl in the distinctive uniform, and Nesta felt herself blushing as the occasional low whistle was directed her way.

Her heart raced as she saw Gwilym waiting for her at the ticket barrier. His belted raincoat emphasized his broad shoulders and slim hips and he had the look of a man at the peak of physical fitness, she thought, as she studied the lean contours of his face and the firm set of his chin.

He greeted her warmly. The touch of his lips against hers sent shivers of longing meandering through her.

'What have you got planned?' she asked breathlessly.

'First, I'm taking you to meet a friend, as I promised,' he told her. 'Afterwards . . .' he left the rest of the sentence unfinished, but the desire in his green eyes left her in very little doubt as to his intentions.

They walked quickly through the main streets of Liverpool. When she wanted to stand and admire the splendid facade of St George's Hall he hurried her on. They finally stopped outside a bookshop and entering a side door went up a dimly lit staircase. Gwilym paused when they reached the second landing and knocked sharply on one of the doors before going in.

The front part of the room was furnished as an office with desks, telephones, typewriters, several dark-green filing cabinets and a long trestle table piled with pamphlets. As she looked round, Nesta saw that one of the walls was covered with Plaid Cymru notices. Before she could read any of them, Gwilym had taken her arm and was propelling her towards the far end of the room where two leather couches and several armchairs were grouped round a small coffee table.

Nesta's heart missed a beat.

A man was sitting in one of the armchairs, writing something into a notebook. The dark shock of hair, the set of the shoulders both stirred up memories. When he looked up she held her breath. The dark beard that hid the lower part of his face made her unsure. Then, as their gaze locked, she felt powerless to speak or move.

'Nesta?' The questioning whisper tore at her heart.

'Da . . . oh Da!' She stumbled forward, almost collapsing into his arms, tears streaming down her face.

Rhys Evans was trembling as he stood up and gathered his daughter close, burying his face in her hair, murmuring her name over and over. Then he held her away, hungrily feasting his eyes on her, his face softening with pride as he saw how the dark-haired solemn child had grown into a beautiful woman.

'I thought I would never see you again,' he shuddered, his gaze never leaving her face.

Nesta felt too choked to speak. Ten years had changed him. His face was thinner, the full beard made him appear older, and his dark hair was flecked with grey at the temples.

His slate-grey eyes, though, still had the same piercing quality she remembered so well. Now, though, there were myriad fine lines around them. His face seemed to have a haunted look, like that of a man who had suffered deeply and now trusted no one's judgement except his own. And there was a grim firmness to his mouth and a hard edge to his lilting voice.

'Would you like to go for a beer, Mr Evans?'

Gwilym's voice startled them both. Nesta had been so overcome by the meeting with her father that she had momentarily forgotten Gwilym, or even where they were.

The pub was bright, noisy and smoky. Nesta sat toying with a glass of sherry, feeling shy and unsure of herself. She felt a sense of relief when Gwilym suddenly looked at his watch, then jumped to his feet and let out a low whistle.

'Will you two be OK if I leave you for half an hour or so?' he asked. 'I have to pop into the *Echo* office to file some copy.'

Nesta smiled up at him gratefully. She suspected it was just an excuse to leave her alone with her father and she was touched that Gwilym should be so sensitive to their feelings.

For a few minutes after Gwilym left they were silent, unsure of what to say to each other.

'There's a couple of seats over in the corner, shall we move . . . it might be more private?' her father suggested.

'You are the Dragon, aren't you?' she whispered softly, once they were settled.

For a moment she thought he wasn't going to answer her. His mouth became a hard line above the beard and his eyes gleaming chips of grey slate. His long thin fingers

grasped his beer glass so tightly that his knuckles shone
like polished ivory.

'Has that reporter chap put you up to this?' His tone
was harsh, the sonorous lilt masked. 'I've seen him before,
he is often at Plaid Cymru meetings.'

'I know. That is how I first met him,' Nesta explained.
'But I was looking for you long before that.'

Briefly she told him about the meetings she had gone to
in Cardiff, and how Tecwyn Phillips had told her about
Saunders Lewis and the Dragon.

'Why should I be the Dragon?' he asked, his eyes glittering.

Nesta hesitated for a long moment. She didn't want to
embarrass him by telling him she had read the contents of
letters he had written to her mother all those years ago, yet
it was the only proof she had.

Knowing he was watching her, ready to deny his identity,
she remembered his friendship with Blodwyn Thomas and
realized how important it was that she placed all her cards
on the table.

Hesitantly she began to relate what had happened.

Rhys Evans said nothing. Even when she mentioned
Blodwyn Thomas, his face remained expressionless. She
held nothing back, except that she had found out it was
Blodwyn who was selling off cottages.

'Have you something else you want to tell me?' His gaze
locked with hers.

'How friendly are you with Blodwyn Thomas?'

She felt uncomfortable the moment she had spoken.
What right had she to question him like this? Supposing he
got angry and left before she could explain her reason for
asking. She felt her cheeks redden. Nervously she looked
away as she saw his eyes harden and his mouth tighten.

'She grumbled because you didn't turn up to help with
the harvest or with the early lambing,' she explained
quickly.

'So?' he shrugged. 'I go there when it suits me. I haven't a lot in common with Blodwyn. It was the Major I used to go to see. Have you met Powell Thomas?'

'No!' Relief washed over Nesta like cool spring rain. It was suddenly all coming together. If it was the Major her father was friendly with, not Blodwyn as she had been led to believe, then she must certainly tell him about the cottages.

She took a sip of her sherry, searching for the right words.

'That wasn't what was on your mind, was it?' Rhys asked, his tone lightening. 'There's no romance between us, if that was what you thought.'

'The cottages . . . the ones that are being sold off to the English . . .'

'Yes?' His voice had hardened again, the wary look was back in his eyes. He put down the glass of beer that he had been about to raise to his mouth and waited for her to go on.

'I . . . I think I know who is selling them off.'

'Who is it?' His grey eyes were flint hard and alert.

'Blodwyn Thomas.'

'Are you sure of this?'

'Cara Pugh told me. She's the daughter of Aneurin Pugh, the MP. They farm nearby. She said the Major had given Blodwyn the power of attorney. If any of the tenants die or move out, it seems Blodwyn sells the cottage the moment it becomes vacant. It's all done through a London agent. Cara says this is why they are fetching such high prices.'

Rhys Evans's face was inscrutable as he absorbed the information. He found it hard to believe that this slim, dark-eyed girl, the daughter he had long given up hope of ever finding, was supplying him with the evidence he had been seeking for years.

'Does Gwilym Vaughan know about this?' he asked cautiously.

'Yes,' Nesta nodded.

'Damn! That means it will be all over the paper before we have a chance to do anything,' Rhys muttered angrily.

'Not so,' Nesta defended. 'Gwilym has known for quite a while and he hasn't published a word?'

'That's not like him! He doesn't usually pass up a good story,' Rhys Evans stated cynically.

'Well, he has kept this one to himself! And, what is more, he has helped me to find you so that I could warn you. He thought it might look like some sort of collusion if it was found out that, all the time you were protesting through Plaid Cymru about cottages being sold to the English, it was your friend Blodwyn Thomas who was responsible.'

'Perhaps he wants the news to break! A great inside story,' Rhys pronounced disparagingly. 'Just think of the headline, "The Dragon's daughter acts as go-between!"'

'So you are the Dragon,' Nesta breathed softly, her eyes shining. 'I'm so proud of you and of what you are doing,' she added, reaching out to cover his hand with hers.

'You mean you are in favour of Plaid Cymru?' he exclaimed in surprise. His slate-grey eyes probed hers questioningly, softening as they met her frank and open stare. She was truly a daughter to be proud of, he thought, and his heart ached that they had been separated for so long. The ten-year void could be bridged but nothing could ever make up for those lost years.

He would never be able to forget the frustration he had felt when he had been stranded in Calcutta, wracked with fever yet his mind sharply alert, worrying about how he could get in touch with Nesta so that she wouldn't think he had deserted her. Or the harrowing sense of futility when he had finally returned to Cardiff and learned that Mr and Mrs Greenford were both dead.

He had been sure Alice Roberts would know what had happened to Nesta. But the pub in Adelaide Street had changed hands and the new landlord had no idea where they had gone.

In desperation he went to see the headmistress at the school Nesta had attended but all she could tell him was that Nesta had gone to live with an aunt.

He knew so little about Eleanor's family that he didn't know where to start looking. For months he had scoured the length and breadth of South Wales but there was never a trace. It was as if Nesta had vanished off the face of the earth.

Each time he went back into hospital the harrowing sense of frustration returned. He would lie there wondering where she was, remembering every minute they had spent together.

Only the thought that Nesta needed him and that some-day he would find her gave him the willpower to return to hospital time and time again for treatment. As the years went by and there was no trace of her, he began to give up hope, knowing that by this time she would have left school and made a life for herself.

It was then that he turned to politics.

Lonely and bitter, his health impaired, he had begun to devote his energies to Plaid Cymru. His love of Wales seemed to be all that he had left.

He had been sceptical when Gwilym Vaughan had told him he knew where Nesta was and would bring her to see him. For several weeks Rhys had prevaricated, weighing up the odds. Ten years was a long separation. She would have changed from the child who had adored him and hung on his every word. Supposing she was disillusioned when she saw him . . . rejected him even!

At their first meeting he could hardly believe that the tall, beautiful girl with the thick dark hair and oval face standing in front of him really was Nesta.

It was like seeing a vision.

He had tried to remain calm, though inwardly he had known an intense euphoria as he held her close. The sudden, blinding, wonderful knowledge that she was alive and well confused him. Gradually, as they talked, he calmed down and shrewdly decided that the situation was one which he must handle with care.

He fought against his inclination to hold on to her, not let her out of his sight again for a moment. Instead, he remained a little withdrawn, giving her space, determined not to encroach on either her freedom or her feelings.

21

Easter was cold but bright. Flurries of snow had left their imprint, delicately sprinkling the fir trees and coating sheltered dips in the cwms with crisp icing. The tops of the mountains still wore their white mantles which sparkled in the bright sunlight as they stood etched against the skyline.

Nesta had never worked harder. Lambing was almost over, but many of them were still so tiny that they were vulnerable to predators and had to be watched over and guarded against foxes and carrion crows.

Normally, scrambling over the lower slopes of the Glyders, with Shep and Bob, the two well-trained, brindled sheep-dogs, was work she enjoyed. Now, she barely noticed their obedient response to her signals. Her own personal problems were absorbing all her attention.

She had seen her father only twice since the New Year and on both of these occasions it had been Gwilym who had made arrangements for them to meet in Liverpool.

Not knowing where to contact him created an invisible barrier between them. After so many years of separation, she wanted to see him as often as possible and recapture the closeness she had known as a small child.

If only he would tell her where he lived, she thought uneasily, it would set her mind at rest. He wouldn't even say how he earned a living, though she had probed as tactfully as she could. Yet, for all that, she felt they were slowly closing the gap and getting to know each other again. It was like re-reading a much-loved book. Reviving and sharing memories so deeply hidden in her subconscious that they were half-forgotten, was a constant source of delight.

As he listened with understanding and sympathy to her

anecdotes about life with the Jenkins family in Pontypridd, and the Lewises in Cardiff, the years of separation rolled away. Yet he became reticent when she tried to question him about his life since he had stopped going to sea. He refused to come to the farm and would say nothing further about his friendship with Blodwyn and Major Powell Thomas.

There had been no further development over the cottages. Nesta had tried several times to prod her father into action but he was reluctant to make any move without positive proof.

'Isn't there anyone in London who could find out something from the estate agent?' she questioned.

'It's in hand,' he told her laconically.

Knowing that her father didn't completely trust Gwilym, Nesta took care to keep the two of them apart. Even when nothing had appeared in the *Liverpool Echo* about the Dragon after either of their meetings in Liverpool, Rhys Evans was still convinced that Gwilym was only acting as a go-between in the hope of a scoop.

When Aunt Wynne told her that her father would be visiting them on Easter Monday, Nesta had a presentiment of trouble, knowing that Gwilym was also coming the same day.

As Nesta had feared, the Bank Holiday was not a success. Finding Gwilym already at the Morgans' cottage, Rhys announced he was going for a walk.

'Can we come with you?' Nesta asked eagerly.

'I'm going for a walk ... and I intend going on my own,' he told her firmly. 'You stay with your boyfriend.'

'We had arranged to see each other today long before you said you were coming,' Nesta explained apologetically.

'Enjoy his company then,' her father told her curtly. Thrusting his hands deep into his trouser pockets he turned away. Nesta stood watching until he was out of sight, willing the tears that stung behind her eyes not to spill over. She wondered if he was going to see Blodwyn Thomas and the possibility left her uneasy.

Her distraction made her an edgy companion and for the first time since they had known each other she found herself snapping at Gwilym. Like her, he speculated that her father might have gone to Gwyndy Farm and even suggested that perhaps they should follow him.

'I can think of better places to go on my day off,' she reminded him huffily.

'I only suggested it because I thought you were concerned about him,' Gwilym retorted angrily.

'You might get a good story out of it, of course. Do they pay you overtime for spying?' she asked tartly.

The moment the words were out she felt appalled at her own rudeness. She had never meant to say anything like that.

For a moment Gwilym stared at her speechless, then with quiet dignity he stood up, took his car keys from his pocket and walked to the door.

'I think it is time I was leaving,' he said, abruptly. 'Say goodbye to your aunt for me.'

Nesta wanted to stop him, to rush into his arms and beg forgiveness, but pride kept her silent. As she heard the car start up, she ran to the door to call him back. Through the blur of her tears, she saw him disappearing into the distance.

'He'll be back. Lover's tiff, nothing more. You've heard them say the path of true love never runs smooth,' Aunt Wynne comforted, as she made a pot of tea, her cure for all ills.

'Here, cariad, take this up to your Uncle Huw. He's in that old shed of his pricking out seedlings ready for planting now the weather is a bit warmer. Take him a couple of bakestones as well. I'll leave dinner for another hour, or so, give that father of yours time to get back.'

Rhys didn't return for dinner and a gloom hung over the cottage as they all waited and wondered.

'Where does he go, Aunt Wynne, when he's not here? Does he live in Liverpool? Is he doing some sort of war work?'

'I don't know what he does nor where he goes. I think my Mam has an address where she can contact him if ever she should need him.'

'Would she give it to you?' Nesta persisted.

'She clams up like an oyster whenever I mention it, cariad.'

'We are a strange family, Aunt Wynne! You are afraid that Grandfather might find out about my father visiting here and Grandma won't even tell you where you can get hold of him. It seems silly somehow.'

'We are all doing what we think is best, Nesta,' Wynne Morgan sighed. 'Rhys and Dad are so alike in some ways and yet so completely different. Dad is taken up with religion and his work, Rhys scorns both. Yet Rhys is just as fanatical about Plaid Cymru. That's work *and* religion to him.'

'Don't you believe in what he is trying to do, Aunt Wynne?'

'Oh, I think he's right about a lot of things, but with this war going on there's more to worry about than selling off a few houses to the English. Who wants to live in them old cottages anyway? Damp they are, and falling down. People that buy them will have to spend a lot of money getting them put right. Farmworkers and quarrymen couldn't afford to put in new plumbing for bathrooms and indoor toilets. Most of *them* would much rather move into one of the new council properties where all these things are done, and where they have tiled kitchens and nice rooms without old beams that harbour spiders to worry about.'

'So you think my father is wasting his time trying to keep Wales for the Welsh?'

'Not really, but I think he's worrying about the wrong things. More to the point is to stop them ruining the mountainsides. Nothing grows underneath pines and firs so it leaves nowhere for the sheep to graze, see.'

'Have you tried telling him this?'

'Me tell our Rhys! Don't make me laugh, cariad. I wouldn't dream of trying to tell him anything. Not that he'd listen anyway. Our Mam tried telling him he ought to keep up the Welsh when he left school but he wouldn't take any notice of what she said.'

'Why not? I would have thought that was one of the things he would approve of. It's part of keeping Wales Welsh.'

'Of course it is. But our Rhys couldn't see that. Mind you, I think that was because of our Da. He does his preaching in Welsh, you see, so our Rhys shut his ears to it. Very eloquent my Da can be. I'll take you along one Sunday to hear him preach.'

'He'd probably have me thrown out,' Nesta grinned.

'I don't know. He might feel differently towards you if he thought he'd managed to convert you,' Wynne said thoughtfully.

'He's not likely to do that!'

'Still a practising Catholic, are you?'

'No! I haven't been to Mass since I left Cardiff. What I meant was that I wouldn't be able to understand a word Grandfather was saying if he was speaking in Welsh.'

Nesta delayed going back to Gwyndy Farm for as long as possible, hoping that any minute her father would return. It was almost dark before she put on her duffle coat and said goodbye.

'Huw had better walk along with you,' Wynne told her. 'Perhaps you will meet your Da on the way.'

They didn't meet him and the farm looked strangely deserted when she and Huw reached there. Blodwyn had left a note on the scrubbed kitchen table to say she wouldn't be home until late.

Nesta was in bed, but not asleep, when she heard the front door open and footsteps on the stairs. She tried to make out if it was one pair of feet, or two, but the thickness of the farmhouse walls made it impossible. She lay for a long time straining to hear if there were any voices but the velvet stillness was unbroken.

When she woke next morning, Blodwyn was already working out in the yard. Several times Nesta tried to ask if her father had been there the previous day, but each time her courage deserted her. Even though Blodwyn seemed to be in a particularly good mood, Nesta didn't think she would react kindly to being questioned about her private life.

As spring advanced, so Nesta's working day grew longer. In some ways she was glad. It took her mind off all her other niggling problems. She had not heard from either her father or Gwilym since Easter. And, to add to her loneliness, Cara Pugh was away, staying with her father in London.

When Gwilym did turn up she was bringing some sheep down from the pens half-way up Glyder Fawr, so that they could be dipped. She heard someone calling her name and her heart raced when she saw him standing there, tall and broad-shouldered in a smart blue tweed jacket and grey flannels. As their eyes met she knew that her feelings for him were stronger than ever.

'Hello, Nesta,' he said awkwardly. He ran a hand through his fair wavy hair as though wondering what to say next. Then as he saw the love shining from her large dark eyes he seemed to relax. Tentatively he stretched out a hand, resting it gently on her forearm. When she made no protest he pulled her towards him, his mouth claiming her lips hungrily.

'I thought perhaps you had gone into the army when I didn't hear from you,' she exclaimed breathlessly when he released her.

'No, but I have been given a new date for my call-up and I don't think there will be any deferment this time. Anyway, I feel it's time I went and did my bit.'

'Is that why you've come ... to say goodbye?' Nesta asked wistfully.

'No ... there's another reason. Something you'll probably find far more serious.'

'What?' A sense of foreboding swept over her as she saw his green eyes narrow. 'You've brought bad news?'

He hesitated. She was so sweet and vulnerable that he didn't know how to begin to tell her the reason for his visit. It was hard to believe she had been brought up in a city, she was so innocent and trusting. He dreaded the thought of seeing the hurt in her soft dark eyes when he told her his news.

He had known many girls but not one of them had touched his heart in the way Nesta did. He would never forget his first sight of her at the Plaid Cymru meeting in Dolgellau, standing tall and slim, her dark eyes huge with fear, nonplussed by what was happening.

When he had first heard her sounding off he had been struck by her forcefulness and for one moment had thought she was a political agitator deliberately trying to inflame the crowd. It was only later, when she had told him her name and who her father was, he had understood why she had spoken up so passionately about something she believed in without thinking what the consequences might be.

'It's something to do with my father?'

'Yes,' he nodded, biting his lip, his brow furrowed. 'There was a fire, two nights ago. A cottage near Trawsfynydd power station was burned down. The police think . . . the Dragon is their number one suspect. I thought you might want to warn your father,' he said quietly. 'If I could talk to him . . .' his hand rested on her arm but she shook it away angrily.

'So that was why you came was it!' Her eyes blazed. 'It would make a good story, wouldn't it? A real scoop for that paper of yours.'

'No, it isn't like that at all,' Gwilym shrugged helplessly. 'I want to help.'

'Well, I don't know where he is,' Nesta muttered. 'I haven't seen him since he walked out of Aunt Wynne's cottage at Easter. Come to that, I haven't seen either of you since then,' she added bitterly.

'I'm sorry. After the things your father said to me I thought it was better if I stayed away,' Gwilym told her.

'He hardly spoke to you!' Nesta flared.

'He was waiting at the bottom of the lane. I gave him a lift back to Liverpool.'

'You mean he didn't go to see Blodwyn Thomas!'

Nesta felt almost light-headed with relief. For weeks now she had been torturing herself unnecessarily. Blodwyn had been in such good spirits, going out most evenings, dressed up as if she was off somewhere special, that Nesta was quite convinced that Blodwyn must be meeting her father. If it was anyone else, she reasoned, then Blodwyn would have brought him back to Gwyndy Farm.

Now that her suspicions seemed to be quite unfounded, she felt overjoyed. Even Gwilym's grave allegation didn't completely swamp her elation.

'Why . . . why do the police think he is responsible?' she asked, staring at Gwilym hostilely.

'The cottage belonged to a Liverpool shipping magnate and he owned the boat that left your father stranded out in India ten years ago.'

'And they think my father would harbour a grievance all

these years!' she exclaimed, her eyes wide with astonishment.

'It makes him a prime suspect,' he told her gravely. 'After all, it resulted in his career at sea coming to an end, didn't it?'

22

'Your place is here, on this farm, not chasing around the countryside with your boyfriend,' Blodwyn stormed when Nesta asked for some time off so that she and Gwilym could try to find her father.

'He's in danger ... don't you understand?' Nesta blazed.

'Rhys Evans is always in trouble,' Blodwyn sneered. 'Unreliable, like you,' she spat angrily, a hostile gleam in her blue eyes.

'Are you sure you don't know where I might find him?' Nesta pleaded. Inwardly, she felt ashamed of her wheedling tone. She loathed having to ask any favour of Blodwyn.

'I haven't seen sight nor sound of him since you arrived here. And how long ago is that, six months ... seven months?'

'I promise I will be back, just as soon as I can,' Nesta told her as she crammed some clothes into a holdall and made for the door.

'Don't be too sure that your job will be waiting for you. This is one of the busiest times of the year, and if you are not here by the time I am ready to start shearing then I intend to report your absence. If you were in the army you'd be court-martialled for deserting your post.'

'I don't suppose your aunt has any idea where he is but it is a starting point,' Gwilym commented, as they drove away from Gwyndy Farm and headed for the Morgans' cottage, with Blodwyn's abuse still ringing in their ears.

'She told me once that he had given my grandmother an address where he could be contacted in an emergency,' Nesta confided.

'Then why don't we go straight to Blaenau Ffestiniog and save time.'

'I think it would be better if Aunt Wynne came with us. She knows how to handle my grandparents better than I do.'

They found the Morgans' cottage deserted. Shonti, the cat, was dozing on the doormat, her white paws tucked beneath her.

'Even the back door is locked,' Nesta said gloomily, 'which means they intend to be out for some time.'

'Well, that decides it,' Gwilym told her. 'We will have to go to Moel Road after all.'

The look of alarm on her grandmother's face, when she answered the door and saw who it was, warned Nesta that she had not picked a good time to call.

Before she could say what she wanted, Caradoc Evans appeared in the hallway behind his wife.

'Who is it then? he rasped, looking over her shoulder.

His craggy face turned puce with anger when he saw Nesta.

'I told you to stay away and leave us in peace,' he snarled.

'I know you did,' Nesta admitted quietly, 'but I need your help. Can I come in?'

'Let the girl in,' Gwyneth Evans urged. 'We don't want the whole street knowing our business, now do we!'

Scowling angrily, Caradoc Evans shuffled back into the living room.

'Sit down, both of you, and I'll put the kettle on,' Gwyneth Evans urged. 'No need to go rushing things. He forgets he is retired now and that he has all the time in the world.'

'Just say your piece and be on your way,' Caradoc Evans growled tetchily.

'This is my friend, Gwilym Vaughan,' Nesta told them. 'We've come to ask if you can tell us where I could get in touch with my father.'

Nesta saw her grandmother's face blanch and caught the quick warning shake of her head but it came too late. Caradoc Evans had risen from his armchair and was towering over her. 'Get out of here. Mistake it was on my part to let you over the threshold. I'll not have his name mentioned in this house, do you understand? We're upright God-fearing people and I disown him completely.'

'This isn't the time for personal feuds, Mr Evans,' Gwilym said firmly. 'The police are looking for Rhys Evans. Unless we can warn him he may end up in prison.'

'Which is where he belongs,' roared Caradoc Evans, red anger creeping above his collar.

'What has he done?' Gwyneth Evans clutched at the edge of the table, looking bewildered.

'We are not sure that he has done anything,' Gwilym said quietly. 'The police think he was responsible for setting fire to a cottage near Trawsfynydd. He's wanted for questioning.'

'Playing the Dragon again, is he?' Caradoc Evans said bitterly.

'So you do know!' Nesta exclaimed in astonishment.

'Know, of course I know! It's not something I'm going to shout from the rooftops though, is it?' her grandfather snarled. 'Ashamed of him, I am. Ashamed of my own flesh and blood. Brought disgrace on us all.'

'Rubbish! He's fighting for what he thinks is right. As a Welshman you ought to be proud of him,' Nesta defended.

'Welshman! He's no Welshman, just a politically minded fool. He hasn't the tongue. Hasn't the sense either to see he is being used. Plaid Cymru! Upstarts, that is what they are. Bringing trouble on us all, causing unrest and dissatisfaction amongst the workers.' Tight-jawed and trembling, his breathing became laboured as he struggled to hold his temper in check.

'Some men are born to be bosses and to lead, others to follow and do as they are directed. Rhys could never take orders. That was why he wouldn't work in the quarries. My family have mined in those quarries for generations. Men of standing, proud of their place in the community. Then Rhys gets these high and mighty ideas about us scarring the mountains! Unable to see that it was what God intended. How else would we make a living, or feed and clothe our children, and provide a roof over our head all the days of our life.'

His voice rose and fell and Nesta remembered the "*hwyl*", the mesmeric chanting her Aunt Wynne had described. As she saw the fanatical gleam in her grandfather's eyes she understood what her aunt had meant. He was capable not only of enthralling an audience but of transporting himself into a state of trance.

And he was doing that now. His head was up, his eyes glistening as they looked into the far distance. For a brief spell he had forgotten her and Gwilym, he was in another world filled by the sound of his own voice.

Abruptly, his entire body began to shake and rock until it seemed incredible that he could maintain his balance. His gaze became transfixed, his sparse frame shook like an aspen in a strong breeze. Then he crashed to the ground, clutching at his chest, a harsh cry emitting from his ashen lips.

Gwilym dropped to his knees beside the prone figure. With deft fingers he undid Caradoc Evans's flannel shirt, slipping his hand inside to feel for a heartbeat.

The colour drained from Gwyneth Evans's frightened face as Gwilym looked up, shaking his head. For one terrible moment, Nesta thought her grandmother was going to collapse as well. Holding her firmly by the arm, she helped her into an armchair and fetched her a glass of water.

Nesta tried to comfort her grandmother while Gwilym went off in his car to notify the doctor and to fetch Wynne and Huw. She wondered how she would explain what had happened to Tudor or Hwyel if they came back first.

Her grandmother seemed to be in a state of shock so Nesta made her some tea. She wished Mrs Evans would cry, or at least speak, anything except sit there looking expectantly at her husband as if waiting for him to sit up and talk to her.

She rallied slightly when the doctor arrived. She answered his questions in a low voice, shaking her head from side to side as if she couldn't understand what was happening.

After the doctor left, Gwyneth Evans sat staring fixedly into space, folding and unfolding the edge of her lace-trimmed apron. The room was uncannily quiet, only the ticking of the clock on the mantelpiece breaking the silence. As she looked up at it, Nesta could hardly believe that only an hour had passed. It seemed like eternity.

She desperately hoped that Gwilym would be back soon. Although the doctor had covered Caradoc Evans's body with a blanket, Nesta still felt that her grandfather's presence dominated the room.

'Grandma!' As she leaned forward and gently touched Gwyneth Evans' arm, Nesta was conscious of how old and wrinkled her grandmother suddenly looked. Lines furrowed her brow, her cheeks were sunk and there was a new sharpness about her mouth and chin.

'Gwilym will be bringing Aunt Wynne any minute now,' she said gently. 'Hwyel and Tudor will be home soon, too. We ought to send for my father . . . for Rhys. We must tell him about Grandfather. Do you know how we can get in touch with him?'

Her plea went unanswered. Gwyneth Evans shook her head repeatedly, her blue eyes vacant as they met Nesta's.

Even after Wynne arrived and took charge, persuading her mother to go upstairs and lie down on her bed and rest, Mrs Evans still refused to tell them how to contact Rhys.

'A piece in the *Echo* about your grandfather's death may help. Your father may see it and get in touch with you, or with someone in the family,' Gwilym told Nesta. 'Perhaps you should go on back to Gwyndy Farm in case he tries to contact you there.'

Nesta found it difficult to concentrate on her work. She was on edge, expecting all the time to hear that her father had been seen or, even worse, arrested.

Everyone was talking about the fire at the cottage, from the postman to the man who delivered the animal feeds. Nesta listened to their theories but steadfastly refused to say anything.

The day Caradoc Evans's funeral took place was one of April showers and sunshine. A crisp wind blew down from the mountains tugging at the women's hats as they gathered round the grave in the hillside cemetery.

Nesta stood slightly apart. The chapel ceremony was strange to her and she felt like an onlooker rather than a participant. Her aunt and uncles lined the edge of the grave, supporting their mother between them, while the body of Caradoc Evans was committed to the earth.

Inside the chapel, the preacher had already eulogized, in both Welsh and English, over Caradoc Evanss' many attributes. Remembering her grandfather's harsh domineering manner, the fury with which he had greeted her visit, his uncompromising refusal to let her stay in his house, Nesta had listened in deepening anger, knowing that not one quarter of what was being said was true.

Sickened by the hypocrisy, she decided to leave and began to pick her way between the grass on either side of the graves towards the road.

It was then that she saw him.

. At first glance she thought it was merely an onlooker watching from the cemetery gates. Something about the man's height, the set of his shoulders seemed familiar, and as she looked again she was horrified to see that it was her father. Afraid to hurry, in case it drew attention, she walked across to him.

'Da!,' she called in a soft whisper. 'Da, what are you doing here?'

His face looked drawn and his slate-grey eyes narrowed as he stared back at her.

'I could ask you the same thing.'

'I came for the funeral . . . I don't understand what is going on, though. The service is strange . . .' she shrugged helplessly. 'But you shouldn't be here, the police are looking for you. They think you started the fire that gutted the cottage at Trawsfynydd.'

'Your boyfriend brought me here.'

'Gwilym did! How could he do such a thing, knowing the risk?' she exclaimed angrily.

'Don't blame him, he wasn't too keen. I had a job persuading him but I had to come, Nesta.' His face softened. 'He was my father, after all.'

'Leave now . . . right away, before anyone sees you,' she urged. She felt almost in tears her concern for him was so great. The disgrace of him being sent to prison, following so closely on the death of her grandfather, would be heartbreaking for her grandmother. Haltingly, she tried to explain this to him.

'I must let her know I am here,' he insisted. 'Just a word with her when the service is over and then I'll vanish.'

'Supposing someone sees you and informs the police . . .'

'It's a chance I will have to take. Go and wait in the car with Gwilym, I'll join you as soon as I can.'

'I only wish I could. I have to get back to Gwyndy Farm. Blodwyn has gone into Chester and I have to see to the animals.'

'I understand. I'm glad you came, Nesta,' he added gently.

'Oh, Da!' Her tears began to surface and she dashed them away angrily. 'How . . . how will I know you are safe?'

'Don't worry, I will be. I'll send a message by Gwilym.'

He reached out and squeezed her arm. 'I was wrong about him, Nesta . . . you've got a good friend there.'

Her mind was a hubbub of confusion as she turned away. The relief of seeing her father, and knowing he was safe, was almost over-shadowed by what he had said about Gwilym. She had hoped that one day they might tolerate each other but it was beyond her wildest dreams that they would ever be friends.

'I can only stop for a moment or I shall miss my bus,' she said breathlessly as she reached Gwilym's car.

'Get in and I'll give you a lift back to the farm,' he offered.

'No! You must wait for my father. Surely, you haven't forgotten the police are still looking for him!'

'You know I haven't. He wants to stay until the funeral ends so that he can speak to his mother, and that means at least another twenty minutes or so. I could run you to Gwyndy Farm and be back again in that time.'

'I would much rather you stayed here,' she smiled. 'It's a comfort to know you will be on hand should my father have to leave in a hurry.'

The realization of the danger her father was in haunted Nesta all the time she did the milking and penned up the animals for the night.

Dark storm clouds swirled over the tops of the mountains shrouding their peaks as though wrapping them in grey shawls, and for the first time they did seem threatening. She was glad when her chores were finished and she could go indoors. She felt vulnerable to the isolation of Gwyndy Farm and even longed for Blodwyn to return.

She had just finished preparing a meal for herself when she heard the scrunch of car wheels outside followed almost at once by a peremptory knocking on the back door. Heart in mouth, she went to answer it.

'Can I come in?'

Her relief at finding it was Gwilym was momentary. Her

eyes searched his face, fearful that he was bringing bad news.

'Is something wrong?' she asked, as she led the way into the beamed sitting room.

'No! Why should it be? I've just taken your father to Chester to catch the London train.'

'And then you came all the way back again!' She turned to put another log on the fire so that he wouldn't see the fear in her eyes.

'He wanted you to know that he was safe and this seemed to be the quickest way of doing it. Also,' he went on with a grin, 'I remembered you had said that Blodwyn would be out. I thought you might like some company.'

Her father's words, 'you have a good friend in Gwilym', sang in her head as she reached up to kiss him.

His arms went round her, pulling her closer. The brief kiss became a long embrace that stirred her blood and set her pulse racing.

Flushed, she pulled away, straightening her mussed-up hair, smoothing her sweater back into place.

'Have you had anything to eat?'

'Come here.' His hands reached out for her again. 'It's not food I'm hungry for,' he whispered, his lips nuzzling into the warmth of her neck. 'When are you expecting Blodwyn back?'

'She won't be home until quite late.'

'An evening to ourselves!' He pulled her gently back on the settle until she was lying in his arms. His hands were firm but gentle as they slipped beneath her thick jumper and began to explore the soft warm flesh of her body.

After her first shyness was overcome, Nesta found herself as aroused as Gwilym. As his lips brushed against her forehead, she raised her face eagerly and felt the soft rush of his warm breath fan over her. For a moment she stopped breathing, then, as his mouth settled over hers, communicating his need for her, she relaxed with a tiny whimper of happiness.

As his hand slid down to the small of her back, pressing her against the hardness of his body, she arched towards him, her own desire heightened by the solid beat of his heart thudding against her breasts.

Piece by piece they shed their garments until flesh was pressing against flesh. Her hand spread over his muscled back, moving ever lower until she was caressing the hard mounds of his buttocks, returning the same sweet thrills as had delighted her minutes before when his hands had sensuously massaged her back.

Gwilym's response was more immediate. His embrace hardened, his mouth demanded, and she felt a scorching desire that melted her resistance, leaving her not just powerless but eager for what was to follow.

'Gwilym, I'm scared,' she breathed as she realized their emotions were carrying them both to a point of no return.

His reply was unintelligible. His breath was coming in short, hard gasps, echoing the movements of his body. As his muscled thighs cradled her own, she found herself experiencing an ecstasy beyond her comprehension. His hands held her body to his so that his movements rippled through her, creating an ever-rising tide of sensations until she drowned, with a lingering moan of joy, in a sea of exquisite harmony.

Their lovemaking seemed to release the tension built up by the shock of her grandfather's death and her fear for her father's safety. She felt no guilt, only a wonderful sense of comfort. Happiness pervaded her entire being, flowing through her, lulling her into a state of complete euphoria.

The crackling of the logs and their own breathing were the only sounds in the room as they lay together in the flickering firelight, cocooned from the world in their love for each other.

Her reverie was broken when Gwilym propped himself up on one elbow, his green eyes intense and unfathomable as he gazed down at her.

'Nesta, I do truly love you, you know.'

'And I, you,' she murmured, pulling his face down to hers, her lips trailing kisses down his cheek.

A sudden burst of brilliant sparks, as the topmost log collapsed into the glowing hollow of the fire, was like a firework display to celebrate the joy in her heart. It must be a dream, she decided. Things didn't happen like this in real life. No one could feel as deliriously happy as she did.

23

Nesta's face became more and more perplexed as she read through the report in the newspaper Blodwyn Thomas tossed across the table towards her.

'Why didn't you tell me that your father would be at the funeral?' Blodwyn snapped, her blue eyes blazing.

She had risen from the table, ready to resume work outside, and stood with arms akimbo, towering over Nesta who was still eating her breakfast.

'I didn't know he was going to be there! He arrived at the cemetery towards the end of the service ... and he didn't stay.'

'Did you speak to him?'

'Only briefly. I had to leave before the service ended to catch the bus. You had gone out and I had to do the milking and see to the animals ... remember?'

'But you didn't tell me you had seen him!'

'I never thought to do so. I've been too concerned about how upset my grandmother was to think of much else.'

'Bah! You don't even know her! The few times you've been to visit her she has more or less turned you out of the house. Funny lot your family and no mistake – and your father is the strangest one of them all!' she added spitefully.

Nesta didn't answer. She was reading and re-reading the report in the *Echo* and wondering who had sent it in.

'Was that boyfriend of yours there?'

Blodwyn's question hatched the doubt already niggling at the back of Nesta's mind. Her next remark crystallized it.

'Do anything for a story, wouldn't he!'

'He didn't write this,' Nesta snapped, stung to Gwilym's defence. 'He was with me . . . here.'

'Straight from the funeral!' Blodwyn's eyes narrowed.

'Well, no. While I was seeing to the animals, he took my father to catch the Liverpool train.'

'And turn in his story! The *Echo* has an office in Chester.'

For the rest of the day Nesta tried to shut her mind to Blodwyn's insinuations but it was impossible. Everything fitted as neatly into place as pieces in a jigsaw.

He probably came back to see me to clear his conscience after filing his copy, she thought bitterly after she had re-read the piece for the sixth time. How could he have written such a story? It wasn't so much a funeral report as an exposé of Rhys Evans!

Everything was there, starting with how he had broken his father's heart by going to sea, instead of following the family tradition of working in the slate quarries, to his association with the Plaid Cymru Welsh Nationalist movement, where he was known as the Dragon.

Just one detail seemed to be missing, Nesta noticed. Nowhere in the entire report, not even in the list of mourners, was her name mentioned. And there was only one person who could have been so sensitive, she thought wretchedly.

Remembering their magical evening together, she was at a loss to understand how Gwilym could have made love to her immediately after writing like that about her father.

Her dismay turned to frustrated anger. It took all her willpower to control the rage in her mind and in her heart. Her face burned with shame as she remembered his lips on hers, his hands caressing her so intimately, and the way she had responded.

She felt betrayed.

Once she was over the initial shock of her husband's sudden death, Gwyneth Evans rallied well. No longer having to be careful in what she said or did, in case she roused her husband's wrath, she became more relaxed, more mellow. The sharpness went from her face and voice. She was anxious to make up to Nesta for the hurt she knew had been inflicted when she had first arrived in North Wales.

The reconciliation between the two of them culminated in a suggestion from Mrs Evans that Nesta might like to come and make her home with her.

'I know you live in at Gwyndy Farm and that you can go and stay with Wynne and Huw whenever you want to, but it would be lovely for me if you thought of my place as your *real* home. You could come whenever you liked, have your own room, feel you belonged, like. I'd find it such a comfort, cariad, so give it some thought.'

'I would love that, Grandma, but what about Hwyel and Tudor. They might not like it.'

'No need to worry about them,' her grandmother chuckled. 'I haven't said a word to our Wynne yet, but Tudor is getting married. It seems he has been walking out with a girl from chapel for months, years in fact. He never plucked up the courage to tell us because he thought his Da wouldn't approve. Silly, if you ask me. A grown man to be afraid of his father. Still,' she sighed resignedly, 'we were all afraid of him, me as well as the boys. Our Rhys was the only one who stood up to him . . . and he was turned out!'

'And what about Hwyel?'

'Oh he's going into the forces. He has always hated it at the quarries. First thing he did after the funeral was to go down to the Labour Exchange and ask to be taken off the reserved list. Then he signed on for the army.' Her eyes twinkled. 'All this talk about the D-Day invasion has him on a knife edge. He's worried in case the war is over before he gets through his training.'

Blodwyn received Nesta's news that she intended moving in with her grandmother with surprising equanimity. There had been tension between them ever since the funeral. Even so, Nesta was completely taken aback when Blodwyn suggested that perhaps the time had come for her to quit Gwyndy Farm altogether.

'It would suit me if you did,' Blodwyn told her. 'Gareth Pryce who used to work here has been invalided out of the army. He would like his job back and I need a man around the place.'

'If I leave here, the Land Army might send me to some other part of the country,' Nesta said dubiously.

'If you want to stay in North Wales I will get you fixed up,' Blodwyn promised. 'Most of the farmers around here are crying out for help.'

'I would want it to be somewhere close to Blaenau Ffestiniog so that I can live with my grandmother,' Nesta reminded her.

Blodwyn wasted no time. By the end of the week it was agreed that Nesta should work for Parry Jones at Cynfal Farm. It was on the western ridge of Moelwyn, and within half an hour's walking distance of her grandmother's house.

Gwyneth Evans was overjoyed. She bustled around, spring-cleaning the middle bedroom and prettying it up with net curtains. She dyed one of her best white sheets to make a new bedspread and then edged it with hand-crocheted lace.

Nothing was too much trouble and, for the first time since she was a very small girl and had lived in Cardiff with her mother's parents, Nesta felt truly welcome.

'It really only needs one thing to make my happiness complete,' she told her grandmother the first evening she was there. 'I wish my father could come and live here with us.'

She also wished that she hadn't hung up on Gwilym when he had phoned her at Gwyndy Farm.

Her new life at Cynfal Farm was demanding, so for most of the time she had no time for her own problems. It was only at night that she would start wondering whether or not she had misjudged Gwilym over the report in the *Echo* and wished she had asked him outright if he had been responsible for it.

Parry Jones had a large dairy herd of brown and white Friesians as well as hens and sheep. His wife, Glenys, made butter and cheese, and they supplied most of the shops in the area. Rationing and quotas had doubled the amount of paperwork involved, so when they learned that 'keeping the books' came easy to Nesta she found herself handling most of the office work.

'Would you like to learn to drive the van?' Parry Jones asked her at the end of the first month.

'You mean you want me to do the deliveries as well?'

'You would find it easier than milking and seeing to the sheep, especially when winter sets in again.'

'Would it mean a very early start each day?' Nesta asked cautiously.

'Start early, finish early,' Parry Jones promised. 'No seeing to the animals at night. Milk round, deliveries to the shops, make up the books and then you've done. Cushy little number, I'd say! Think about it.'

'All right, I'll give it a try. There's one problem,' she said dubiously, 'I can't drive.'

'Nothing to it. You'll pick it up in no time. Give you a lesson right now, if you like? Come on.'

'I haven't a driving licence,' Nesta protested.

'Sort that out when you can drive. You don't have to take a test or anything, not with the war on,' Glenys Jones told her.

Nesta couldn't believe her good luck. After the months of heavy farm work, often ankle deep in mud and manure, driving the smart little van seemed like a holiday.

The June mornings were sweet with bird song and flowers, the cool air fragrant. She became a familiar figure around the town. Quarrymen, on their way to start an early shift, called out *'Bore Da,'* as she drove past them. The shopkeepers were equally friendly. They liked the reserved, dark-haired, dark-eyed girl and knowing she was Gwyneth Evans's granddaughter they often slipped her a packet of tea, some biscuits or a bag of sugar to take home.

Working at the farm also meant that occasionally Glenys Jones would give her some butter or cheese. And when Parry Jones went shooting, if his bag of rabbits was particularly good, he would give her one to take home for her grandmother.

'If things go on like this we shall be forgetting there's a war on and be throwing those dratted old ration books behind the fire,' Gwyneth Evans chuckled, as Nesta handed her a plump rabbit. 'This will help to feed our visitors at the weekend.'

'Aunt Wynne never said anything when I saw her this morning.'

'Oh, didn't she?' her grandmother answered, her eyes twinkling. 'She will probably pop in, though, seeing that it is to celebrate your birthday. No . . .'

She left the sentence unfinished so Nesta didn't pry. She knew her grandmother loved springing little surprises.

On her birthday, her grandmother handed her a long, slim package. Inside was an intricately carved love-spoon.

'Your grandfather made that for me to mark our betrothal,' Gwyneth Evans told her with a tremulous sigh.

'It is very beautiful but I can't take it . . . it's yours,' Nesta said gently as she studied the delicately carved, intertwining links. The initials 'G' and 'C' were inlaid in cherry-wood in the twin bowls of the spoon and there were interlocking hearts and leaves uniting them.

'I want you to have it,' her grandmother insisted.

'You should give it to Aunt Wynne,' Nesta protested.

'Huw made her one when they got engaged. Not as fancy as mine, but nice all the same.' She wiped away a tear from the corner of her eyes. 'It's a custom that seems to be dying out, so you look after this one.'

On Saturday, when Nesta arrived home from Cynfal Farm, there was a car parked in the roadway outside. As she let herself into the house she could hear her father's voice and immediately guessed what her grandmother's surprise was.

'This is a wonderful birthday present!' she exclaimed, flinging herself into his arms, hugging and kissing him.

'Look who else is here,' her grandmother chuckled.

As her father released her, Nesta drew in her breath sharply. Standing in the shadows was Gwilym. She felt her throat go dry. It was the first time she had seen him since the funeral, since their memorable evening together and since the report had appeared in the *Echo*. She didn't know who had invited him but she wished he hadn't come.

'What's gone wrong between us, Nesta?' Gwilym asked, the moment they were on their own.

'How should I know? I have not seen anything of you since . . . since the funeral,' she said, fighting to keep her voice steady.

'When I tried to get in touch with you at Gwyndy Farm, Blodwyn said you had left.'

'And you didn't ask where I had gone?'

'She said she didn't know. I thought you must have decided to go back to Cardiff.'

'Blodwyn helped to get me a job at Cynfal Farm . . . she knew I was coming to live here,' Nesta frowned.

'That's not how I understood it or I would have come to see you long before this. By sheer chance I met your father a couple of days ago, and when I asked about you he said he was coming here to see you today. Anyway, why have you never got in touch with me?' he asked in bewildered tones.

She stood for a moment in silence, wrestling with her thoughts, anxious to clear the air between them. She had found it hard to believe that Gwilym would betray her father's confidence. Now, she wondered if Blodwyn had misled her all along and Gwilym hadn't been the one to file that story. The only way to find out, she decided, was to ask him.

The surprise on his face when she did was clear proof of his innocence.

'You thought I would do a thing like that?' he challenged, his eyes suddenly hostile. He cleared his throat angrily. 'I thought you knew me better than that!'

'I'm sorry. I didn't know what to think. I was upset about my grandfather. If we hadn't gone to see him that night he might still be alive. And then, when Blodwyn showed me that report . . . well . . . what else could I believe?'

'You just accepted her word,' he said bitingly.

She nodded miserably, almost afraid to meet his eyes. When she did she saw no reproach in their green depths, only love. Confused, she looked away. Gently he drew her towards him. Once she was in his arms, his hard lean body pressing against her, the old passion flamed anew.

It was the happiest birthday Nesta could ever remember. The rabbit pie was delicious, and afterwards they picked strawberries from the garden and topped them with cream from Parry Jones's dairy. To finish off their feast, they drank a toast in home-made elderberry wine, which was as delicious as the finest port.

'While I have a rest, why don't you all go for a walk? Show them some of your boyhood haunts, Rhys,' Gwyneth Evans suggested when their meal was over and the washing-up done.

'Shall we take the car?' Gwilym asked as they set out.

'Yes, do that,' Rhys agreed. 'We'll have a run round, then you can drop me off and I'll walk home. Give you two a chance to do some sightseeing on your own,' he smiled.

*

As he watched them drive away, absorbed in each other's company, Rhys felt a pang of loneliness. It seemed ironic that now he and Nesta had found each other he was about to lose her yet again. For her sake, he was glad she had found someone like Gwilym Vaughan. He was not only a fine-looking chap but clever and would go far. It was a pity the war would interrupt his career but he was ambitious enough to make up for any lost time, Rhys decided.

He felt a deep sadness that he had missed seeing Nesta grow up into such a fine young woman. With her dark hair and eyes and slim figure, she was like him, not Eleanor. But she had her mother's sweet nature, even if it was spiced with his own fiery passion when it came to things she cared about.

He still couldn't understand why they had never traced him through the shipping agents. He'd been on their books for at least three years after he'd got back from India. He had had every intention of going back to sea once he was discharged from hospital. When they had turned him down on medical grounds he had thought he was being victimized. Now, all these years later, he knew it was not so and he had come to terms with the inevitable.

24

While the rest of the world seemed to be able to think of nothing but the war, peppering every conversation with news about Nazi brutalities and the atrocities that were making the headlines, Nesta daydreamed about Gwilym.

The Japanese invaded Burma, captured Singapore, then were defeated by the US naval forces in the Battle of the Coral Sea, but Nesta still lived in a romantic world of her own.

The whole of July sped by in a haze of long, hot days. Gwilym visited her each weekend and their feelings for each other reached a new peak.

The war seemed to be escalating and, each time she saw Gwilym, Nesta expected him to say that his calling-up papers had come through. There were reports of fierce fighting in the Far East as well as on the Russian front. The Americans had landed in North Africa and linked up with the British Eighth Army. The Allies had also landed in Sicily.

Mrs Evans read her newspaper avidly from cover to cover, passing her own sharp judgement on how Churchill and Montgomery were running the war.

Hwyel and Tudor were now in the army. Although they were in different regiments, they had both been posted to the south of England in readiness for the invasion of Europe. As long as they were still in Britain their mother seemed to take it for granted that they were safe. She knitted constantly, warm khaki socks, gloves and balaclavas, in readiness for the coming winter.

She also began to take a keen interest in local happenings and regaled Nesta with local chit-chat.

Gossiping was a novelty to Gwyneth Evans. When her husband had been alive, and Tudor and Hwyel living at home, her time had been fully occupied with cooking, cleaning, washing and ironing. Now she had time on her hands and was free to indulge in a chin-wag with her neighbours without censure from Caradoc.

'Got to talk about something while we're standing in a queue,' she would retort when Nesta laughingly scolded her.

Nesta enjoyed the snippets of news. She had got to know a lot of the local people while doing her milk round.

What she enjoyed most about working for Parry Jones were her regular deliveries to Betwys-y-Coed, Penmachno, Nantmor and Beddgelert, and along the steep-sided deeply wooded road to Penrhyndeudraeth and Tremadoc.

It gave her immense satisfaction to be able to name the five peaks of the Snowdon range, to distinguish between Glyder Fach and Glyder Fawr, as well as recognize Moelwyn and Moel Hebog and the mountains of the Manod range. As she grew familiar with their ever-changing moods and colours, she began to understand more clearly her father's zealous love for his homeland.

He seldom visited the terraced house in Moel Road. Where he lived or what he did remained a complete mystery. And, although Gwyneth Evans seemed ready and eager to talk about her other sons, she remained reticent when it came to Rhys.

After one or two attempts at questioning her and finding it was impossible to draw her out, Nesta gave up trying. She hoped that if she was patient then, in her own good time, her grandmother would tell her whatever there was to know.

Towards the end of September it seemed that time had come. They had just finished their evening meal and Nesta had started to clear the table when her grandmother stopped her.

'Sit down a minute. I've something on my mind and now is as good a time as any to talk about it.'

'What is wrong?'

'It's about your father. I heard some talk about him today that I didn't like.'

'You know what they say about rumours,' Nesta chided.

For once her grandmother didn't smile. She sat nervously twisting the edge of her pinafore, biting her lower lip and shaking her head uneasily.

'What was it you heard?' Nesta asked gently, aware that this was no idle chatter but something that her grandmother found deeply worrying.

'I was in a queue for that bit of fish we've just had,' Gwyneth Evans told her, 'and I overheard two women talking about Blodwyn Thomas. The moment I heard them mention Gwyndy Farm my ears pricked up. I didn't know either of them, mind you, and they didn't know me from Adam. If they had, they probably wouldn't have said what they did.'

'Go on,' Nesta urged.

'They mentioned something about the man staying there and I heard the words "arson" and "police". Ever since, I've been putting two and two together, and I don't like it, Nesta. People can be very spiteful, you know. Rhys was often up at Gwyndy Farm before the Major went off into the army. There was a lot of talk then, or so our Wynne told me. She was worried in case her Dad heard anything at the quarry. She knew how cut up he'd be if there was any scandal.'

'Why should there be any scandal? There was no talk of arson in those days, was there?'

'It's not the arson I'm concerned about, cariad,' Gwyneth Evans said impatiently. 'No one worries too much about that. It's the other scandal.'

'I don't understand?'

'Him and her! Alone in that house!'

'Oh, Gran! Surely you are not letting *that* upset you. Heaven's above, there's a war on, those sort of things don't matter any more.'

'They matter to me,' her grandmother told her fiercely. 'I brought up all my children to know right from wrong and to behave properly. And it's not right to be living in another man's house, alone with his wife, while he is away in the army!' she added in a disapproving voice.

'But what makes you so sure it is my Da who is there?'

'They said "he" was back again. And since it isn't the Major, who else could it be but our Rhys. Shocked they sounded!'

Nesta didn't answer. Her mind was buzzing. If people knew he was there, then the police could pick him up any time they wanted to. The charge of arson had never been cleared.

She couldn't understand her father choosing someone like Blodwyn as a friend. She was so brash with her brassy blonde hair and strident voice. When daydreaming about her father, Nesta had always imagined that, once they found each other again, they would set up home together ... just the two of them. She had never even considered that she might have to share him with someone else.

For her grandmother's sake she had hidden her disappointment when he hadn't wanted to come and stay at Moel Road after her grandfather had died, but she had expected to see much more of him. She was puzzled and a little hurt by the barrier that still existed between them. He was so self-contained, so withdrawn, as if his love for her had burned itself out. The only fire left in him was for Plaid Cymru and he seemed to devote all his time and energy to furthering its aims.

Even about that he preferred to keep his own counsel. When she questioned him about his long absences he was reticent. He looked thin, almost haggard at times, but he refused to confide in her, or disclose his whereabouts, or let her share his life in any way.

228

'Look, if it will make your mind any easier, I'll go up to Gwyndy Farm and see if he is still there,' she told her grandmother.

It was mid afternoon when Nesta drove down the lane to Gwyndy Farm. Blodwyn was feeding the hens. In a sleeveless blouse, her arms bronzed by the sun, her hair bleached gold and twisted into a knot at the nape of her neck, she had an Amazonian attractiveness. Her solid hips and mammoth bosom filled her tan brace-and-bib dungarees provocatively.

'And what has brought you out here?' she greeted Nesta caustically, balancing the bowl of feed on one hip.

'I wanted to speak to my father. I heard he was here.'

'Did you?' Blodwyn's sharp blue eyes narrowed, an ironic smile touched her lips. 'And did you also hear that I've bought a slate quarry and he is going to run it for me?'

'I don't believe you! He wouldn't even consider such a job. He hates anything to do with quarrying,' Nesta exclaimed hotly.

'Oh, I don't mean using a pick and shovel. He won't have to get his hands dirty.' Her hard blue eyes mocked Nesta. 'I need a manager. Someone who can ensure it makes money. Working for a local magistrate would look good in the eyes of the law,' she added softly.

'That's blackmail,' Nesta exclaimed, shocked.

'Is that what you call it? I would call it common sense . . . and compromise.'

'Yes, it's that all right. You have compromised him! People are talking . . . blackening his name.'

'He did that without any help from me. I'm just trying to save him . . . from a prison sentence.'

'What do you mean?' White-faced and furious, Nesta grabbed at Blodwyn's arm. The bowl of feed that was balanced on her hip went crashing to the ground, splattering both of them.

'Does that boyfriend know what a temper you've got?'

Blodwyn asked angrily as she brushed the bran from her dungarees.

'I'm sorry,' Nesta muttered contritely. She turned away, tears stinging, angry that she had fallen into Blodwyn's trap.

'I've left a message for him to come and see us,' she told her grandmother. She didn't mention the slate quarry, preferring to believe that it had been something Blodwyn had made up simply to annoy her.

For the remainder of the week they seemed to be sitting on the edge of their chairs waiting for a knock on the door.

'My Mam is like a cat on hot bricks,' Wynne confided in Nesta when she popped in to see them. 'She can't sit still for two minutes together. And knit, knit, she's going at it like a machine.'

'I know, but she has to do something to keep herself occupied.'

'Oh dear,' Wynne put an arm round Nesta's shoulder and gave her a warm hug. 'It can't be very much fun for you, cariad.'

That night Rhys Evans came to Moel Road.

Nesta was already in bed. Her early morning start of five-thirty meant she liked to be in bed just after nine o'clock. As usual, she had left her grandmother pottering around downstairs, filling the kettle and putting it on the trivet in front of the banked-up fire so that the water would be hot next morning, and laying the table ready for breakfast.

Nesta was almost asleep when she heard a knock on the front door, and then a man's voice. When she slipped on her dressing-gown and went downstairs she found her father there. He was sitting in the armchair by the fire and her grandmother was bustling about making tea and buttering some of the bakestones she had made earlier in the day.

'He's come. She did give him the message,' Gwyneth Evans exclaimed delightedly.

'Message, what message?' Rhys Evans asked puzzled.

'I sent Nesta up to Gwyndy Farm last week to ask Blodwyn Thomas to tell you we wanted to see you.'

'She told me that you were going to work for her ... manage a slate quarry she had bought,' Nesta blurted out angrily.

'All lies!' His face darkened and his mouth tightened. 'I haven't seen her since the Major went away.'

'But . . .'

'Let it rest,' he signalled towards his mother with his eyes and Nesta said no more. Deep inside her she felt a crawling fear. What had she done? Why had Blodwyn said what she had? And why was he here if Blodwyn hadn't given him the message? She watched in silence as her grandmother poured out tea for the three of them.

'I've got some nice lamb chops. It wouldn't take me long to cook you a meal, Rhys,' his mother told him. 'And you've no call to feel you'd be eating up our meat ration,' she added, fetching them from the larder for his inspection. 'Lovely, aren't they? Nesta brought them home. She does a bit of swopping.' She pulled a face. 'Black market I suppose you would call it, but since the sheep are home-grown on our mountains I can't see that it's so dishonest, can you?'

Before Rhys could reply a hammering on the front door startled all three of them.

'More visitors . . . at this time of night?' Gwyneth Evans exclaimed, flustered.

'I'll answer it,' Nesta said quickly. 'You go and put those chops out of sight.'

'You can't go to the door in a dressing gown!' her grandmother exclaimed shocked.

'Leave it to me. You do as Nesta said and put the meat away,' Rhys told her.

As he opened the door they heard a scuffle and Nesta ran down the hall to see what was happening. She found her father struggling in the grasp of two uniformed policemen.

'Da!'

'What's going on out there?' Gwyneth Evans called.

Nesta turned quickly to try and stop her grandmother coming into the hall but she was too late. Gwyneth Evans's quick intake of breath rattled in her throat as she saw the policemen on either side of her son. With an anguished cry she crumpled into a heap on the floor.

'Please ... help me,' Nesta pleaded as she knelt beside her grandmother, loosening the neck of her dress and chafing her hands.

'I'll call an ambulance,' one of the policemen said, releasing his hold on her father.

'You'd better get dressed, miss,' the other one instructed. 'Someone had better go along to the hospital with her.'

'I ... I think it should be my father,' Nesta told him.

'Sorry, miss. Our instructions are to take him in ... there's a charge of arson against him.'

The week that followed seemed endless. Nesta and Wynne took it in turns to sit at the hospital bedside as Gwyneth Evans's life ebbed away. Fleetingly, she regained consciousness and knew them. She kept asking for Rhys and was unable to understand why he didn't come to see her.

Nesta was at her bedside, cradling one of the thin, blue-veined hands in her own, when the end came. For a brief spell, her grandmother was completely lucid. Her eyes opened, wide and clear, and her voice was thin but steady.

'You must help your father, Nesta,' she entreated, clutching Nesta's hand fiercely and pulling herself off the pillows. 'Don't let him waste his life. They're using him for their own ends. Make him see sense. He's not strong, he must look after his health ...' her voice suddenly failed in mid sentence.

Nesta felt a moment of blind, whirling panic as her grandmother closed her eyes and, with a shuddering sigh, sank back against the pillows.

Even as she reached out to press the emergency bell to summon a nurse, Nesta felt the life go out of the hand she was holding and knew it was too late.

25

It was as if her whole world had suddenly fallen apart, Nesta reflected as she sat huddled in a corner seat on the train taking her to Cardiff.

She didn't know which had upset her the most, her father being taken away by the police, or her grandmother's death. It had been like one of those frightening nightmares where terrible things are happening all around you but your feet are clamped to the ground and you can't move, she thought with a shudder.

She was glad her grandmother had been spared the shame of knowing that her father had been arrested. After thirty-six hours of non-stop questioning he had been released but he had not been cleared. He remained under a cloud of suspicion. Nesta felt anxious about what it must be doing to him both mentally and physically, he had looked so thin and drawn. Whenever she mentioned it, though, he brushed aside her concern.

She would never forget the moment the ambulance had arrived at Moel Road and they had carried her grandmother into it on a stretcher. A knot of neighbours had gathered outside the gate, curious to know what was happening. They had already seen the police take her father away.

'He'll end up at the Old Bailey,' she heard one man prophesy morosely, as she waited to get into the ambulance. 'Arson is like sabotage, an offence against the King. Especially in wartime. Makes him a Fifth Columnist.'

'If he'd been in the army doing his bit, the same as his brothers, then he wouldn't have ended up in this sort of trouble,' another agreed.

At the time she had managed to shut out their remarks, but they had registered in her mind and she'd brooded over them ever since. She had felt resentful when she saw the same people at the cemetery and silently labelled them hypocrites.

Gwyneth Evans's funeral was a quiet affair. There was none of the flamboyant oratory there had been when Caradoc Evans had been buried, just a straightforward interment on a dull wet day. Nesta had felt too numb to cry.

'You'd better come back to our hourse,' Wynne told her afterwards. 'You can't stay on here. We have to give up this place at the end of the week. It belongs to the quarry-owners, see. They will be needing it for one of their workmen.'

'But what about when Tudor and Hywel are demobbed? It is their home.'

'They are not the tenants. They will have to shift for themselves when the time comes. I'll sort through the bits and pieces and anything I think they might want to keep I'll try and make room for at my place.'

'How will I get to work? I have to be at Cynfal Farm by six each morning, long before the bus starts running.'

'Won't Parry Jones let you use the van? You could park it in the road outside our place. It would be quite safe there.'

The new arrangement worked well, although, when the winter weather set in, Nesta sometimes found the early morning drive treacherous. Once or twice, when there were some really severe snowstorms, she stayed the night at Cynfal Farm.

'It's not just your neck I'm worried about,' Parry Jones told her, 'it's my van. Can always get a new Land Army girl but vans are in really short supply.'

The winter had seemed to drag by and, although she was kept busy, Nesta felt lonely. She missed her grandmother. They had grown very close in the short time she had been living at Moel Road. With no one else at home, Gwyneth Evans had been glad of her company and had enjoyed spoiling her. There had always been a hot cooked meal waiting for her when she got home, and her washing and ironing were taken care of, even though Nesta protested that she was quite capable of doing it herself.

What she found she missed most of all in the weeks immediately after her grandmother's death was the companionship that had grown up between them. For the first time in her life she had found someone who was interested in her opinion and treated her as an equal. Whereas before Nesta had listened to other people and inwardly rejected or rebelled while outwardly remaining politely submissive, she was now able to air her views.

She had never tired of listening to stories about her father when he had been a boy, and anecdotes about Wynne and the rest of the family. The one area on which her grandmother had refused to be drawn was about what had happened after her father came home from India. Gwyneth Evans would become vague and either change the subject or get up and make a cup of tea.

Nevertheless, it would have been comforting to confide in her after being questioned by the police about her father's disappearance. They had looked askance when, like Huw and Wynne, she had told them she didn't know where he was. There seemed to be no trace of him at all. Complete silence, almost as if he had been spirited away. And just to hear her grandmother's opinion about where he might have gone would have helped to relieve her own anguish.

Nesta also missed Gwilym.

Because he was her first boyfriend she sometimes found it difficult to handle their relationship. Remembering how pushy and bold Bronwen had been with the men and boys who had flocked round her, and how it had all ended up, Nesta tended to hold back. Unwilling to express her own tumultuous feelings of love, she sensed that Gwilym must sometimes feel irritated by her reticence, and she was afraid she might lose him.

This was one subject she hadn't been able to bring herself to discuss with either her grandmother or Aunt Wynne. It was something she was determined to work out for herself. Bronwen had always been more than willing to talk about such matters, and Nesta had always felt sickened that she was so willing to kiss and tell.

Gwilym had been on leave only once since he had been called up, and then it had been just a weekend pass. He no longer had a car, so they had met in Chester and gone to the pictures, sitting close together in one of the double seats at the very back of the cinema. The film had been a third-rate comedy but it hadn't mattered. They were together, bodies and arms entwined. As his mouth had covered hers, memories had flooded back like an incoming tide.

The Pathé newsreel broke the spell.

'When I go back I will be training to take part in bombing raids like those,' he told her, sitting upright, his attention focused on the screen. 'Pay those Germans back for all they've done to our country,' he boasted. He had completed his initial training and was hoping to qualify as a pilot, and he was brimful of confidence.

He insisted on taking her for a meal afterwards to an expensive restaurant in The Rows. She felt out of place in her Land Army uniform. He looked devastatingly handsome in his blue uniform and she noticed a number of women giving him admiring glances, and although she felt bursting with pride, she also felt the stirrings of unease.

While they ate he talked non-stop about his new life. She tried to be interested but the people were just names to her and she felt shut out.

He had promised to write regularly but in the intervening four months she had received only two letters. They didn't sound at all like the Gwilym she had known when he was a reporter on the *Echo*. They were sprinkled with RAF expressions like 'wizard' and 'prang' and incidents that held very little interest for her because she could not in any way identify with them.

Towards the end of the year, when some three hundred bombers had made a mass raid over Germany and, more recently, when there had even been daylight raids over Berlin, her fears for his safety gripped her like a cold hand.

In the New Year, speculation about the invasion was on everyone's lips. Yet the end of the war was still not in sight and, on the home front, life was becoming more and more difficult because most things were in short supply or unobtainable.

She felt so restless and unsettled as the cold winter days gave way to spring that she decided to take a break . . . get right away in the hopes it would help her to sort out the muddle her life had become.

When the train pulled in at Cardiff Central station, Nesta automatically began to walk along Penarth Road in the direction of Grangetown. As she crossed from Aber Street to Corporation Road, she suddenly wondered whether her Aunt Gwen would be willing to put her up. Apart from a card at Christmas she had not kept in touch since she had been in North Wales.

When her aunt answered the door, Nesta was shocked at the change in her. She had always been plump but now she was grossly overweight, her double chin sagging and her eyes like two small currants gleaming from out of rolls of fat.

'Hello, Aunt Gwen. It's me . . . Nesta,' she added as she saw the bewilderment on her aunt's face.

'Nesta!' Aunt Gwen's face creased into a smile and Nesta found herself enveloped in a warm hug that felt like tumbling into a feather bed. 'Come on in. Fancy you calling. Have you got time for a cup of tea?'

'Yes, plenty of time. I .. I was hoping I might be able to stay with you . . . just for a few days,' she added quickly as she saw her aunt looking at her suitcase.

'You are not back for good, then?' Aunt Gwen said, pushing her tangled hair away from her face.

Nesta followed her aunt into the back living room and was appalled at the state it was in. The table was a jumble of unwashed dishes. A newspaper that looked as though it had once been wrapped round some fish and chips was screwed up into a ball amongst the dirty breakfast dishes.

'Whatever is that outfit you are wearing?' her aunt asked, as she cleared a space and reached down a couple of mugs from the dresser.

'Land Army uniform. I work on a farm in North Wales.'

'Funny they should send you there instead of into the ATS. Your father came from around those parts.'

'I know. I've found him.'

'You have! Now there's something strange. Bet he was surprised when you met up again after him disappearing like he did. Still goes to sea, does he?'

'He was taken ill while he was in India. By the time he got home again Gran and Grandad were both dead and no one could tell him where I'd gone.'

'And then you meet up again after all those years. Funny how things turn out, isn't it?' Aunt Gwen murmured, shaking her head in a disbelieving way.

Nesta decided it was pointless to try and explain that she had gone to North Wales looking for her father. Instead, she began to ask Aunt Gwen about the Lewis family, and about Cardiff.

'Oh, a lot has happened since you left,' Aunt Gwen told her. 'Elwyn and Idris have been called up . . . and Dylan.'

'Elwyn and Idris had already gone into the army before I left here.'

'Yes, so they had. Well, our Idris has been killed. In North Africa it was. Only just landed. A sniper got him by all accounts. And Elwyn's been taken prisoner. And we don't know where Dylan is. When he writes to our Gwladys his letters are censored and there's no proper address. All secret, like, ready for this invasion lark.'

'And what about Bronwen?'

'She's still living here. Did you know she had a baby?'

'No!' Nesta shook her head, afraid to ask if Bronwen was married.

'Little boy. Called him Wynford. He's just turned a year. She has just taken him to the park. She goes out for a walk with the pram most afternoons. She will be surprised to find you back.'

Nesta spent the next day revisiting old haunts. Everything seemed different from what she had remembered.

The clanging trams and trolley buses were frighteningly noisy after the quiet of the mountains. Queen Street, St Mary's Street and all the shopping arcades off them were crowded with people looking at the things they wanted to buy but couldn't because of rationing.

The open-air market on The Hayes was even busier. As she caught sight of her Uncle Lloyd, red-faced and sweating as he served the throng of women who pushed and jostled for the meagre portions of meat he was handing out, Nesta compared it with the leisurely pace in Blaenau Ffestiniog and wished she was back there.

In the main library, in St John's Street, she checked to see when the next Plaid Cymru meeting was being held but found only official notices about blackout regulations and rationing.

She saw no one that she knew at the City Hall. She asked for Tecwyn and then felt a sense of relief when she was told he was away ill. With nothing better to do, she wandered up the imposing main staircase to the galleried landing above and sat on one of the long leather couches, studying the larger-than-life marble statues of bygone Welsh heroes.

Bored, she left the City Hall and went to the museum nearby. Many of the exhibits had been put into storage to protect them so it was practically deserted. She rapidly tired of listening to the echoing of her own footsteps and left.

Outside the sun was shining brightly, but a cutting wind whipped round the buildings, making it too cold to linger.

The next day she went to Pontypridd.

It seemed strange to go to the hairdresser's in the High Street instead of to the terraced house crouched against the hillside like a dog cringing at the foot of his master.

Dilys minced over to the reception desk and opened the appointments book before she realized who it was.

'You!' she exclaimed, tossing back her shoulder-length hair. 'For a moment I thought you were a customer. I didn't recognize you dressed like that!' She smothered back a giggle, her green eyes dancing.

'It's Land Army uniform.'

'Aunt Gwen told my Mam that you were going into the ATS,' Dilys said in surprise.

'I was . . . at one time. I ended up in North Wales in the Land Army, though. How are you?'

'Fine!' Dilys extended her left hand displaying a thin gold band. 'Married, now! Still living with my Mam, though. No sense in getting a place of my own until Greg gets out of the army. Saving hard, see. Are you going up to see Mam? She still lives here, in the flat. She'll have a fit. Our Chris is at home. Embarkation leave or something. Go on up and see them.'.

Aunt Betty hadn't changed at all. She was still as thin, angular and tight-lipped as Nesta remembered her.

'You had better come on in and I'll make some tea,' she said grudgingly. 'You staying down in Cardiff with our Gwen? Lucky you've come now, while our Chris is here. He often asks about you.'

An hour later, when Dilys popped up from the shop to have her midday meal, Nesta and Chris were still catching up on each other's news.

'I wish I had known you were in North Wales, I would have come to see you,' he said after she had told him about Blaenau Ffestiniog and the mountains that surrounded it. 'You've brought everything so much alive that I want to be there, breathe in that sparkling air, scale those rugged mountainsides. And some day I will! Once this war is over I'll come and join you there,' he grinned.

When she was leaving, Chris said he would walk to the bus stop with her. 'I'm still in love with you, Nesta,' he told her, as they reached the corner of the road. He turned her to face him, his hand cupping her chin so that he could look down into her eyes. 'I think you still feel the same way about me. What are we going to do about it?'

He had always been her favourite cousin, and for a moment Nesta felt her childhood fondness for him being rekindled.

'Not a lot we can do,' she laughed, her face flushing. 'We're first cousins . . .'

'I haven't been a Catholic for many a long year, nor anyone else in our family, so it wouldn't worry me. You don't still go to church, do you?'

'No.' she shook her head. 'I stopped going to Mass when I came to Pontypridd. When I went back to Cardiff I occasionally used to go with Bronwen. Father O'Malley wouldn't let us in the church dances unless we had been to Mass that Sunday.'

'Blackmail!'

'It was really. Anyway, I haven't been since I've lived in North Wales. They are all chapel up there. The hellfire and brimstone type,' she added with a grimace.

'So what does it matter if we are first cousins? We can be married in a Registry Office. What about this weekend?'

'Chris, you are a crazy idiot!' Tears and laughter mingled in her voice. 'I shall be back in North Wales by then.'

'You mean I am not going to see you again?'

'You could come to Cardiff tomorrow. Aunt Gwen asked me to invite your mother and Dilys to tea. I am sure she would have included you, if she had known you were home.'

To her astonishment his arms suddenly went round her, crushing her close. She struggled breathlessly to free herself but she was no match for his strength.

She felt excitement stirring as his hands moved down her spine, his touch sending ripples of pleasure through her. As the moist tip of his tongue crept into her mouth, her senses were spinning, and strange heats began to flame inside her. She closed her eyes, imagining that it was Gwilym's arms that were holding her, Gwilym who was kissing her so passionately.

The realization that it was Chris came flooding back and she broke free, panting and wild-eyed.

He looked at her strangely, as if aware that her responses had been for someone else.

Too embarrassed to speak, she turned and walked blindly away.

26

Nesta spent a restless night, tossing and turning, her dreams invaded by both Gwilym Vaughan and Chris Jenkins.

She woke at dawn, as fingers of light began filtering through the bedroom curtains. She bitterly regretted what had taken place between her and Chris.

It was Gwilym she loved.

Every fibre of her being ached for the day when the war would be over and they could be together again. Her feelings for Chris were warm affection and tenderness, the same as she would have felt for a brother whom she had grown up alongside.

She regretted coming back to Cardiff. She and Chris had never corresponded and she was sure that it was the unexpectedness of seeing her again that had brought about his declaration of love and proposal of marriage. He was all keyed up for D-Day and whatever lay ahead once his leave was over. She remembered the fleeting terror in his eyes, and the way he had squared his shoulders, when she had mentioned that Idris had been killed.

As she helped Aunt Gwen to tidy up the house in readiness for their visitors, Nesta was still unsure how she should handle the situation. She wished there was someone she could confide in. Bronwen was too full of her own problems.

The air force sergeant, who was Wynford's father, had disappeared without a word, leaving her penniless and pregnant. She had wanted to have an abortion, but Father O'Malley had threatened her with eternal damnation, so she had been too scared to go through with it.

'Can't see me ever getting married, now,' Bronwen had sighed, when she had finished telling Nesta what had happened. 'Who'd want to be saddled with some other fella's kid? Suppose I'll have to try and get my old job back. Mam says she'll look after Wynford if I do go back to work.'

Nesta's hopes that perhaps Chris would not come were dashed when she opened the door to find him standing there between Aunt Betty and Dilys.

'I haven't seen any of you for years,' Dilys exclaimed breezily as she pecked Aunt Gwen's cheek. She gave a self-satisfied smirk and ostentatiously smoothed her tight-fitting dress down over her slim hips. 'I'm married now,' she said, holding out her hand to show off the slim gold wedding band. Greg comes from the south of England. His father has a garage business in Maidenhead.'

'I think you were about twelve, Bronwen, the last time we all came to Cardiff on a visit,' Aunt Betty commented, 'and to think that now you have a baby.'

'Greg and I decided to wait until after the war before starting a family,' Dilys said brightly, reaching out to take the baby's hand and make cooing noises at him.

'You are still living here with your Mam, are you, Bronwen?' Dilys remarked, looking round the cluttered room with raised eyebrows. 'We haven't got our own place yet, either. We thought it was much more sensible for me to go on working so that we could save up for a nice home and give our children a proper start in life.'

Although she didn't particularly like Brownen, Nesta found it embarrassing to hear Dilys putting her down, so she went into the kitchen to make the tea.

Chris followed her.

'Have you thought any more about what I asked you?' he whispered, slipping his arm round her waist and kissing the nape of her neck.

'Chris, not here!'

'It's the only chance we are likely to get. Unless we leave them all to their gossiping and go for a walk on our own.'

'We can't do that!' She tried to keep her voice casual, to treat the matter lightly.

'I need to talk to you . . . plan for the future. It would mean a lot to me, Nesta to know you were waiting for me.'

'No, Chris, it isn't possible.'

'Give me some hope,' Chris begged, his blue eyes pleading. 'I love you, Nesta. I always have . . . always will. Even if you turn me down you won't stop me loving you. I'm twenty-five, not some callow youngster. Why do you think I've never married?'

When she made no reply, he pulled her into his arms, his lips covering hers in a fierce kiss that left her breathless and shaken.

'I've always wanted you. I will never be happy with anyone else,' he insisted.

The intensity of his gaze touched her heart. She couldn't bring herself to hurt him, to see the hope in his eyes fade.

'I . . I don't know, Chris. I haven't even thought about marriage . . . I'm not ready for it,' she prevaricated.

'You can't be a Land Army girl for ever,' he argued, 'but if farming is the sort of life you want then that's what you shall have. I never want to work at the pit again.'

'I'll think about it . . . I'll write to you Chris . . .'

'That won't do,' he said harshly. 'You said once before you would write to me but you never did. I must know where we stand, I want a definite answer.'

'I had better make the tea. They will be wondering what we are up to out here,' she said, gently pushing him to one side and taking the teapot over to the bubbling kettle.

'And your answer?'

'I'm fond of you Chris but I'm not in love with you. Let's just leave it,' she pleaded gently.

'All right. As long as you tell me there is hope and that you are not in love with anyone else.'

His eyes narrowed as a long sigh escaped her but, to her

relief, he didn't press her any further. The kiss he gave her on the cheek was light and brotherly.

'Here, help me carry some of these in,' she said, handing him two plates of sandwiches. 'Go on, I'll bring the tray with the tea things on it.'

Aunt Gwen was giving Bronwen's baby a bottle, so Nesta poured out the tea and passed it around. As he helped himself to sugar, Chris rose to his feet, cup and saucer in hand.

'Have you ever drunk a toast in tea?' he asked, grinning round at them all. 'Well, here's your chance. Nesta has promised to marry me after the war is over, so you can drink to our engagement.'

In the stunned silence that followed, Nesta could hear her heart thudding. She looked round the room and was stunned by the reaction on everyone's face. Bronwen's lower lip was pulled down in a sneer and Aunt Gwen's mouth had dropped slackly from amazement. But it was the look on Aunt Betty's face that dismayed her the most and left her feeling shaken.

'You two can't marry each other,' Aunt Gwen gasped, her double chins quivering with indignation. 'You are first cousins! It's against the church to do such a thing.'

'We gave up being Catholics a long time ago,' Chris told her cheerfully.

'You might have done, but I don't think that Nesta has,' she told him indignantly. 'She went to Mass every Sunday as regular as clockwork while she was with me. None of your heathen chapel in this house, I can tell you.'

'Chapel isn't heathen,' snapped Aunt Betty. 'All those crosses and rosaries and statues and holy water don't mean a thing. My Dai was a deeply religious man and he saw to it that all our children were brought up to go to chapel twice every Sunday.'

'You needed to do something to atone for your sins,' her sister challenged. 'My Lloyd always says it was downright wicked the way you changed your religion as soon as you went to live in Pontypridd. Our Mam must have turned in her grave when she saw you trooping off to chapel instead of to Mass on a Sunday.'

'Well, she would do more than turn in her grave if she thought that Nesta and Chris were intending to be married,' Aunt Betty shrilled. Tears began to spill from her eyes, making runnels down her powdered cheeks, as sobs shook her thin frame.

Passing the baby back to Bronwen and heaving her bulky frame out of her chair, Gwen went over to place a consoling arm around her sister's shoulder.

'Don't take on so, Betty. They'll come to their senses.'

'I am not so sure,' Aunt Betty sniffed. 'I think she is leading him up the garden path.' Her small deep-set eyes flashed an angry look at Nesta.

'Miss high-and-mighty, with her airs and graces, won't marry the likes of you, boyo,' she declared sourly. 'I know what she's like. Dancing and carrying on! It's her fault that poor Bronwen is saddled with a young baby.' She turned and clutched at Gwen's hand. 'If Nesta hadn't egged your Bronwen on to go dancing at the RAF place at St Mellons, it would never have happened,' she declared wildly.

'Bronwen's older than Nesta, she has a mind of her own, hasn't she?' Chris said angrily.

'Nesta turned her head with that silver tongue of hers, just as she is turning yours,' his mother shrilled.

'Drink up your tea and have another cup,' Gwen said placatingly. 'Come on, Dilys, pass your mother a sandwich or a piece of seed cake. Nice it is, even if I do say so.'

'I can't eat anything when I'm this upset,' Betty sniffed, as she put her empty cup down on the table with a clatter. 'All this carry-on has really upset me. Fetch me my coat Chris, and take me home.'

'I . . . I don't want to go yet, I want to stay with Nesta,' Chris protested stubbornly.

'You see! Mesmerised him, she has. Poor boy, he doesn't know what he is doing or saying,' Aunt Betty exclaimed triumphantly.

'For such a thing to have happened on his last day at home,' she added, breaking into fresh sobs. 'As if it isn't bad enough that they're taking him away from me.' She blew her nose loudly and dabbed at her eyes.

'Never know if you'll see them again or not, do you?' Gwen added morbidly. 'Look at our Idris. Home on leave and large as life, then three days later a telegram to say he'd been killed. Shot down by a sniper and that was the end of him. Tragic!' She sniffed loudly. 'Terrible thing, this war. You mustn't add to your mother's troubles,' she added noisily, rounding on Chris.

'I think you had better go with your mother, Chris . . . she needs you,' Nesta said worriedly.

'See what I mean!' Aunt Betty's tears stopped abruptly. She looked round at them all exultantly. 'Sanctimonious little bitch! Pretending to care! Get back to North Wales, to your gaolbird father, you deserve each other!'

Nesta felt herself trembling, as she felt the waves of hate directed towards her. With a cry like that of a frightened animal, she pushed her way towards the front door and rushed out into the street.

She had no idea where her feet were taking her as she ran along Corporation Road towards the docks. Tears were streaming down her face.

By the time Chris caught up with her, she had reached James Street bridge and was leaning against the railings, trying desperately to stop the deep gulping sobs that racked her body.

'Don't let them get to you, Nesta,' he begged. 'I don't know what came over my mother. She's not herself. I know she's upset about my going away. And then Aunt Gwen talking about Idris being killed . . . it just got to her.'

'Deep down she must have always felt that way about

249

me,' Nesta whispered unhappily. 'All those years I lived at your house, Chris, and I never knew,' she sighed. She made no resistance when he gathered into his arms, gently stroking the back of her head and murmuring consolingly.

'You'd better go,' she gave him a gentle push. 'You'll only upset your mother even more if you stay here with me.'

'There is no hurry. Dilys is taking her to the station. They will wait there for me.'

'Please go.' She kissed him lightly on the cheek and turned away.

'Will you marry me, Nesta?' he begged, holding her arm and forcing her to look at him. 'Tell me, so that I know I have something to come home to.'

'I can't promise, Chris. Perhaps your mother was right, perhaps I have been leading you on. If so, it has been unintentional,' she added quickly.

'You mean there is someone else?'

'There is someone I care for very much. He is in the air force. At first we kept in touch but I haven't heard from him for months now. I think perhaps he has forgotten me.'

'But you intend to go on waiting?'

'I don't know.'

'Then give me my answer. Say you will marry me when all this is over,' he pleaded.

'I don't love you, Chris, not in that way,' Nesta said wretchedly.

'You will. I can wait. We'll live in North Wales if that is what you want. And you'll never have to see my mother again,' he added with a small grin.

'You deserve someone better than me, Chris.' She reached up and stroked his hair, letting her fingers move gently down the profile of his face. 'You are a wonderful person, Chris. You made life so much easier for me when I first came to Pontypridd. I'll always be grateful to you.'

'So how can you let such a nice person go out of your life?' he smiled jokingly.

'It wouldn't work out, really it wouldn't,' she murmured, shaking her head sadly.

'No, you are wrong, Nesta,' he told her earnestly. 'I love you, I want you. There will never be anyone else for me.'

As her gaze locked with his and she saw the pleading in his blue eyes, Nesta felt her defences crumbling. He was her favourite cousin and she liked him enormously. He was kind and friendly and quite good-looking. She could imagine him in twenty to thirty years' time, his fair hair beginning to thin and turn grey, his waistline gone as he put on weight and settled into middle-age, a contented family man . . .

Life with Chris would never be exciting but she would be well cared for and he would do everything possible to make her happy. If only it was him she loved, she thought wistfully, but the spark wasn't there.

'There is too much at stake, I could never be the wife you deserve,' she said humbly. 'It is not just religion. There's the feeling your family have about me, that would always be there, and would get worse with the passing years,' she explained, trying to let him down gently.

'Nonsense!' He held her face between his hands. 'I know it would work. I believe in us, so whatever you say I shall go on hoping.'

27

Nesta stared unseeingly out of the carriage window as the train raced northwards, her mind in turmoil.

As she remembered how vitriolic Aunt Betty had been towards her, tears stung her eyes so that she had to blink quickly to stop them spilling down her cheeks.

She could understand why they had resented having to bring her up. With families of their own, an additional child must have been a tremendous burden. Uncle Dai couldn't have earned very much as a miner and, although Uncle Lloyd was probably a bit better off, Aunt Gwen had always been a poor manager.

What had really upset her was when Aunt Betty had said, 'Get back to your gaolbird father'. She was still mystified as to what her aunt had meant.

She puzzled over it until the train reached Abergavenny. The sight of the Sugar Loaf stirred a longing for the mist-clad awesome mountains which had become part of her daily life in North Wales. Carnedd Llewellyn, the Glyders, Moel Hebog, the Arenigs, the five peaks of the Snowdon range topped by the Eyrie. She'd be back amongst them soon, feeling as safe as Owain Glyndwr had when he had taken refuge amongst them over four hundred years ago.

Resolutely she stood up and reached down her suitcase to find the book she had packed. It would at least help to take her mind off her problems. She was getting as bad as her father, romanticizing about Wales and its past.

As she replaced her case on the rack she caught sight of the newspaper the man sitting opposite her was reading. A chill went through her as she read the headline: 'THE DRAGON TO STAND TRIAL FOR ARSON'. In a blinding flash it became crystal clear what her Aunt Betty had meant.

Nesta tried to concentrate on her book but it was impossible. The headline seared her brain, dancing in front of her eyes so that the print was a blur. Shock and panic mingled. When the man folded up his paper, and dropped it on to the seat beside him, she leaned forward eagerly.

'Excuse me. Could I have a look at your newspaper. I . . . I didn't have time to get one.'

'Of course.' He passed it over to her with a broad smile. 'Nothing very startling. The date for the invasion is still not fixed. Are you in the services?'

'Yes, the Land Army.'

'Aah, that's what the uniform is. I did wonder. Where are you stationed?'

'North Wales.'

'Aah! The headline about this chap they call the Dragon setting fire to that cottage caught your eye, did it?'

Nesta could feel herself colouring up and wished she had never asked him for his newspaper.

'The people up there seem to be making a lot of fuss about outsiders moving in,' the man went on. 'I wonder how they would like it if their families were being bombed out.'

She smiled non-committally. She had no intention of entering into a dispute with a complete stranger and one who was obviously opposed to what Welsh nationalists were trying to do.

'Sounds quite a character,' the man went on with relish. 'A fanatic by the sound of it. This is my station,' he said, standing up. 'You can keep the paper!'

By the time she reached Chester every detail was imprinted on Nesta's mind. In an interview, Blodwyn Thomas had described her father as a casual labourer she had hired to help out on the farm and said that, by the time she discovered he was an active supporter of Plaid Cymru, he had moved on. Later she realized that he had only worked for her so that he could spy out the countryside.

The case was likened to that of Saunders Lewis, who had resorted to arson as a weapon against the British government in the Llyn Peninsula case.

The newspaper article stressed how important it was to stamp out vandalism and went on to make the point that, had anyone been in the cottage at the time, the crime would have been even more serious.

'I can see you've already heard what has happened,' Wynne greeted her, when she arrived back at the Morgans' cottage. 'We had the police round here the day after you left for Cardiff. Not that we told them anything, mind you. Huw thought it was best for us to stay out of it.'

'You could have told them my father wouldn't do a thing like that,' Nesta said wearily.

'What would be the good of us speaking up for him, girl?' Huw said angrily. 'Probably only make matters worse. These London lawyers twist your words, anyway. Real evidence is what is needed!'

They were still talking about it over breakfast the next morning when there was a hammering on the front door.

'Postman probably,' Wynne said, getting up from the table.

She returned in seconds with someone following her.

'Look who is here, then! There's timing for you! A day earlier and Nesta would still have been down in Cardiff.'

'Gwilym!' Nesta stared in disbelief. In his officer's uniform, with its gold braid and glittering wings, he looked even taller, broader and even more masculine than she remembered him.

'I've managed to get special leave so that I can be a witness at your father's trial,' he told her. 'We've got to act fast. I have information that will prove conclusively that he didn't set fire to that cottage.'

'You mean you know who did?'

'That's right!' He paused, enjoying the suspense he was creating.

'There was an air raid over Liverpool that night. A German bomber dropped some of his load as he made his get-away, and a stray bomb set that cottage on fire. I've been over it several times and my commanding officer was able to get it officially verified.'

'What are we going to do about it?'

'Take our evidence to the defending counsel, of course.'

'The date for his trial hasn't been fixed yet,' Nesta said bewildered.

'Oh yes it has! That's why I am here. It's at ten o'clock tomorrow morning, in Liverpool. I've come to collect you so that you can stay at my home overnight, and then we can see the lawyer who is representing your father first thing in the morning, before the trial starts.'

'I've only just come back from Cardiff.'

'Right! Well just pack your suitcase again and we'll be off,' he said with a confident grin.

'I can hardly believe this is happening,' Nesta told Gwilym in a piqued voice. 'You haven't been in touch for months and then suddenly you pop up with all this.'

'I know. I have been meaning to write to you but I've spent every spare minute collecting this lot together. When we are not flying sorties over Germany we are on permanent standby.' His hand reached out and took hers. 'I've thought about you a lot . . . about us,' he said with deep conviction.

Now that Gwilym was back at her side she wondered why she had been so lacking in trust. There was no estrangement. He was as warm and loving towards her as he had ever been. Remembering Chris, a wave of embarrassment swept through her. She must have been out of her mind. There was no question at all about her feelings for Gwilym, there never had been.

On the way to Liverpool, Gwilym went over the evidence he had amassed, convincing her that it would prove conclusively that the Dragon was innocent.

It wasn't until they reached the suburbs of Liverpool and were pulling up outside Gwilym's home that Nesta gave any thought to the fact that she would be meeting Gwilym's parents for the first time.

She knew practically nothing about his background, except that he worked on a newspaper, and she was taken aback by the obvious signs of wealth. The well-manicured front lawn and gravelled driveway leading up to the double-fronted detached house looked like something from the front cover of a glossy magazine.

Inside, it was tastefully decorated and elegantly furnished. From the wide hallway, doors led off on both sides and a wide staircase, carpeted in rich bronze Wilton which glowed warmly against the pastel-green walls, led up to the bedrooms.

An agony of nervousness gripped her.

Apprehensively, she slipped her hand in Gwilym's as he opened the front door. His reassuring squeeze did nothing to dispel the goose-bumps she felt breaking out all over her.

Mr and Mrs Vaughan were expecting them. A meal was waiting in the panelled dining room, and afterwards Sara Vaughan took Nesta upstairs to the guest room with its pink flowered wallpaper and matching floor-length curtains.

Mrs Vaughan hovered, folding and refolding the fluffy pink towels, straightening the pink and white candlewick bedspread and checking the drawers and wardrobe to make sure there was everything Nesta might need.

Nesta liked her immensely but was surprised at how young she was. A slight, attractive woman with sea-blue eyes and soft brown hair swept up in a French plait, she hardly looked old enough to have a son in his twenties.

Her elegant pale-blue dress showed off her slim shapely figure to advantage.

'She was Dad's secretary when he married her,' Gwilym explained, as they sat talking long after his parents had gone to bed. 'She's in her forties but he's almost seventy.'

'She is very lovely and terribly glamorous,' Nesta sighed enviously, remembering the matching sapphire pendant and earrings and exotic perfume she had been wearing.

'Not nearly as lovely as you are,' Gwilym murmured, drawing her into his arms. 'I've dreamed so often of the day when we could be together again,' he breathed, burying his face in the softness of her hair.

As their lips met in a sweetly tender kiss, her need for him flared. Trembling with desire, she returned his kisses, thrilling to his every touch.

Because they were in his parents' house, she reluctantly drew away. 'I'd better go up to bed,' she whispered, placing her fingers over his demanding mouth.

'I suppose so.' He stood up and pulled her to her feet. Gently his lips touched hers. 'See you in the morning. And Nesta . . . don't worry. Everything is going to be all right, I promise.'

'You have both decided to go in uniform, I see,' Sara Vaughan commented next morning as they sat down to early breakfast in the sunny morning room that looked out on to the terrace at the rear of the house. 'Probably a wise choice. It should attract sympathy from the judge if you have to give evidence.'

Sara herself was wearing a swansdown-trimmed cream satin negligée with matching satin mules. She looked very feminine and lovely. Even at that early hour her face was carefully made up, her hair in a soft chignon in the nape of her neck. Beside her, dressed in her Land Army uniform, Nesta felt like a country hoyden.

The courtroom was packed. Nesta was anxious to visit her

father before the case started but was not allowed to do so.

'It would help to reassure him if he knew we were here and that you had some fresh evidence,' she grumbled.

When they finally managed to see the lawyer representing her father he listened without comment to Gwilym's disclosures.

'I'll arrange for you to be called as a witness,' he promised, making a note on the clipboard he was carrying. 'Just wait in the corridor outside the courtroom.'

'We won't be able to see or hear what is going on if we are out there,' Nesta said anxiously.

'You go inside then, and I'll join you as soon as I've given evidence,' Gwilym suggested.

When her father was brought into the dock, Nesta's heart ached. He looked as gaunt and hunched as his father had looked when he came home at the end of a working shift in the quarries, she thought sadly.

As the evidence against Rhys Evans built up, and his exploits on behalf of the Plaid Cymru movement were catalogued, Nesta grew increasingly alarmed.

She felt furious when Blodwyn Thomas took the stand. Nesta had never seen her looking so smart. Her blonde hair was in a neat roll, and she was wearing a blue tweed suit and a crisp white blouse. She gave evidence in such a confident manner that every word carried conviction.

She succeeded in making Rhys Evans out to be a spy for Plaid Cymru, a man who touted for casual work in order to find out what future plans for the countryside the local farmers might have.

By the time Blodwyn had finished speaking, Nesta was almost in tears. She felt sure that after such defamation of his character the verdict was bound to go against her father.

They took so long to call Gwilym that Nesta was afraid he was not going to be allowed to give evidence at all. Once he was in the witness stand, however, she saw the ploy behind the delay. Her father's lawyer had allowed the case to build up to its peak and then, when the Dragon's guilt seemed to be proven, he was using Gwilym's irrefutable evidence to prove conclusively that the Dragon was innocent.

Gwilym had done his research well. He had all the facts at his finger-tips and was even able to give the exact time of the air raid over Liverpool. His documented evidence on how the German bomber had jettisoned its bomb load, trying to make its escape when chased by a British fighter plane, brought gasps of surprise from the body of the court.

From where she was sitting, Nesta could see hope gradually transforming her father. As his name was cleared, his bowed shoulders squared and the hang-dog look went from his face. He was listening with a new awareness as the case against him was dismissed.

Outside the courtroom they were surrounded by pressmen. Good-natured banter was directed at Gwilym by reporters who knew him, while searching and in-depth questions were fired at Rhys Evans.

When it was all over, Gwilym insisted that the three of them went back to his home.

'My parents are expecting you and they hope you will stay with them for a few days now that you are free,' he told Nesta's father.

Sara Vaughan made it an excuse for a party.

Neighbours and friends crowded in. Nesta was too overjoyed by the turn of events to even feel embarrassed because she was in Land Army uniform whereas the other women were wearing pretty dresses.

She felt proud of her father. In the charcoal-grey suit he had worn in court, he looked like a distinguished scholar or philosopher. To her surprise, he seemed quite at ease being lionized by the bank managers, accountants and Liverpool business men who made up the gathering. As she watched, she found herself wondering how many of them owned weekend cottages in North Wales and whether they would have been so supportive had her father been found guilty.

After dinner, when everyone seemed to be relaxed and enjoying their drinks and cigars, Gwilym and Nesta wandered out into the garden to the summer-house half-hidden by a rustic pergola.

'I have to leave first thing in the morning,' he told her regretfully.

'Me too! I don't know what Parry Jones will say when I get back. I should have been at work yesterday. I hope Huw explained where I was.'

'I should think that by now everyone around Blaenau Ffestiniog will have read it all in the *Echo*, so he will know, anyway,' Gwilym smiled.

'Your evidence clinched the case,' she told him gratefully.

'Well, I had to do something dramatic to save the man who is going to be my father-in-law, now didn't I?'

'Your what?'

'You always said I was good with words,' he grinned. 'Isn't that an original proposal?' His face became grave, his tone earnest, 'Will you marry me, Nesta? I've thought of little else while we've been apart. I meant to wait until the war was over but now this has brought us together again . . .'

'Oh Gwilym, are you sure? You went away without a word . . . the separation would have been so much easier to bear if I had known you cared,' Nesta breathed, raising her face to his.

'So your answer is "Yes",' he murmured, as his mouth hovered fractionally above hers.

Their lips met and a warm sense of fulfilment ebbed through her as she relaxed in the arms of the man who had been so much in her thoughts.

Their background differences, her father's political struggles, even his own ambitions for the future, all now paled into insignificance for Gwilym, overshadowed by the bliss that was his at that moment. A sense of achievement, an inner glow, seemed to fill him, making him oblivious to everything except his overpowering love for Nesta. His strength, his compassion and understanding all melded into tenderness towards her.

There was such an air of innocence about Nesta that he wanted to shield her from the harsher realities of life. He had felt protective towards her the moment he had witnessed the crowd's anger against her at the meeting in Dolgellau. He had tried to excuse his feeling by telling himself it was the trusting look in the huge brown eyes dominating her heart-shaped face that had broken through his defences.

Each time he had seen her his feelings had grown stronger until he could no longer ignore the fact that he was in love. Marriage, and all its responsibilities, were not part of his scheme of things. He was ambitious. He wanted to reach Fleet Street and an editor's chair. So, he had kept silent.

When he had received his call-up papers he had expected their friendship to end. It would be a different life, a complete break. They would forget each other.

His training had been strict and tiring. At the end of the day he was so physically exhausted he couldn't wait to reach his bunk. Always, though, before he fell asleep, he thought of Nesta. He remembered her gentleness, her courage in tackling the arduous farm work, her loyalty to her father and her pride in the cause he was fighting. Memories of her clear expressive voice and light bubbly laugh lulled him to sleep. And each night he promised he would write to her next day . . . and tell her how he felt.

In the cold light of reveille, his caution and reserve returned. If he took a wife it could well stultify his chosen career. His father would use marriage as a lever to persuade him to give up journalism and work for him, something he had been fighting against since the day he left school.

Now, as their kiss deepened, pulses throbbed through his entire body as Nesta responded. With a fierce, desperate urgency his hands moved intimately over her.

His lips were gentle as they tenderly explored her throat, then his whole body was suddenly aflame as her arms encircled his neck and she pressed against him with trembling eagerness.

28

'Airmen certainly get treated a lot better than soldiers,' Wynne Morgan remarked, when Nesta, her face wreathed in smiles, looked up from the letter that had arrived while they were having breakfast and announced that Gwilym would be home on leave in ten days' time.

'Take our Trevor,' Wynne went on. 'Not seen sight nor sound of him for over a year now, not since they sent him out to North Africa. Air force boys seem to be able to do as they like.'

'Not all of them,' Nesta grinned. 'Only the aircrew. It's because they do such a dangerous job,' she added smugly.

'They are all doing their bit and taking risks whichever of the services they are in,' Wynne exclaimed huffily.

'Oh, I know that,' Nesta said contritely. 'I didn't mean that Trevor wasn't . . .'

'She's teasing you, silly,' Huw guffawed. 'Pulling your leg! I can't wait for Gwilym to come on leave. Perhaps once this wedding is over we'll be able to get some sense out of you. Mooning around the place ever since your father's trial. Don't know how old Parry Jones puts up with it. Bet you get half the orders wrong.'

'No I do not,' Nesta said quickly. 'Is that the time?' she gasped, as she looked at the clock on the dresser. 'Parry Jones will think the van has broken down.'

Her heart was singing as she drove the six miles from the Morgans' cottage to Cynfal Farm. The early spring sunshine was already creeping high over the mountains, promising a fine, warm April day. Sheep and lambs dotted the slopes, the birds were singing, it was a perfect time to be happy.

And in ten days she would be married!

She still couldn't believe it. So much had happened in the last few months that she felt as if she was in a constant whirl of excitement. Not all of it had been good. She had been saddened by her grandmother's death, and her father being brought to trial had been a frightening experience and she couldn't bear to think what the outcome would have been without Gwilym's evidence. At least her grandmother had been spared the strain of that ordeal.

The brief visit to Cardiff had been disastrous, too. The raw hatred in Aunt Betty's eyes was something she would never forget. Her stomach churned just remembering her aunt's vicious words and she felt angry, ashamed and bitter over the scene that had ensued.

As the road dipped towards Ffestiniog, she feasted her eyes on the cavalcade of mountains, towering like silent sentinels. Everything about the scenery appealed to her. She hoped that when the war ended she and Gwilym could live here, amongst the mountains and streams, the wooded cwms and gushing waterfalls. Towns like Cardiff, Liverpool and Chester were all very well for the occasional visit, the big day out shopping, but they were not places to live in.

Guiltily her thoughts switched to Chris and his promise that they would live in North Wales if she would marry him. It hadn't been fair to raise his hopes when she knew her feelings for him could never be anything more than friendship. Knowing the hurt and despair she had felt when she thought Gwilym had gone out of her life, she owed it to Chris to put the record straight. It would be a hard letter to write but not to do so would be both cowardly and unfair.

Her good intentions went completely out of her mind once she arrived at Cynfal Farm. There was work to be done in the dairy and so many orders to be taken out that she hardly had time to snatch a sandwich at lunch-time she was kept so busy.

'Time off again, is it?' Parry Jones said worriedly when she told him that she was to be married. 'And after that, what?'

'Well, I shall be back at work again. Gwilym only has four days' special leave. He probably won't get home again until the war ends. They talk about the invasion taking place this spring, you know.'

'This spring! Why, it is the end of April already. Soon be summer! I don't think we can stand this old war going on much longer. What with the rationing and all the other shortages, the country is on the brink of starvation. Things must come to a head soon.'

Nesta was sure he was right but found it hard to be really concerned about it all. She certainly wanted the war to end, and for Gwilym to come back home as quickly as possible. For the moment, though, she was deliciously happy, her mind buzzing with plans for their wedding, and she could think of little else.

Gwilym would not arrive home until the morning they were to be married, so she had agreed to go to Liverpool the day before and stay overnight with his parents. Goronwy and Sara Vaughan would then drive with her to the registry office and act as witnesses. Wynne and Huw had been invited along for the ceremony and also to the celebratory meal afterwards at the Vaughans' house.

Nesta had told them so much about Sara and Goronwy Vaughan and their home that they were reluctant to attend, and she had to plead with them to accept the invitation.

'I don't know, I'm not much for high-class company,' Huw told her. 'Rough and ready sort, me. Perhaps Wynne will go, but not me, I wouldn't fit in.'

'Of course you will,' Nesta insisted. 'Please, Uncle Huw. It matters a lot to me. Otherwise, I shall be surrounded by Gwilym's family and friends and no one of my own.'

'Is your father going to be there?'

'I am not sure.'

'Lying low these days, isn't he? Once his name was cleared I thought we should be seeing a lot more of him. No need for him to hide himself away now, so where is he?'

'I really don't know. I have sent a message to the Plaid Cymru headquarters to let him know about the wedding. I hope he gets it in time because I very much want him to be there,' Nesta added wistfully.

In her suitcase when she left for Liverpool, the day before she was to be married, was her wedding outfit, an elegant light-blue two-piece suit. It was a present from Wynne and Huw and she knew it must have taken most of their clothing coupons for the coming year.

'You can't be married in that Land Army uniform,' Wynne had said in shocked tones. 'A girl's wedding day is special, one to be remembered. Dressed up like a farm worker isn't the right sort of memory for a bride to have.'

'Gwilym will be in uniform.'

'Well, that's different. Anyway,' she added with a teasing smile, 'I've always said they spoil those air-force boys. Their uniform is pretty enough for weddings or anything else. Not like the poor soldiers in their drab khaki, now is it?'

It wasn't until she was in bed, in the Vaughan's pretty pink and white guest-room, that Nesta remembered she hadn't written to tell Chris she was going to be married. The thought made her uneasy. It was almost as if she was doing something dishonourable behind his back.

When she had come up to bed she had been happily tired. All evening she and Sara had been talking about Gwilym's homecoming and going over the plans for the next day. Now she was so full of remorse and misgivings about Chris that she knew it would be impossible to sleep. Sitting up in bed, she began to compose a letter. It was the hardest thing she had ever had to write. It was well after

266

midnight before she had finished and all around her were screwed up balls of paper showing how many times she had started and then re-started.

With a tremendous feeling of relief, she sealed the envelope ready to post next day. Now that she had written to Chris she could go to her wedding with a clear conscience.

Gwilym arrived home before she was up next morning. She could hear his mother insisting that he ought to have his breakfast in his bedroom and stay there until it was time for him to leave for the registry office.

'It will bring bad luck if you and Nesta see each other before the ceremony,' she warned.

Gwilym brushed his mother's protestations aside with a laugh.

'We are having a registry office wedding not a church service,' he told her in exasperated tones. 'I'm going to have little enough time to be with Nesta as it is. I've only got four days' leave.'

In the end they all sat down to breakfast together and they were still lingering over their second cup of tea when Wynne and Huw arrived.

'Goodness, we didn't expect you to come all the way out here, we thought you would meet us in Liverpool,' Sara Vaughan greeted them. 'None of us are ready yet,' she added in a flustered tone.

'Sorry if we are putting you out,' Wynne apologized, 'but there was a telegram for Nesta, and when we opened it we thought she ought to have it right away.'

'From my Da to say he can't make it?' Nesta asked, her voice sharp with disappointment.

'No! It's not from him.'

Frowning, Nesta took the yellow envelope Wynne held out. As she read the contents the colour drained from her face.

'What is it?' Gwilym was at her side, taking the slip of paper from her shaking fingers.

'CHRIS SERIOUSLY INJURED. ASKING FOR YOU. COME AT ONCE.'

'It's my cousin . . . Chris Jenkins,' she whispered numbly. 'I'll have to go.' Her dark eyes mutely appealed to Gwilym for understanding.

He stood shaking his head, unable to believe what was happening. His mouth tightened and there was a hardness in his green eyes as he stared at her questioningly.

'You can't go now,' Goronwy Vaughan protested. 'We have to be at the registry office in an hour. There is only just time for you to finish getting ready. Come on,' he said fussily, 'the car will be here in half an hour. We've got to get into the centre of Liverpool, remember.'

'I must go to Chris, he needs me,' Nesta protested, her chin jutting stubbornly.

'You can't do this,' Gwilym told her, taking hold of her shoulders and shaking her angrily. 'If I go back to my unit and say that I haven't got married I'll be on a charge. I had to get special permission to be here at all!'

'They will understand if you tell them the reason . . . you're good with words,' Nesta said, pulling away.

'The car will be here any minute,' Goronwy Vaughan grumbled. 'Let's get the ceremony over with now we've got this far. You can both go and see this cousin of yours afterwards. Go to Cardiff, or wherever it is, for your honeymoon,' he added jocularly.

'No! I can't get married knowing that Chris is lying ill and asking for me,' Nesta repeated, her cheeks flushed. 'I'll get my things together. When the car arrives it can take me to Lime Street station,' she added defiantly.

'Nesta, you can't run out on me like this. You can't do it,' Gwilym bristled. He felt stunned and bewildered by her behaviour. How could her cousin, or anyone else, mean that much to her.

'Gwilym, I must.'

'I forbid it!' Danger flags blazed in his green eyes as they pinned hers.

'You can't stop me ... we're not married yet!' she flared.

'Nor will we ever be if you go ahead with this crazy idea,' he stormed.

'Please Gwilym, we're wasting time. I must get to the station. It will take me at least three hours to get to Pontypridd!'

'Don't do it, Nesta. Don't fall into the same trap as your father,' Gwilym said angrily. 'He's always making stands because he feels it is his duty to do so. You can't take on the cares of the entire world, you know. Today is our wedding day, for God's sake! Doesn't that mean anything?'

'I've already told you, I can't go through with it. Chris needs me, don't you understand?' she pleaded, tears of frustration trickling down her face.

'And obviously you care a great deal for him!' Gwilym's voice rasped with resentment.

'I do, but not in the way you mean. Chris was kind to me when I was a child,' she explained patiently. 'He took me to school and walked home with me afterwards, and stood up for me when other kids bullied me. I was nine years old and felt all alone in the world. Can't you understand?'

'No! The only thing I can understand is that you are walking out on me. If it was a church wedding it would be tantamount to deserting me at the altar,' Gwilym declared in outraged tones.

'Well, it is a civil ceremony, not a church wedding, and all we do is sign a legal document. All I am asking is that we postpone doing so.'

She stood there trembling, knowing all eyes were on her, choking with emotion and inwardly praying that Gwilym would support her. Surely he must understand. Chris was seriously ill. It was within her power to help. No matter what anyone else thought, she knew it was her duty to do that.

'It's that damn religion of yours, isn't it?' Gwilym said heavily. 'You have to make an act of contrition because you feel guilty at having chosen me and not him.'

She stared at him blankly, frowning and repeating his words in a flat toneless voice.

'Don't deny it!' There was sadness and scorn in Gwilym's voice. 'Is it always going to be like this? I know something about the Catholic church, the need to atone for your sins. You can't go through life seeking forgiveness from those you feel you might have hurt or wronged, Nesta. You've got to learn to stand by your decisions.'

'Is this really the right time to be having a theological discussion?' Goronwy Vaughan asked with heavy sarcasm. 'You two might know what you are arguing about but I don't.' He looked around at the bemused faces of his wife, Wynne and Huw for support.

'Nesta knows what I mean,' Gwilym said firmly.

She looked up into his face, her brown eyes desperately pleading with him to understand what was in her heart, but his green eyes were as hard as emeralds. Her gaze raked his face, and she found herself shuddering as she saw the stubborn set of his jaw, the grim tightness of his mouth. She had never seen Gwilym looking so harsh and uncompromising.

Even if she hadn't let Chris go back to his unit half-expecting her to wait for him, she would still feel that she ought to go to him if he was wounded and asking for her. She owed it to him as a friend. Gwilym might think she was being silly and sentimental but years of loneliness had taught her the importance of having someone you could depend on.

'I knew things would go wrong when you insisted on having breakfast together,' Sara Vaughan twittered in peeved tones. 'Everyone knows that the bride and bridegroom shouldn't see each other before the service.'

'It's too late to worry about that now, the car is outside, so what are you going to do?' Goronwy Vaughan demanded. His pointed grey beard waggled aggressively, his watery grey eyes looked bewildered behind his gold-rimmed glasses and his small mouth was screwed up into a disapproving moue. His podgy hands toyed nervously with the gold watch chain that spanned the waistcoat that strained over his portly stomach.

'I'm going to go to Lime Street station in it,' Nesta said, taking a deep breath. 'I'm sorry, Gwilym, it's something I just have to do, otherwise I would never be able to live with myself.'

'I'll come with you and see you on the train.'

'Gwilym!' A chorus of surprised voices greeted his decision.

'Someone must explain to the registrar what is happening,' he said wearily.

Like strangers they sat side by side yet worlds apart as the limousine took them into the centre of Liverpool. Each time Nesta glanced at Gwilym she saw his face was set grimly, his eyes staring fixedly out of the window, determined to avoid her.

'Tell me you understand ... please,' she begged as he carried her case as far as the ticket barrier when they reached Lime Street station.

'You must do as you think fit,' he replied stiffly, shaking off the hand she had laid pleadingly on his arm. 'As I said before, you can't be responsible for the entire world. You must make your mind up whether you want him or me.'

29

Nesta felt a choking, spinning nausea grip her as the pungent smell of disinfectants and medications mingled on the air as she entered the hospital. She took a long, deep breath to try and control her heaving stomach as the ward Sister led the way to the screened-off bed, her grey print dress and starched white apron rustling ominously.

'He's been asking for you for days,' she told Nesta, in a reproving tone. 'He's very weak, so try not to excite him.'

'I came as soon as I received the telegram from his mother,' Nesta said timidly.

'Well, you are only just in time.'

'You mean . . .' Shock choked Nesta. She had sensed that Chris might be desperately ill but now she was faced with the reality that he might be dying, she didn't want to believe it.

As the Sister pulled aside the striped curtain, Nesta saw that Aunt Betty was already at the bedside. Chris lay propped up against a mound of pillows. Bandages completely covered his head and part of his face. One arm was lying on top of the bedclothes, encased in plaster. A cage supported the bedclothes and kept them from touching the lower part of his body.

Nesta felt her throat go dry as she bent to speak to him.

'Chris, it's Nesta,' she murmured in a low, strained voice.

The mummified form on the bed lay motionless, only a faint groan emitting from the cracked lips as he laboriously breathed in and out.

'You'll have to speak louder than that or he won't hear you,' her aunt told her. 'Both his ear drums were damaged in the blast.'

'What happened?' Nesta asked, fighting back the sour taste in her throat.

'He stepped on to a mine and it exploded. One of his legs was blown right off. It's a wonder they brought him home, he was that smashed up. Might have been better if he'd died out there,' she added morosely.

'Don't say that!' Horror struck her like a giant fist. She felt so helpless as she stood there at his bedside.

'It's true. He will never be able to walk or work again, so what sort of life is that going to be?' Aunt Betty said bitterly.

'There's plenty he can do. Chris has a good brain, he loves reading . . . there's lots of things he can still enjoy,' Nesta protested weakly.

'Take up politics like that no-good father of yours,' her aunt sneered.

Before she could reply Chris stirred and gave a laboured groan of pain.

'Go on, then . . . let him know you are here,' her aunt ordered.

'Chris . . . Chris,' Nesta bent closer, tears stinging her eyes as she repeated his name more loudly and took his hand.

'Nesta!' His voice was a desperate croak. The hand she was holding twitched convulsively, then the fingers clung tenaciously. 'Nesta?' He bit down on his lower lip to stifle a moan of discomfort. 'Is it you?' he gasped.

'Yes, Chris.' She gave his hand a reassuring squeeze.

His eyes fluttered open, staring up at her. His hand gripped hers as if trying to reassure himself that she was not just a figment of his feverish imagination.

'Try and rest . . . I'll be here when you wake up,' Nesta told him softly.

'Promise you will stay.' He sighed deeply, his grip on her hand relaxing as he drifted into semi-consciousness.

'I don't know what you said to him last time you saw

him but he seems to think you are going to marry him,' her aunt told her as they kept their painful vigil.

'You were there when he asked me,' Nesta reminded her. 'You were the one that made such a fuss and was so much against it.'

'But what did you say to him afterwards?'

'I didn't promise,' Nesta said evasively.

'He thinks you did.'

'No.' Nesta shook her head sadly. 'I realized it wouldn't work. It would only turn you all against him.'

'You mean you had someone better in mind, don't you?' Aunt Betty sniffed. 'Our Dilys always reckoned you were a dark horse. She wasn't kidding.'

A groan from Chris claimed the two women's attention.

'He's dying, you know,' Aunt Betty repeated resentfully.

'Don't say that! He's young and strong, he will pull through,' Nesta insisted.

'No! I've already told you, he is just a wreck. It would be for the best if he was to slip away now,' her aunt insisted. 'The only reason I sent for you is that I want him to die happy,' she added fiercely.

'What do you mean?'

'I thought I had made myself clear, already. Chris thinks you promised to marry him. Next time he rallies, tell him that's why you are here. Do you understand?'

'But that wouldn't be the truth!'

'What does the truth matter, it's what he wants. Don't worry,' she added bitterly, 'you won't have to go through with it. I can guarantee that.'

'I don't feel for him in that way . . . I don't love him!'

'I don't give a damn about your feelings, or whether or not you love him. I just want him to die happy,' Aunt Betty said curtly.

As Chris's eyes flickered open, his mother gripped Nesta's arm. 'Tell him you do . . . and that you will marry him. NOW!'

274

Tears scalding down her cheeks, Nesta took Chris's hand between her own again.

'Chris . . . can you hear me?' She choked back her tears and tried to steady her voice. 'You've got to get better . . . I've come so that we can be married.'

'Nesta!' His voice croaked, his eyes glittered feverishly. The grip on her hand tightened as his swollen lips gaped in a smile. Then came a choking gasp, a gurgling deep in his throat and his entire body twitched as if in the throes of an immense convulsion.

'Chris!'

The panic in her voice conveyed itself to her aunt. Dragging back the curtains she began calling for help. The ward Sister and a nurse were at the bedside in seconds.

Gently but firmly they loosened the grip Chris still had on Nesta's hand and the nurse moved her away from the bed.

'I am afraid your son has gone, my dear,' the ward Sister said as she straightened up and laid a hand briefly on Betty's arm.

'I . . . I only did what you asked me to do,' Nesta murmured heartbrokenly as she walked out of the hospital with her aunt.

'Yes, you did what I asked,' Aunt Betty agreed in a toneless voice. 'You can go now.'

'But the funeral . . . I must stay for that!'

'I'd rather you didn't attend. You are not family any more. It would be upsetting to have you there.'

Nesta turned away feeling dejected and forlorn. She was too unnerved by the cold bitterness in her aunt's voice to argue. Perhaps she shouldn't have come in the first place. It would have been far better if Chris had remained in her memory as she had last seen him, strong and handsome in his uniform. Or even to have remembered him as a schoolboy, shy but caring, ready to defend her against the taunts of the other children because she was a misfit.

*

Where did she fit in, she wondered as the train carried her northwards once again. Was Gwilym right after all? Was she like her father, a fighter of lost causes, someone who was destined to drift through life searching for an anchor?

When she changed trains at Chester she phoned Gwilym's home to let him know she was on her way back. The crisis had ended so swiftly that there was still time for them to be married before he went back off leave.

Sara Vaughan answered the phone and Nesta had difficulty in getting her message across. Sara sounded distraught, as though she had been crying, and knowing the upset she had caused them Nesta felt a sharp twinge of regret.

'Is Gwilym there? Let me speak to him,' she begged.

'He's gone.'

'What do you mean? He had four days' leave. It doesn't end until tomorrow,' Nesta said, bewildered.

'They sent for him. Haven't you heard the news?' Her voice rose hysterically. 'The invasion has started! We don't know when we will see him again ... if ever,' her voice broke and all Nesta could hear were her racking sobs before she hung up.

D-Day! That would mean Gwilym taking part in bombing raids over Germany again. A shiver of apprehension went through her as his mother's words, 'We don't know when we will see him again,' echoed through her head.

If only she could have spoken to him, made things right between them, she thought with a pang of despair. The memory of Chris lying covered in bandages filled her mind. In the brilliant May sunshine it was hard to believe that Chris was dead. She couldn't bear to think of Gwilym like that. It mustn't happen.

If only the war would end, she thought resentfully. Chris was the second of her cousins to be killed and the war had only just reached its peak. Four years of death and shortages and who knew what lay ahead.

A feeling of desolation swept over her at the thought

that Gwilym was facing this new ordeal without them even having had the chance to say goodbye. It was as if God or fate or something was punishing her for her decision to go to Chris.

'Gwilym was right, I am guilt-ridden,' she thought bitterly, as she journeyed back to Blaenau Ffestiniog.

'Well, and how did the wedding go?' Parry Jones asked cheerfully when she reported for work at Cynfal Farm the next morning.

'There wasn't any wedding,' Nesta said dully.

'Oh! What went wrong? He didn't jilt you, did he?'

'No!' Nesta felt reluctant to explain just what had happened. The memory of Chris lying in the hospital bed, so horribly wounded, still scarred her mind. 'Gwilym was called back. He was needed for D-Day,' she added laconically.

'Big push forward, it's to be. The newspapers are full of it,' he agreed. 'Still, seems a pity you didn't get married first. Reckon these young lads need a family behind them so that they know what they're fighting for.'

'I'm sure you are right,' Nesta agreed wearily. 'Still, it was not to be. I'll get on and catch up with the deliveries.'

'Just a minute!' Parry Jones cleared his throat uncomfortably. 'It's like this, girl, I wasn't sure what might happen once you were married. You might be starting a family in next to no time and then you'd be no good to me. The work round here would be too heavy, see. Sorry, and all that.'

'I don't understand.'

'Well, think about it,' he went on defensively, 'you've been taking a lot of time off lately. Upsets routine, that sort of thing. I need someone dependable, see.'

'Are you telling me my job has gone?'

'I'm afraid so.' He looked away quickly. 'Hired a chap to do the work here instead. He has just been discharged from the army. Shot through the foot or something.

Anyway, he's as strong as a horse and he's been doing the round for me while you've been gallivanting off to Liverpool. Since he is a local man and has a wife and child to support, I felt it was my duty to let him have the job permanently, like,' he added defensively.

'You want me to leave altogether?' Nesta gasped, a sense of deep bewilderment making it difficult for her to believe what she was hearing.

'That's about the height of it.'

'You can't just sack me like that,' she said angrily. 'The Land Army sent me here . . .'

'Aah, well, that's all taken care of. I had a word with Blodwyn Thomas, her being a magistrate and the one who got me to take you in the first place. She said she would sort all the paperwork out with the government. Said you should go up and see her and she'd tell you what you had to do next . . .'

The thought of having to face Blodwyn filled Nesta with abhorrence, but pride wouldn't allow her to admit that to Parry Jones or let him see her distress.

'Twm Richards, the chap I've taken on, will give you a lift up to Gwyndy Farm,' Parry Jones offered.

'No, it's all right. I'll walk. I want to go home first.'

'Twm Richards can take you to the Morgans' place then, no trouble.'

'I'll walk.'

'Goodbye then, cariad. No hard feelings?'

Nesta didn't bother to answer. At that moment she hated the smug rotund little farmer, standing there so full of righteousness because he had found work for a man who had been wounded.

She felt as if her whole world was collapsing. Her grandmother was gone, she had no idea where her father was and she had lost her job. Now that Chris was dead she never wanted to see any of her cousins ever again, so she would never go back to Cardiff or Pontypridd.

Her heart ached for Gwilym. If only she had been able to speak to him, admit she had been wrong to postpone their wedding and rush off to see Chris as she had.

The May sunshine was hot on her back as she turned up the lane towards the cottage. She found Wynne in the garden hanging out some washing.

'Back already! What's happened now?' she asked as she saw the tight set of Nesta's face.

'My job's gone. Parry Jones has taken on a chap called Twm Richards.'

'That's his wife's cousin,' Wynne told her. 'Wounded, so I heard.'

'Shot in the foot but he's as strong as a horse and he needs the work to support his wife and child,' Nesta said caustically, repeating, word for word, what Parry Jones had told her.

'I see! Bit of a shock for you, though, cariad. Let me just peg out these last couple of shirts and I'll make us a nice cup of tea.'

'You finish what you're doing and I'll make the tea,' Nesta offered.

As she waited for the kettle to boil, Nesta looked round the cottage kitchen as if seeing it for the first time. It no longer felt like home. The polished black range with its shining steel fender, the dresser with its array of decorative cups and plates, the rocking chair with its chintz cushion and the Welsh shawl that Wynne had woven spread over the back of it, seemed strangely unfamiliar. Even when Shonti came purring round her legs, his white paws reaching up as she filled his saucer with milk, she felt unmoved.

'Well, what are you going to do now, then?' Wynne asked as she sat down at the table and stirred sugar into her tea.

'Parry Jones said I had to report back to Blodwyn Thomas. When he told her he was taking on Twm Richards, she said to tell me to go and see her when I got back.'

'Why don't you leave going up to Gwyndy Farm until this afternoon? You'll be feeling better about it by then,' Wynne advised.

'No, I don't think I will. In fact, I'm not going to see her at all.'

'What are you going to do then?' Wynne asked, her voice sharp with anxiety.

'If you had asked me that five minutes ago I would have said I didn't know,' Nesta told her. 'I do now. I've just made my mind up!'

'Oh?'

'I'm going to do what I should have done years ago,' Nesta said decisively. 'I'm going to join the ATS.'

'Do you think you'll get in . . . just like that, I mean?'

'Now the invasion is under way, I'm sure they'll want every able-bodied person they can get.'

'And what about Gwilym? Don't you still want to marry him?'

'Yes, of course I do. More than anything in the whole world, but he's not here and I don't suppose he will get home again until the war is over. Anyway, I'm not ready to settle down yet,' Nesta said firmly. 'For the first time in my life I'm going to do exactly what I want to do, not what other people think I should do.'

'You will keep in touch with us though, Nesta?' her aunt said worriedly.

'Of course I will. And I'll come to see you if I get any leave . . . where else would I go? You and Uncle Huw are all the family I have now . . . except my Da! And half the time I don't know where he is.'

'I do!'

The tone of her aunt's voice brought Nesta up sharply. Aunt Wynne was rubbing her forefinger round and round the rim of her cup in a troubled way.

'Where is he? Has he been to see you?'

'No!' With a tremendous effort her aunt looked up and let her eyes meet Nesta's. 'He is in hospital.'

'Do you mean he has had an accident?' Visions of Chris's mutilated body swam into her vision before fear numbed her.

'Not an accident . . . he's ill. They've sent him away to a sanatorium. He . . . he's got TB.'

'What's that?' Nesta exclaimed, her brown eyes misting with shock.

'Tuberculosis . . . some people call it consumption. He has had it for ten years but never told any of the family . . . except my Mam. All those times when he seemed to just disappear he was in hospital for treatment. He's been gradually getting worse. This is his last chance. They're going to try out some new medication . . .'

'Will he be cured?'

'Probably, if he completes the treatment. In the past he's tended to neglect himself. Now, if he stops in the sanatorium for six months, follows their instructions to the letter, he has every chance of making a complete recovery,' Aunt Wynne assured her.

'Where is he? I must go and see him.'

'No.' Her aunt laid a restraining hand on Nesta's arm. 'He doesn't want that. He said he couldn't bear for you to see him with tubes and drips and such like . . .'

'But I won't be able to rest until I see him . . .'

'Don't fret, cariad. It is all going to be all right, I know it is,' Aunt Wynne assured her, smiling confidently. 'You go off and join your ATS. When this war is over, and you come back home, it will be a fresh start for us all.'

A selection of bestsellers from SPHERE

FICTION

JUBILEE: THE POPPY CHRONICLES 1	Claire Rayner	£3.50 ☐
DAUGHTERS	Suzanne Goodwin	£3.50 ☐
REDCOAT	Bernard Cornwell	£3.50 ☐
WHEN DREAMS COME TRUE	Emma Blair	£3.50 ☐
THE LEGACY OF HEOROT	Niven/Pournelle/Barnes	£3.50 ☐

FILM AND TV TIE-IN

BUSTER	Colin Shindler	£2.99 ☐
COMING TOGETHER	Alexandra Hine	£2.99 ☐
RUN FOR YOUR LIFE	Stuart Collins	£2.99 ☐
BLACK FOREST CLINIC	Peter Heim	£2.99 ☐
INTIMATE CONTACT	Jacqueline Osborne	£2.50 ☐

NON-FICTION

BARE-FACED MESSIAH	Russell Miller	£3.99 ☐
THE COCHIN CONNECTION	Alison and Brian Milgate	£3.50 ☐
HOWARD & MASCHLER ON FOOD	Elizabeth Jane Howard and Fay Maschler	£3.99 ☐
FISH	Robyn Wilson	£2.50 ☐
THE SACRED VIRGIN AND THE HOLY WHORE	Anthony Harris	£3.50 ☐

All Sphere books are available at your local bookshop or newsagent, or can be ordered direct from the publisher. Just tick the titles you want and fill in the form below.

Name _____

Address _____

_____

Write to Sphere Books, Cash Sales Department, P.O. Box 11, Falmouth, Cornwall TR10 9EN

Please enclose a cheque or postal order to the value of the cover price plus:

UK: 60p for the first book, 25p for the second book and 15p for each additional book ordered to a maximum charge of £1.90.

OVERSEAS & EIRE: £1.25 for the first book, 75p for the second book and 28p for each subsequent title ordered.

BFPO: 60p for the first book, 25p for the second book plus 15p per copy for the next 7 books, thereafter 9p per book.

Sphere Books reserve the right to show new retail prices on covers which may differ from those previously advertised in the text elsewhere, and to increase postal rates in accordance with the P.O.